Confide in Me

BELLA ROANE

Confide in Me

First published in 2022

Copyright © Bella Roane 2022

ISBN: 978-1-7391679-0-5

Cover Design by Michelle Catanach

Published with the support of:

DEDICATION

For my daddy, my hero, my confidant, my biggest fan. I
did it!

And to Lucy. Simply, I love you, sis.

PROLOGUE

Fate. What a load of shit! Whoever thought it up was a fool.

Fate didn't play a hand, wasn't tempting, and didn't happen for a reason. You make your choices; you make your bed, and you lie in it.

That's what happened. A bad choice had led her here, and now she was completely alone.

She had screwed it all up. Her marriage, her family, her reputation. She had to control her indignation, though, as she had brought it all on herself. It was no good being angry or bitter—she had no right to feel like that.

Who was Carrie Pritchard anyway? She thought she knew, but how much does someone really know themselves?

Twenty years ago, she was a beautiful young woman leading a carefree life, surrounded by an abundance of friends and the centre of *the* social circuit. She was on the cusp of an exciting career and finally leaving her tempestuous family behind her. Years later, she had blossomed into a wife and mother, lovingly bringing up her children with a devoted husband who made sure she and the kids didn't want for anything.

And now? She was still in the marital home, but he wasn't.

The kids still lived with her, but her son spent as little time with her as possible, hiding in his room and only venturing out for school or the occasional snack. He went to Matthew's as often as he could, catching the bus at the bottom of the street, and Matthew would bring him back a few days later. The twins needed her, but only because they didn't understand what had happened. Matthew saw them at weekends, taking then swimming and to the park, dutifully dropping them off on Sunday evenings after a boisterous schedule of fun. Of course, this was the highlight of her week. Not only getting the kids home but also seeing Matthew.

At 4 p.m., she would get a shower and make sure she used the expensive perfume that he had bought her for her birthday last year, an indulgence then but now an investment. She made herself up, but not too much, as Matthew didn't like that. He had always complimented her on her flawless complexion and the fact that she didn't need a lot of makeup to look radiant, just a smudge of eyeliner and mascara, a quick flick of blusher and a splash of shiny lip gloss. She wanted those times back and desperately tried to erase the complications that had engulfed them. But the radiance had been replaced by a glassy tint; the makeup was a mask. She had cried so much over the past few months that she didn't think she could ever repair the creases that now made up her face. Hooded eyelids hung like heavy hammocks over her once sparkling eyes, and her pretty mouth had taken on a perpetual downturn. He would knock on the door, and she would open it, trying not to kink and forcing her unyielding mouth into a smile.

The twins would run in and smother her with hugs, excitedly recalling the events of the past few days with Daddy, and their love would momentarily hush the dull aching pain of reality. Luke would push past her, straight up to his room and slam the door, twisting the knife a little further as he did so.

Matthew wouldn't even look up. He'd mutter something about collecting them next weekend, turn and go back out into the world—his world, without her. Every time he did this, the fragile fragments of her broken heart splintered and frayed. She'd had to endure this for four lonely weeks, but it was her fault. No wonder her son hated her, and no wonder her husband couldn't bear to look at her. She had been so stupid, selfish, and swayed by a little bit of attention. She was a slut. She was ashamed.

Glancing at the clock, she saw it was just after six. He'd be here soon. With her weekly routine complete, she went to wait patiently by the window for the car to pull up outside. Even though it was a cold winter evening, she felt hot.

Across the road was a small park; it was late on a Sunday, but it was still brimming with young families. The streetlights highlighted flashes of colour peeping out through the patchy yew hedge that separated the park from the street. A few kids were racing around on swings, roundabouts, and slides as their parents stood chatting under the fairy lights adorning the gates. Someone had brought a flask, and they happily shared the contents between themselves—a pretty little scene on a crisp, cold evening in late January.

Memories of that summer, playing hide and seek with the girls and football with her son filled her head. They were a lifetime ago, her life before she crushed it. A tear danced on her eyelashes, but she brushed it away along with her thoughts. They would be here soon; she didn't deserve to feel sorry for herself, mourning her past life.

Then he was here. Luke reluctantly got out of the front seat and opened the door for the twins, who clambered out excitedly. As they raced up the small path to the front door, Carrie checked her appearance in the hallway mirror once more and opened the door, greeting the girls with open arms. They bowled straight into her as she bent down to embrace them, almost knocking her off her feet. They had armfuls of craft that they wanted to show her and stories of a fantastic trip to the beach where they had even braved the sea!

Suddenly there was a squeal from Jen as she remembered what they had been doing before Daddy had picked them up on Friday.

"Lego school! Let's go and play with it, Hannah!"

Two raucous little whirlwinds soon disappeared up the stairs scattering an intermittent trail of lolly sticks and pipe cleaners along the hallway. Picking up the mess, she noticed Luke had returned to the car while Matthew trudged up the path with the bags. He casually told her that Luke would not be coming home for the week and would be staying with him.

She swallowed hard and tried not to let the tears form again on her eyelashes. A pang of guilt ricocheted inside her, slicing through every raw nerve it could find. What could she do? What could she say? It was no use protesting. At least Luke had tried, but he just couldn't do it anymore. He was fifteen; it was all so hard on him. She had done this.

Matthew told her that he would take him for the week, have the girls back at the weekend and see if he wanted to come home the following Sunday. He was looking up at her now, and she almost felt a softening in his gaze. It was fleeting, but she was sure it had been there. Her heart fluttered slightly. He didn't feel sorry for her, but maybe he felt sad about the attrition that his family was suffering.

Not waiting for a response, he turned and called back that he would see her on Friday and was down the path and out of her life for another week.

* * *

As he drove away from the house, *their house,* it struck him how wounded she had looked. Like a delicate flower being driven down by the beating rain, he thought she had been on the verge of collapsing on the floor. Like soft petals weighed down by the affliction of consequence, she had looked utterly beautiful in that moment. He could see beyond the makeup and forged smile. She was devastated, and it had taken everything he had not to reach out and comfort her. Losing Luke was just another chink in the marital armour she was determined to keep wearing. It was the same every week, and he had to remind himself of the deceitful thing she had done to him and the family. He had to stay strong and in control. He couldn't be taken in by the sweet mirage of memories from their shared life before.

Matthew knew he could never love anyone as much as he had loved Carrie. It had been a deep love that radiated through the surface of his skin to his heart—his heavy heart. Did he still love her? It was now all in the past tense to save his sanity. She was all he had ever known and all he had ever wanted. Yet, he was not all she had ever known, not anymore—their special connection, destroyed by her betrayal.

He cursed himself because he still wanted her, even after everything she had done to him. He had to stay true to himself, but what about the family? Who was being true to them? He hadn't been entirely honest with them either. He turned this thought over and over in his mind, then pushed it back where it had been buried. Nobody knew about that. No, this was about *her*, not him.

Luke stared out of the window as they drove along the dark streets. Matthew was flattered that his son had taken his side but was also crushed by what it would do to Carrie. Luke was so like her with his striking auburn hair and walnut-coloured eyes. She adored him. They enjoyed similar interests, like mountain biking, chess, and tennis. Carrie had been a fantastic athlete at school, and Luke was shaping up to follow in her footsteps. He had an active schedule during the week, which Carrie had managed expertly. However, with this latest turn of events, it would be down to Matthew to juggle rugby, football, cricket nets, and a recent introduction of basketball. Luke had made it clear that he didn't want to see his mum for a while, so work would have to take a back seat, at least for this week anyway.

This is what irked him. She didn't work; he did. He paid the bills, gave her an allowance for the kids, and let her live in the family home. He sacrificed his family time so she could give them this colourful upbringing. The twins were at school now, so she didn't even have to look after them during the day. Now with Luke staying with him because of her, *she* had denied two little girls their brother. Matthew gripped the steering wheel a little tighter as they approached the red traffic light. He couldn't help but lurch from profound, sentimental devotion to revolt and disgust. For the trillionth time, he asked himself, why?

Luke hadn't said a word since they'd left the house. Beneath his stoic expression, Matthew knew that it hurt his son deeply to turn his back on his mother. She had let him down in a way he had never imagined, and now Matthew had to try and put his son back together. The jigsaw of a broken teenager was a riddle for a better man than him.

His irks germinated little sprouts of annoyance. Now the whole week would be disrupted by early finishes in the office and working into the small hours at the flat. However, he couldn't give her the satisfaction of knowing it would be an upheaval. He couldn't bear to think that she might propose to help, and no matter that it could be an excuse to see her again, he didn't need anything from her. What could she offer that he couldn't do anyway? No, he and Luke were going to have the best week together. The absent father label was ripped off and thrown away as quickly as it had been applied.

CHAPTER 1

Three months earlier....

Carrie snuggled further down into her cosy bed as the rain beat down hard on the windows. This was her safe place. He couldn't get her here.

The blankets and duvet were tucked under every part of her body; no cold air could slither in to spoil her refuge. No cruel words or icy glares could penetrate these pacifying walls. Briefly, she relaxed, for it wouldn't be long before he joined her in this temporary shelter she had built from him.

For now, she welcomed the rain and wind. It reminded her of childhood stories her father told her about the fisherman out at sea bravely battling the elements to bring in the catch for the following day. She allowed herself to close her dry eyes. She imagined a tiny trawler being tossed around by towering waves and men hiding out below deck nervously waiting until the storm had eased, silently praying their ship would hold strong. The thuds and groans from the wind outside intensified the scene. The fierce pictures in her head were strangely comforting and familiar.

The storm will always pass, her father would say. The men would soon be safe on land, reunited with their families, daredevil voyagers who had taken on the sea and won. These men risked everything to provide for their families—heroes from a simple life.

Soon she would become that tiny trawler, and he would be the storm. Raging and tormenting her round and round, over and over, until finally releasing her from the struggle, there would be calm. An unsettled content, leaving her in an apprehensive state. Would the storm bite back, or could she settle for the night? Was the worst of it over?

That was what her husband wanted, a simple life. But she wasn't satisfied. She didn't know why but she fought it with every breath in her body until it exhausted them both. She loved Matthew intensely. Fifteen years married, and three wonderful children had bounced into their world. Yet even with every new wrinkle that formed around his eyes or a grey strand that peaked out amongst his thinning hair, she loved him.

He could cut her deeply with his profound silences or burn her with his dismissive remarks, yet she still went back for more. Like a rejected lamb seeking some sort of comfort from its contemptuous mother, she craved his attention and affection like a drug.

Matthew didn't feel the same, and her transparency was reflected in his eyes like a ghost in a mirror. He no longer looked at her but beyond to some faraway place they had once explored together. They had both snatched for the key to that place from time to time but had never tried to unlock it.

He was just acknowledging her presence, or maybe he was suffering it? He muttered when he replied, kept his head low and rarely made eye contact unless they were fighting. Years of petty battles had forced him to retreat, waiting in the shadows until she had worn him down to the point at which all he could do was rain down his bullets of accusations and arrows of leverage to expose her weaknesses. He would relentlessly drive her away, stop her from penetrating the bastille of who he really was. Recently, though, his new tactic of manoeuvring her off course was working particularly well, igniting and stoking the flames of irritability before she had even lit them. She wondered, fleetingly, if she had made him like this. Tonight, she knew what was coming.

It hadn't always been like this. They had first met at school and gradually became friends through a huge social circle. Matthew had noticed Carrie from their first day at high school together but had been too shy to approach her. She was immensely popular with everyone, including the teachers and was often asked to accompany the piano, singing beautifully as the teaching staff and pupils entered the hall. It was in these moments that the tone and texture of her voice lifted him up, and they drifted away together like they were the only ones in the room. The lines of his surroundings blurred into one another like an Impressionist painting. He imagined that he was her muse, and she was magnifying his existence with every note.

Finally, as they entered their GCSE year and he found himself in the same maths class as her, he finally plucked up the courage to ask her for a walk one breaktime. They talked and talked. About what? She couldn't remember, but it was lovely. He had been so attentive and sweet. He had listened to her without just nodding detachedly and pretending not to stare at her breasts through her blouse, unlike the other boys in her year. Here was a boy who showed her respect and liked her for who she was. She had found someone she could see a future with, and it had felt perfect. A smile tickled her lips at the sweet memory, and then it was replaced by confusion and shame.

The familiar dull footsteps could be heard ascending the stairs. *Pretend to be asleep, pretend to be asleep*, she repeated as she pulled the covers around herself even tighter. The door handle to the bedroom turned with its usual squeak. Her heart was beating so fast she thought it might deceive her dormancy. He cleared his throat.

"I got the email about Luke's homework." Silence. He tried again. "Can't believe that he hasn't done it again for a second week."

She held her breath. He went into their little bathroom to brush his teeth. Maybe he would forget? After a few minutes, he came back out.

"Why have you let this happen?" There it was, the accusation, the bait tempting her into a fight. Why have YOU let this happen?

Luke was beginning to test the boundaries; she had been the same at his age. Matthew had been a nerd, not the 'cool' kid. Maybe that was why she hadn't noticed him for so long. He had been so hung up on succeeding at school that he forgot to kick back and enjoy himself. Obviously, that had changed when they met, and for five glorious years, they really lived. She had followed him here to university, and whilst he studied, she worked two part-time jobs until she had enough to fund her nursing career.

They both worked hard but played harder. His parents were disappointed and said that she was a bad influence on him. Even on their wedding day, his mother, Felicity, shed a tear. She would tell anyone who would listen that it wasn't joy she felt watching her son marry his sweetheart but anguish. Carrie had always and would always be a stain they couldn't remove.

"Don't you think it's important? Do you not check his homework? I don't understand how this has happened again, especially after last week."

There was no point; sleep was no excuse. He would not give up. Not until she had explained herself. She leaned over, switched on her bedside light, and then sat up propped against her pillow.

"What do you want me to say?" she asked tentatively.

Now he had her attention, and in the dim light, he seemed to grow immensely. She took a sharp intake of breath. *Here we go*, she thought, feeling the dread dropping down to the depths of her stomach like a stone.

"We were here last week, Carrie. I thought it was made clear. You must be on this. His exams are not too far away, and he must do well in them."

This was the second week that Luke had not done his chemistry homework. Carrie had had a text from the school, and she had confronted Luke about it that evening. He was sorry and said that he would catch up. Carrie had been satisfied with his response, and it was case closed as far as she was concerned. Then she made the fatal error of mentioning it to Matthew.

Luke was hauled into the kitchen and subjected to a barrage of questions as to why he hadn't done it. Then at 9 p.m., after Matthew had hammered his point home, Luke sat at the kitchen table and completed it. He then did a further ten questions to ensure his understanding of reactive acids and chemical changes had really gone in. Every now and again, he would look across at Carrie and she could see the bewildered look in his eyes. She had let him down. He thought his mistake had been reprimanded by a slap on the wrist from her. He didn't blame his dad for this. He blamed her. She should have said more to Matthew to protect him, but she didn't, and his disappointment was her punishment.

Matthew wrote an email to his teacher, apologising for the oversight and requesting that in future, all communication to do with his son's work came via him. He then marked Luke's work and ordered him off to bed.

"Well?"

"Erm, I don't know. I thought he had done it. I asked him and he said he had done everything."

"What? You trust a fifteen-year-old boy's word? Are you mad? We agreed that he would show you. Why didn't you check?"

She tried a different approach. "I hoped that after last time, we could trust him."

"Well, *obviously* not," he snapped. "Do you have any idea how embarrassing it was to receive an email after the promises I made last week?"

She folded her arms. *Just apologise, and it'll stop*, she thought. She patiently waited for him to finish. He kept repeating his point over and over just to make sure she had really understood. She wasn't going to cry, but anger was starting to bubble up inside her; the pressure cooker was rapidly reaching boiling point. She tried to calm herself with a deep breath. The responsibility did lie on Luke's shoulders, after all.

"I mean, this is what we agreed. You manage the home and I work. I thought you accepted that?"

"Yes, I do." Carrie just wanted it to end.

"It doesn't sound like it to me. Do you not acknowledge some of the liability?" She almost laughed then. It was as if Matthew was addressing one of his business associates. She could imagine him speaking to his colleagues in the same way when he was reprimanding them.

"Liability?"

"Yes, liability. You know what it means, don't you?"

The anger flooded through her; the lid was coming off; this comment had pierced the skin. She felt hot. *Are you fucking serious?*

He had done it, unleashed the beast, touched a raw nerve, hit her where it hurt. He had got the reaction that he wanted. He always did this. He pushed and pushed until she snapped. Why? It was like a small child taunting their pet hamster over and over until it finally bit them. He was the one with the degree, and she wasn't allowed to forget it.

"For God's sake, he's a teenager. We must let him fail to succeed. He must learn from his mistakes."

"Don't twist this around, Carrie. We were talking about *you*. Do you not accept some liability?"

"No, I don't! He *must* learn! Let him get into trouble at school; he needs to understand the consequences!"

Matthew raised his eyebrows.

"Whoa! Don't shout at me. You really need to calm down and not get so hysterical." He turned down his tone while climbing several rungs on the ladder of superiority. "Don't bother yourself with it. I'll find time to phone his teacher tomorrow and smooth things over." Excellent, he had reached the top.

She was seething, but there was nowhere to go with this now. She wasn't going to cry. Not this time.

"Ok, well, I'll speak to Luke then," she offered.

"No, leave it to me." He got into bed and switched off the light. "Leave it *all* to me."

Gloom engulfed the room like the beginning of a nightmare.

* * *

He left without saying goodbye. This was all part of the ritual, and it would carry on for days—hours and hours of a thick, dense pressure suffocating their house. It was only punctured now and again when he had to be civil in front of the children just to keep up the illusion that everything was fine. This was her greatest fear, the effect their bickering and sniping had on her three kids.

Jen and Hannah were only five and had just started school. They were too wrapped up in this fascinating daily adventure to be the slightest bit interested in what Mummy and Daddy were doing. Even though they were not identical twins, their personalities were staggeringly similar. There was not a quieter and more reserved one; they were both loud, confident, bundles of energy in equal measures.

It was Luke who was the sensitive one. Not an ideal trait when you're a fifteen-year-old boy navigating your way through the choppy seas of puberty, trying to be the perfect big brother, son, and pupil. They had to be careful. Luke did not need any more unsettlement in his life right now.

She would put a stop to it tonight. Either by trying to talk it through or just apologising. The latter was the preferred tact most of the time—it was much easier. She cursed herself for not doing it last night because apologising every time caused little or no offence and dissolved the conflict instantly like sugar in tea. Yet it left a bitter taste in her mouth, at the very least.

She looked across the kitchen counter. Her son was mindlessly crunching his way through an overflowing bowl of cornflakes whilst the girls bounced around him like ping pong balls. They were screaming, giggling and chasing each other around, but he didn't flinch.

What was he thinking about? What *does* go on in the mind of a teenage boy?

She imagined an empty space where his brain should be with her shouting into it, hearing her own voice echo back to her through. A vast cavity of nothingness with the occasional cloud of interest drifting in; football results, a good song on the radio, a text message. She stifled a giggle when she saw how tired he looked.

"Did you not sleep too well last night, love?" She leaned towards him so she could be heard over the noise of the girls.

"Hmm?" Luke seemed to snap back into the real world. "What?"

"Are you ok?"

"Yeah." He shrugged. "Just got a test today, that's all."

"It's not a chemistry test, is it?" She narrowed her eyes, leaving the gate open for him to explain last night's homework oversight. Nothing. He just ignored her, and she dropped it. After all, Matthew was going to deal with it.

He suddenly got to his feet. "Gotta go, Mum, see ya!" He put down his half-eaten breakfast, grabbed his bag and headphones and was out of the door.

"Bye, love," she said as the door closed behind him. Luke was becoming more and more aloof. Hormones had a lot to answer for, she thought.

"Right, girls, are you ready for another action-packed day at school?"

"Yeah!" they both yelled in unison.

"Come on then, let's go!"

* * *

Traffic. It was getting worse. The roadworks didn't help or the fact that the traffic lights had failed on the dual carriageway. It was bedlam! Every man for himself, negotiating the four lanes of traffic without any lawful direction. Thank goodness he wasn't turning right. The queue was a mile long!

His phone pinged—the bank.

A familiar message illuminated the screen.

'You have gone into an unarranged overdraft and your account is now in arrears. Please phone us on…we will be happy to discuss the matter with you….'

Shit!

He thought he'd fixed this last month by jiggling the

accounts around. Had *she* gone and bought something and not told him again?

Although he was annoyed with Carrie for not having Luke under control, he couldn't be angry with her for spending money that she thought they had. Carrie was very generous. She didn't buy anything for herself. It was usually for the kids or him: a new shirt or book, thoughtful little gifts. Last month though, it had been a garden swing for the girls and the price was extortionate! Yet, it had been for their birthdays, and they loved it. It was one of those swings where they could sit opposite each other, was it called a see-saw swing? Made from hardwood and what looked like old gymnasium rope, it was not about to blow down in a hurricane. Safety was her priority, not price. That was how it should be. He could just picture them squealing with delight as he pushed them higher and higher, challenging them to touch the sky with their fingertips. She had been right about that purchase, he smiled.

Matthew had been good at hiding their problematic financial situation from her. Carrie only knew about the joint credit card, not the undisclosed ones he had been forced to take out year on year. The debt was mounting, and he was struggling to meet the minimum payments. Now even his day-to-day account was looking unhealthy. They would have to tighten their belts. It would be subtle; she wouldn't even notice. Just cancel a few direct debits on unnecessary luxuries. He had already cancelled their usual trip to France this year. He had told Carrie there had been a mix-up with the booking, and she had bought it. She hadn't asked a single question. He knew he could turn things around without arousing any hint of suspicion; it wasn't that difficult.

The traffic ahead came to a halt. Maybe Carrie could get a job? She was clearly bored at home. Even with family life, a dog, and the house to run, she couldn't settle, and she still craved more. He couldn't understand it. No job, no worries, no pressure! What he wouldn't give for that! Maybe it was empty-nest syndrome now the girls were at school every day.

She had been an excellent senior staff nurse and was loved by everyone she looked after. Nurse Carrie was a saint. But then came Luke, a happy accident after their honeymoon. Having a baby of her own to care for changed everything. Carrie gave up her career to concentrate on her little family, and he couldn't have been prouder of her. Despite the pleas from the hospital for her to come back, even offering her part-time work, she refused. She felt she couldn't have a foot in the door of two places. She had committed to raising her family and that was what she would do. Maybe part-time work would be good for her now, though? She could re-train. She had only been out of nursing for fifteen years, do things really change that much? Without the kids at home, he wondered what she did all day.

He pondered on this. However, he liked having her at home, and it was comforting to know where she was.

His phone rang, it was Johanna.

"Where are you? We've got this presentation to do in half an hour." She was whispering. There was no need to alert the rest of the open plan office.

He was grateful to Johanna for that. He could do without any tittle-tattle from the gossips today. She was a godsend to him. His right-hand woman, whom he turned to when he needed a second opinion or was having a crisis of confidence as her judgement was always bang on. He could trust her with any job delegated her way, and if he were being honest, he sent her tasks more often than maybe he should, as she would probably have done a better job anyway. Considering this, he asked himself how he was the accounts director, and she was the team leader, not vice versa. He really admired her, not just as a colleague but as a good friend too. She had this incredible ability to cast no shadow and turn every daunting challenge into an exciting opportunity.

"Traffic, sorry," he said after a short pause, momentarily distracted by a zebra crossing. "ETA ten minutes."

"Ok. I'll finish putting the last few slides together. Are you happy with the content? Did you get a chance to look over them last night?"

He took a deep breath; he knew he could tell her. She understood.

"Carrie and I had another fight last night; I didn't get a chance. Sorry, Jo. It all just...*consumed* me."

"Oh, are you ok?"

"Yes, it was over one of the kids. It'll blow over. They're just becoming a bit more frequent, you know?"

"Ok, well, don't worry about the presentation. I'll sort it. Just come straight over to my desk when you get in so I can brief you on the updates. Hopefully, we'll be having a celebratory coffee in a few hours. We can talk then…if you want to."

And just like that, she made it all better. A huge weight slid from his shoulders. She was a ray of sunlight and a breath of fresh air.

"Thank you so much, Johanna. I owe you."

"I know. You always do."

He smiled to himself as he hung up the call.

* * *

September was creeping into October. The sunshine was still strong enough to cast a warm glow through the trees. Acorns were cracking underfoot, and squirrels busily prepared their drays for the impending winter. The storm last night had left its mark. Branches littered the ground, and puddles obscured the way. It would be quite challenging to keep a steady pace as she mentally prepared herself to run.

She loved this time of year. After the craziness of the summer holidays, it was a welcome reset. She would walk the girls to school and then take the dog through the woods that would eventually lead to a dense forest of pine, oak, and birch, riddled with trails corkscrewing their way around a dramatic sandstone ridge that protruded out of the tree-line. This was her favourite time of the day, complete escapism. At the very top of the ridge was a viewing point where you could look out over the estuary. Today that view would be amazing, and she couldn't wait to take the familiar path.

Betty was a flat-coated retriever. She had a narrow, elegant head with a glossy, shaggy coat and was as black as a panther with the energy and agility to match. She certainly kept Carrie fit. It was because of the dog's excess energy that Carrie had taken up running. She wasn't particularly competitive. Time or pace didn't matter to her. She just enjoyed the thrill of the chase along twisting paths, weaving gracefully through the ragged ferns and brambles with her dog at her side.

There was a pristine brook running adjacent to the forest edge. She had to pick her way carefully amongst the undergrowth and loose cobbles that had once marked out an elaborate road. Carrie wondered if it had once been Roman, as the local countryside was riddled with historical evidence from that period. Betty darted in and out, chasing anything that moved, occasionally bounding into the brook to cool off and steal a few laps of water. Carrie could forget about the fight here. She could be reminded of how lucky she was to be surrounded by beautiful nature. It was so good for the soul. She felt completely at peace as her feet moved effortlessly along one after the other, pounding out an even rhythm across the rustic carpet of the forest floor. She smiled and felt like she could conquer the world with this positive vibe. Maybe the Romans had felt the same as they trudged along this ancient road thousands of centuries earlier.

She would talk gently to Matthew that evening and smooth things over. He must be under a lot of pressure at work. He never talked about it as he preferred to close the door on his job once he crossed the threshold of his home. He didn't bring his worries to her door, and she was thankful for the protection, but she also wanted to help. If he did have troubles, was it not her job to ease them?

He had never been one to cause a fuss or complain, not like when she was working at the hospital. She hadn't heard him mention anything to do with work for months now. She felt guilty about these carefree, happy moments she had to herself that cut through the boredom of her repetitive week. She wished that she could share them with him. It seemed almost selfish of her to enjoy them whilst he was saddled with all the worries. No wonder he got cross. She had dropped the ball again.

Over the last few years, communication had become a rare luxury in their relationship. It flirted with them now and again when they had something interesting to talk about. Otherwise, the conversations were just the usual mundane logistical chit-chat that parents exchanged daily. Can you collect Luke from football tonight? Did you see that the twins can write their own names now? When's parents' evening? And so on. She would make him talk once the kids had gone to bed. They owed it to them and their marriage. These petty fights were ridiculous and getting out of control. Salvaging scraps of pride and virtue were not as important as wiping the slate clean and moving on. She would instigate the apology, and hopefully, they'd have a happy house again.

Suddenly, she was aware that Betty was missing.

"Betty! Betty! Bets! Where are you, girl?" she called clearly and then waited a few moments before calling again. Why hadn't she brought the dog whistle? She had begun to rely on it more and more these days.

"Betty! Come on!" Nothing. Just a gentle rustle of leaves on the breeze and the soothing trickle of the brook filled the air.

Betty often did this, vanishing for what felt like an eternity, reappearing as if nothing had happened. She must have caught the scent of a badger or a fox. Carrie wasn't particularly worried; she would be safe enough as there were no roads nearby. It was just a bit annoying. She decided to sit down on a mossy log to wait and enjoy the warmth of the autumn sun. She closed her eyes and turned her face into the comforting rays, wrapping their arms around her like a bear hug—total bliss. Images of sun-drenched shores and an aquamarine sea twinkled in her mind, replacing the acidic recollection of the previous night. The holiday they were supposed to have gone on in August teased her thoughts.

A few twigs snapped to her left, and she was plucked from her daydream like a fish from a stream. The great black dog leapt out of the thicket, covered in a foul-smelling substance.

"Oh Betty, you really stink!" Carrie crinkled up her nose and got to her feet quickly so as not to have the stench smeared all over her. "You need a bath, girl! We'll have to go up the hill another day. I've got to get this off your coat before it becomes too dried on."

Betty was already trotting off in the direction of home. It seemed she'd had enough of playing chase today and couldn't wait to parade her putrid filth through the village where they lived like a badge of honour. Gross! Carrie chuckled, picking up the pace to follow her canine friend back to civilisation.

CHAPTER 2

The reflection in the mirror was not improving. A puffy face with bulbous eyes. Carrie looked just like one of those ridiculous goldfish that people had as pets. She often wondered why they bothered because they were hideously ugly. That was how she felt right now, hideously ugly. Inside and out.

However, it didn't matter. Carrie didn't have to go anywhere or see anyone if she didn't want to. Today was like all the rest—one day after another of monotonous tasks and menial housework.

She washed her face and brushed her teeth. The kids were eating breakfast downstairs while Matthew had already left. In the space of a few days, they had reached rock bottom, and there didn't seem to be a way out. She had only asked if he wanted to meet for lunch one day and became a little defensive when he had said no. She just thought it would have been good to talk and make some plans.

They always used to meet for lunch, about once a month. They didn't go anywhere fancy. Once, they even went for a quick bite in McDonald's as Matthew hadn't much time, but at least he found a little bit from somewhere for her. Sometimes she would take the train and come back with him in the afternoon in time to pick up Luke from nursery.

Wow! That was eleven years ago. They seemed to have daydreamed through Luke's childhood, and then they had the twins. They were a secure family unit now, but it had come at a price. The sacrifice of being a happy couple? She knew this was common, especially after so long together; nevertheless, there should be room within the anarchy of family life for some adult time without feeling guilty. She strongly felt that children shouldn't crowd a marriage; they should enhance it.

Carrie put her toothbrush back in the pot and resisted the urge to look in the mirror. She didn't need to feel any worse than she already did. She collected her glasses from the bedside table and headed downstairs. At least those hideous bulbous eyes would not look so shocking from behind her lenses.

The noise coming from the kitchen was unbearable. The two girls were screaming at each other over who should eat the last of the cereal. Betty was joining in barking at them, thinking that this little human game was great fun and how clever she was to make as much noise as they were. This included leaping on her water bowl and paddling the contents all over the kitchen tiles.

Amongst all the chaos, Luke sat scrawling through his phone. He was picking at a bunch of red grapes, completely oblivious to the pandemonium engulfing the room. He looked grey and unwell. She was glad he was getting some fruit into him as he could do with an injection of vitamin C.

Carefully avoiding the puddle on the floor, she leaned over the counter and grabbed the cereal box from Hannah's hand. The noise immediately stopped.

"Really, girls, it's too early for all this shouting. You're exciting Betty and look at the mess."

The girls dropped their heads. "Sorry, Mummy," they said in unison.

"Now go upstairs and brush each other's hair to show me what big sisters you are and how you both are sorry for shouting. I'll fix you some cereal when you come back down. No big deal." She gestured towards the door.

The girls walked up the stairs solemnly, followed by the dog. Even Betty had lowered her head. Carrie turned her attention to the wet floor and to her son.

"I'm surprised you could hear yourself think over that racket! You ok, love?" she asked.

"Uh hum," he said, not looking up.

She retrieved the mop and bucket from the utility room and filled it with hot soapy water. She would have to put Betty outside until they left so as not to repeat the same mad paddling situation all over again when the dog came back downstairs.

"I heard you last night, you know." Luke looked at his mum. Piercing eyes, staring hard at her trying to read her thoughts. "You kept me awake."

Carrie's heart sank. No wonder he looked so tired. They had been arguing until two in the morning when she finally gave in, defeated. Pangs of guilt delved deep and swirled around the depths of her stomach. She didn't want this.

"We weren't arguing, buddy. Just discussing a few matters about the holiday. You know, with the mix-up this year." She busied herself with the mess on the kitchen floor.

He ignored her response. "It makes me sad when I hear you. Are you going to split up?"

Carrie let out a snort of nervous laughter. "No," she replied. "Sometimes parents need to talk seriously, and when emotions are involved, it can become a shouting match. We don't always see eye-to-eye, but we work it out. We stick together for you guys."

As soon as the words had left her mouth, she regretted them. The transparency of her remark revealed the fragility of her marriage. This was something that she didn't want her fifteen-year-old son to know. He searched her face, willing her to say more and tell him it was going to be ok.

Eventually, he said, "I want you to stick together for *you*! Not for me!"

His words ruptured her feeble defence.

She opened her mouth to force some sort of reply, but

the moment was broken by the sound of the dog thundering down the stairs, followed by two giggling five-year-olds. She was quite relieved. What would she have said? There were only so many times that you could reuse a sticking plaster. Obviously, he could see what was really going on. The bickering had to stop, and as Matthew was too stubborn to apologise and speak up, it would be up to her. For the sake of the children, she had to do it. She couldn't let her marriage slip through her fingertips. She had to regain some sort of authority, even if that was staying silent and putting up with the outbursts.

The girls ran into the hallway to put on their coats and shoes, forgetting about the cereal their mother was supposed to prepare.

"Listen," she started reassuringly. "Relationships ebb and flow. It's not always rosy in the garden like these TV shows would have you believe. I love your dad, and he loves me, and we both love you kids. There's nothing to worry about, ok?"

Getting up from the kitchen counter, he seemed to accept this. "Mum, I just want *everyone* to be happy." He sighed.

Her marriage might be in turmoil, but one thing that Carrie was certain of was the love she had for her brave boy, who was maturing into a fine young man right before her eyes. He was wrestling with the role of son and peacekeeper. The latter was a self-appointed job he didn't deserve and shouldn't feel the need to do. She was so proud of him but at the same time sorry that her actions had made him feel this way.

He grabbed his school bag. "Anyway, better get going, or I'll miss the bus."

"Have you had enough breakfast?"

"Yes, Mum, bye! See ya, sisters!" He high-fived the girls as he passed them in the hall and then was gone—the breezy life of a teenager. She hoped that she had reassured him enough and that he could shrug off the diplomatic shackles he'd placed on his adolescent shoulders.

* * *

After taking the girls to school, Carrie started on her usual run into the woods with Betty. She had decided to take a longer route today and conquer that hill. She also needed valuable thinking time to review the events of the night before.

He had behaved inexcusably. It had taken every ounce of strength to be positive in front of her children this morning when all she wanted to do was hide away from the world and be forgotten about. His cruel words had carved themselves into her subconscious and were gnawing away at what self-esteem she had left.

"Look at you now! You're hysterical! You're a mess!"

"Why does it always have to come to this? You push and push and push until finally, I snap and push back. Is that really what you want?"

"I'm working late, and all the hours' God sends for you all. I'm a proud man who wants to provide the best for his family. Why don't you understand that?"

"It's all right for you with your carefree lifestyle. You don't have to worry about anything important, do you?"

"I'm the one with all the stress. You know how busy I am at work. Money doesn't grow on trees, you know! One of us has to pay for all of this." And then the crescendo. *"I really don't know why you wind yourself up so much about nothing. Your life is so easy, don't you agree? Do you have anything to say for yourself?"*

A pathetic 'Sorry' had been the response from the timid figure crouching in the doorway of their bathroom as Matthew paced the bedroom like a captive beast. At first, she had been cross. All she had wanted was to spend a little time with him. She had stood her ground, determined that they would make time for each other and sort this out, but how come she was now slumped on the bathroom floor, choked up with tears and utterly exhausted from an argument about apparently nothing? Confusion fogged up her mind. His twisted response had altered the content of the original altercation from being about them to being about *her*. She was the selfish one. How dare she?

Once the apology had slipped out, he seemed to relax.

"Can we go to bed now, then? You know I have that important meeting in the morning." She didn't. "I've got to get my head straight for tomorrow."

She heard him pull back the covers and get into bed. He switched off his bedside light, plunging the room into darkness. She had waited a few moments, contemplating the spare bed, as the last thing she wanted was to be near this man who was happy to leave her in a dishevelled state, quietly sobbing away. She thought of the children; she couldn't excuse another night in the spare room.

Out in the forest, the flashback stabbed at her, and her breathing suddenly became difficult. She couldn't maintain an easy rhythm. Memories of last night swirled around and around, and she couldn't focus. She tripped on an exposed tree root; her heart was dragging her down. She felt so desperately sad and hopeless. Her legs became heavy, and every step was a challenge. Somehow, she pushed on as she wanted to channel this negative emotion to keep going. Tears streamed down and burnt her cheeks in the chill of the crisp morning, but the hill was in her sights. She was going to achieve something today, and she could own this moment right now. He wasn't here; he couldn't get in, and she could run away from it all.

As determination replaced desolation, she felt herself coming out of the mist. Nearly there. Even Betty seemed to be willing her on as she ran at her side, temporarily forgetting the rabbits darting in all directions, clearing their path.

She reached the summit, breathing hard. What a sight! It had been worth it.

The river snaked away towards the sea, peppered by white gulls snatching at the surface to steal an unsuspecting fish. The pattern of trees became irregular along the bank, eventually giving way to brush, samphire and scurvy grass as it reached the riverhead, then the vastness of the open sea. She could just make out an oil tanker on the horizon, and the low October sun shimmered across the water.

Her heart rate slowed to a regular tempo as she took in the view. She had done it, and she had not stopped. She had conquered the nemesis of the hill, and so, it would seem, her emotions, for now.

After a few moments, she turned to look behind her beyond the forest and the wood, past the station and the girls' school, in the direction of her street, her house, her little corner of the world, her sanctuary. So how come this rugged, untamed expanse of water to her left felt more like home to her right now?

Betty jumped up and barked at her impatiently. Carrie was suddenly aware of the cold, and she shivered. "Come on, little lady, let's go back."

* * *

The office was stifling hot. Beads of sweat were forming on his forehead, and through his suit jacket, he could feel his shirt clinging to his back. He took a sip of water, but it did nothing to soothe his dry mouth. Matthew glanced at his watch, five to nine. Nearly time.

He reminded himself that he wasn't nervous; he was ready. This would change his and their lives forever. The promotion was in his grasp, he just had to nail it today, and it would all be ok. That grip of pressure would loosen around his neck a little, maybe a lot. Then he could concentrate on his family. They all needed a break.

On reflection, maybe Carrie had been right. The kids deserved some time with him just as much as she did. He had been very neglectful of the family's needs recently. Once he had got this boost, things could change. Hopefully, it would filter down from the kids to his marriage, and he would be riding high on success once again. He needed her patience, and he needed her trust in him.

He walked over to the window and looked down at the busy street below. Everyday people going about their everyday lives. A woman chatting on her mobile phone whilst attempting a run-hobble in sky-high shoes to flag down a taxi. An older gentleman in a suit, weaving his bike in and out of the traffic, not even stopping for red lights or crossings. A group of teens, a little older than Luke, smoking as they dawdled casually along the high street late for school. All with a purpose, all with somewhere to be. All with responsibilities in their own little way. Matthew sympathised with the woman and the older gentleman, but he felt envious of the teens. Meandering along, free of urgency and accountability. What he wouldn't give to be that age again.

His thoughts turned back to Carrie. He had been hard on her last night. Just like the people below the office window against whom he shouldn't judge his own life, he couldn't do it to her either. Let's face it, he couldn't do this job without her sacrificing her own career to keep the day-to-day routine ticking along smoothly. This was not the first time he had been up for a promotion. Last year he had met the board to discuss a possible new role but had not quite cut it in their eyes. He had been devastated, not just for being unsuccessful but for letting down his family. Carrie had been unwavering in her support. She stayed up with him until the small hours listening to him droning on about what he would do differently if he had his chance again. She had encouraged him to respond to their critical feedback, ready to build a case to challenge them if the opportunity for promotion ever came around again. Here it was, today. Fifteen months of him (and Johanna, to be fair) working late nights, even Saturday mornings, to win back the prospect of a better future for them. Maybe he should tell Carrie about the debt. That way, she might understand the strain he was under. No, if all went to plan today, he wouldn't need to.

The office door opened abruptly, and the board members filed in. There were only three of them. Charlie Harvey, the managing director and chairperson, was a plump stocky man with a jolly round face. He liked Portugal, red wine, and golf. Matthew hoped he would have a lifestyle like Mr Harvey's in a few years. The office staff only saw him four days a week. It was rumoured amongst the secretaries that he would scribe in his diary an all-day meeting off-site, but, in reality, he would be on a golf course somewhere. Nice work if you can get it.

The other board members were the opposite of Charlie Harvey. Clarissa Stanton-Peake was in her early fifties. Tall, slim, with a haughty expression. She always talked in a loud voice and was bursting with her own self-importance. Head of sales and new business, she was staunchly dedicated to her job, the first in the office and the last to leave. Matthew had only found out a few years ago, despite working at the company for sixteen years, that there was a Mr Stanton-Peake, and according to Johanna, he was a thoroughly nice bloke. Each to their own, he thought.

Finally, Monsieur Jean-Paul Baudelaire. A thin, balding Frenchman who couldn't look you in the eye when he talked to you. Instead, he chose a spot on the wall behind you or the ceiling to direct his attention. Matthew thought it must have been a habit Baudelaire had acquired through nerves. After all, he had worked closely with Stanton-Peake for nearly a quarter of a century, so he deserved a medal. He was a typical company secretary with meticulous attention to detail and devoid of a sense of humour. Although interestingly, he had six children.

They took their seats.

"Good morning, Matthew." Harvey smiled warmly from the head of the table. "Here begins your interview for Financial Director. Please sit and when you are ready, begin."

CHAPTER 3

Waiting for the girls at the school gates, Carrie noticed a new face amongst the usual crowd. A tall, handsome stranger with a child's flowery coat tucked under one arm leaned casually against the wall. He must be new to the area, she thought. She hadn't seen him before. They had lived in this small village for twenty years, and in that time, she had pretty much seen everybody. Little Browton was the kind of place you only left reluctantly because it was so close to the spectacular coastline and had excellent transport links to two major cities in the region.

All at once, the air was filled with screaming children, happy to be released from the confinement of the classrooms to enjoy the weekend. Weary teachers stood waving them off as they acknowledged the parents one by one. The twins had not come out yet, so Carrie was able to observe this stranger a little more closely. He had a daughter about the same age as the twins. She was beautiful, with tight curls springing out from under her red beanie hat. She watched as her father scooped her up in his arms and nuzzled his face into her cheeks as she squealed in delight. *How wonderful that Daddy could be there to pick you up, little girl,* she thought.

"Mrs Pritchard! Mrs Pritchard! Please may I have a word?" It was Mr Turner, the girls' teacher. He didn't look happy, and the girls were not with him. This wasn't going to be good. "Do you have five minutes to come inside, please?" he enquired. She nodded and followed him back into the building.

Hannah and Jen were sitting at a desk with whom Carrie assumed was an assistant sitting across from them.

"Thank you, Miss Fuller. I'll take it from here," Mr Turner said. Miss Fuller got up to welcome them into the classroom, then promptly left.

The girls looked very glum. Hannah was staring at the floor and swinging her legs backwards and forwards from her chair. Jen had hidden her face in her folded arms which were outstretched on the desk. Carrie took a seat in between the pair.

"Mrs Pritchard, I'm so sorry to have to bring you in like this and on a Friday as well," he began. "The thing is, the girls have had a fight today, and it's not like them, as I'm sure you'll agree."

"A fight? Who with?"

"Each other."

Shocked, Carrie looked from Jen to Hannah and back again. Not a flicker of concern or acknowledgement for the crime they were being accused of, just nonchalant scowls. She looked at Mr Turner, and he continued.

"We had a new girl start today, Delilah. Delightful little thing who was eager to make new friends. Hannah and Jennifer were very welcoming at first, but as the day progressed, they decided they didn't want to share their new friend with each other." He looked from one twin to the other, trying to detect a hint of an apology. They both continued to disengage. Hannah moved her gaze from the floor to the window, no doubt wishing she could be outside, anywhere but here. Carrie sympathised.

"So, Mrs Pritchard, we need to make it very clear that fighting is not something that boys and girls do at Little Browton Primary. Although nobody got hurt, it could have been quite different." He narrowed his eyes to deliver the final blow. "So, I am hoping that I will have your full cooperation in their sanction?"

"Yes, of course, Mr Turner." She thought it would be a missed playtime or even just a verbal apology.

"I'd like the girls to write a letter of apology to each other. They need to say how *very* sorry they are and how it won't happen again."

Carrie scoffed. Was he joking? How could two five-year-old girls write all that in a sentence, let alone in a letter? Frowning, she turned to ask Mr Turner, who was practically patting himself on the back about what he thought was a fantastic idea.

Finally, she said, "But they're five, Mr Turner. How can they possibly do that?"

Sensing the brewing confrontation and the fact that their mother might be about to defend them, Hannah and Jen pricked up their ears and sat up straight like two obedient puppies. They stared hard at Mr Turner, who was still basking in his own brilliance. He was a newly qualified teacher, so this must have been his first teacher-parent issue, and he wanted the upper hand.

"Well, now, that's the best bit. I thought they could tell you what to write, and then you could write it down for them. They can just write their names at the bottom." He smiled. "Won't take long."

She glared back at him. *I could really do without this,* she thought. In her head, she was screaming at him. *So why didn't you do it with them in the first place?* But she couldn't find the words to ask him politely, so she just nodded in agreement.

As the punishment was now out of the bag and no longer his responsibility, Mr Turner got to his feet.

"Could we have the letters in on Monday, please, so we can nip this little matter in the bud? It's important that we move on from this incident as quickly as possible. So sorry to rush you, but I'm late for a staff meeting."

He bundled them out of the door. A staff meeting on a Friday? *Yeah, right,* she thought, and so much for a sanction. Carrie felt like she was the one being punished. The twins wouldn't even put pen to paper to draw a picture! She had only just got them both to write their names legibly before they had started in reception class. The worst thing was, they thought the letter was a fabulous idea. Jen even asked if they could put them in an envelope with a stamp and post them back to school. They started on their journey home.

"Can we have an ice cream?" Jen asked as they passed the corner shop.

"No!" Carrie responded firmly.

"But we were only fighting for some of the day, and Mr Turner did say that everyone deserves a second chance…," she protested.

"What? When did he say that?" Carrie asked.

"In assembly."

"So, before the fighting?"

"Erm…yeah…so…."

Carrie rolled her eyes. What was the point? It had been totally and utterly missed.

* * *

"Congratulations," Johanna quietly said as she rolled her chair over to his desk. "Very well deserved, I'd say."

"Thank you, but I couldn't have done it without you. Cheers." He held out his coffee mug, and she obliged with a firm 'clink.' Their eyes met briefly; then, she looked away.

"Have you told Carrie yet?"

"No."

"Oh. Are things still a little frosty?"

"Yep."

She waited then for more information. None came, so she probed further.

"Well, this will surely be something to celebrate, won't it? I mean, she knows how hard you have worked to get to this position. You need to tell her."

"Maybe, but not yet." He shut his laptop and turned to look at Johanna. She was very pretty. A little older than him, possibly forty-three or four. She always looked immaculate, with her long blonde hair neatly curled up into a bun, rich brown eyes framed by thick eyelashes and a full-peachy mouth. He had always fancied her, just a little. How could he not? He was convinced that she knew. That was why the flirting came so easy to them both. He really enjoyed her company. "Fancy a quick drink?"

"Thanks, but I can't tonight, Matt. I have plans," she said. He hid his disappointment by grabbing his jacket from the back of his chair. "How about next week?" she offered.

"It's a date." He winked at her.

"Now, now, the office will talk." She teased, breaking into one of her award-winning smiles. "Go home." He laughed then. A strange sensation that he hadn't felt in a while. He felt relaxed; he felt happy.

She was right. He knew why she had turned down his offer. He should be sharing this moment with his wife, not his colleague. Johanna's sharp intuition had pushed him in the right direction. He had to seize the moment to try and make things right. He could do that. He had just been appointed Financial Director, and things were looking up. No more money problems for the Pritchards'! He felt the oppressive, frozen ceiling of his monetary constraints was finally beginning to thaw.

He would grab a bottle of wine on the way home as a peace offering. Then he'd surprise Carrie with the good news. He would sort out the bank and then might even re-book their holiday over the weekend to show he was serious about making up. They could put the kids to bed and have their favourite cheese and wine in front of the wood-burning stove surrounded by candles. Carrie loved candles. They'd go for a long family walk on Saturday with Betty, and then he'd cook a hearty roast dinner on Sunday. They would all reconnect. This was the answer he needed. Maybe money could buy happiness after all.

Finally, the downward spiral of despair was curving sharply upwards, and the bitter battle from the night before would be forgotten.

* * *

Betty barked sharply as the door unlocked. He must be home. Carrie took a sharp intake of breath. From previous experience, she was unclear as to which version of her husband was about to come through the front door. Sometimes it would be a sheepish, semi-apologetic edition who would slip in quietly, releasing the elephant from the room with a few soothing words. But often, he'd still be fiercely holding on to his grudge like a king defending his castle. He wouldn't make eye contact when he entered, and she would simply be ignored for a few days when even he had become fed up with his grumpiness.

"Hello, girl! How are you? Have you had a good day? Have you? What a good dog you are! What a good dog!"

She slowly exhaled; he would not play the floundering king tonight. By the sound of his exchange with the dog, he had calmed down from their argument last night, and he sounded happy. Maybe the prospect of the weekend was cheering him up, or the meeting had gone well after all.

Matthew walked into the kitchen and put his keys and the wine down on the sideboard.

"Hello," he said, making his way over to her. He kissed her gently on the cheek. "I'm really sorry about last night. I was quite worried about today. It was all I could think about, and I overreacted."

"It's ok. I'm sorry too. I should have known something was on your mind and not pushed you so far." She smiled weakly, catching his eye, which softened his expression and gave her strength.

"I bought some Rioja on the way home. And I've got good news. Where are the kids? I want to tell you all together." He wandered off, calling their names as she retrieved two red wine glasses from the cupboard. She felt a little apprehensive. It did seem a little too good to be true that the malevolent arguments of the previous week had been dispersed with a few words of justification and some good news. Perhaps it was more of a sedation than a dispersal. Perhaps, this was the calm before the storm.

Once they were all seated in the comfort of their living room, he told them how he had been appointed Finance Director or FD for the girls to remember.

"Well done, love."

"Nice one, Dad. Will you be making a lot more money now?" quizzed Luke.

"Will you have your own office?" asked Jen.

"What does an FD do, Daddy?" Hannah pondered as she played with her hair.

"Can you buy me that new Lego model of the hospital, *please*?" Jen begged.

"Will you take us to France in the summer holidays again?" asked Luke.

It was interesting to hear the various tangents on which the questions were shooting off. Each one expressed what relevance his promotion meant to them as individuals and how it might affect their own agendas. He didn't mind. He knew they meant no harm.

Only Carrie, after her initial shaky words of praise, was silent. She looked vacant and hollow. She was smiling, but the smile was thin, veiling something he couldn't access. He had lost her to her thoughts. He hoped she was contemplating happier days to come just as he was, but something told him she was still hurting from his unkindness. Not for the first time, he felt her slipping away, and he couldn't do anything to stop it. Couldn't she just be happy for him or at least happy for them both?

He broke the spell. "Crikey, girls, it's nearly eight. It's way past bedtime!" Gathering the little ladies in his arms, he started to bundle them upstairs.

"Just a minute. Before you take them up, we've got some news too," Carrie announced. The girls slipped from their father's grasp and attempted to disappear upstairs to safety. "Not so fast. Sit down, girls," she said firmly.

Hannah and Jen reluctantly returned to their seats on the sofa. One pulled a cushion over her little body to form a defensive barrier from her mother's imminent attack. The other, crossing her arms and legs, sulking angrily.

He turned to face his wife. A stern look had replaced the smile. What on earth was she about to say? Was she trying to steal his moment? Endless nights of poring over figures and manipulating spreadsheets, missed dinners and bedtimes, and schmoozing disingenuous clients until the small hours when all he wanted to do was curl up in his warm bed and get a good night's sleep. He'd been slaving away for months on end, and here she was about to stick a pin in it.

Sensing that he might also be subjected to a telling-off along with the girls, Luke retreated upstairs. Matthew released the tension that had filtered through his body and temporarily replaced it with a stab of guilt. How could he have thought to accuse his wife of suppressing his triumph? He was trying to make amends tonight, not start another onslaught. She certainly had something on her mind. What had the girls done this time? Last week they had painted the downstairs toilet in some old silver modelling paint they had found in the garage. They had done quite a decent job of what he understood to be daisy chains and horse people. It had taken Carrie three coats of Pebble Mist to get rid of their masterpiece.

"Mr Turner called me in after school today. Apparently, the girls had a fight over a new girl who has just started," she said.

"A fight?" Matthew interjected.

"Yes, he didn't go into specifics, but he made it clear that that sort of behaviour doesn't go at school. Especially when the two fighters are sisters." Carrie frowned at the two girls.

"She started it!" piped up Jen.

"She pulled my hair really hard!" Hannah replied, uncrossing her legs and flicking one straight out in the direction of her sister. Sensing that their little war was about to reignite, Jen swiped back at her with the cushion.

"Enough girls!" Carrie shouted.

Matthew was astonished. What a twist of events this turned out to be. His two little darlings attacking each other like alley cats had taken his moment away, after all. He switched his gaze from one daughter to the other, trying to catch their eye so they could suffer the disappointment in his eyes. He knew they were feisty and would bicker like an old married couple, but they had never fought.

Finally, when he got little response from their bowed heads, he said, "My two little girls in a fight? What a shame. I was going to take you to the cinema to see that new Doodle Girls film, but I can't do that, now can I?" They both remained silent. "OK, Mummy, how are we going to put this right? Maybe we can have a little talk tonight about how the girls will make it up to us for this unacceptable behaviour." He was beginning to list suitable chores in his head. Tidying out the wardrobe that they tended to throw all their dirty knickers and socks into (according to Carrie anyway), feeding the dog for a week (but could they be trusted with a tin opener?) or sweeping the leaves from the driveway (something he had already put on his own weekend job list).

Instantly, the girls brightened up. It was as if Matthew had flicked a switch, and their limp bodies began filling with air like helium balloons ready for a party.

"We get to write a letter, Daddy!" Hannah shrieked.

"A sorry letter. *I* have to write to Hannah, and she has to write one to me!" Jen chipped in, clapping her hands together in anticipation.

"Then we can post it with a stamp!" Hannah concluded. Carrie rolled her eyes, but Matthew missed it.

"What? But you're five." Feeling confused, he ran his hand through his hair. "Was this your idea?" He swung his words accusingly at Carrie.

"God no, I think it's ridiculous. Especially as it falls on us to write it. They are just supposed to put their names at the bottom!" she replied. "How about you do one letter with Jen, and I'll do the other with Hannah? That way, they won't know what the other has written, and it will be more heartfelt."

Matthew couldn't be bothered. Since he'd arrived home, he'd realised how exhausted he had been this last week and just wanted to fill his weekend with watching the football and maybe tidying the garden. The prospect of a family walk was even a little too energetic now. He could get away with watching telly with his laptop on his knee, pretending to do some work. Why did these stupid things have to eat into your weekend? He had earned a weekend off, surely. His earlier plans evaporated just like his good mood.

"Well, you'll have to do it with them. I want to get my head around my new role this weekend. I have to be ready on Monday morning." He swiftly moved to sit between the girls, who were now bouncing on the sofa, giddy with excitement. He had opted out of parenting this weekend as he switched on the TV.

Carrie shrugged. "Come on, girls. Let's get you two off to bed."

* * *

Later that night, as Matthew switched off the lights downstairs before heading to bed, he remembered the wine still unopened on the sideboard while the cheese was still in the fridge. The walk would be replaced by a stupid letter-writing exercise that would take hours. The roast dinner was still a distant possibility.

The girls had taken an age to get to bed, and Carrie had gone up not long after, complaining of a headache. Luke hadn't come out of his room since Matthew had gotten home. At least he had got to watch that new action movie without any interruptions. It seemed in this game of having a successful marriage, they struggled to get beyond square one.

CHAPTER 4

He was there again, standing at the school gates with his back to Carrie, waving his daughter off.

Hannah and Jen squealed with delight when they saw Delilah and went tearing into the playground after her, waving their apology letters around like flags greeting the queen—little buggers. She could only hope that this was not the start of round two.

It had taken at least two hours to write those blasted letters. Getting blood out of a stone didn't even come close. Jen wanted to draw pictures of dragons while Hannah wouldn't lift her head off the table for thirty minutes. Carrie wrote the letters herself. She even signed Hannah's because she was rapidly losing faith and her weekend. Matthew, on the other hand, had a lie-in, a bike ride and then disappeared to the driving range with Luke.

"I'll take the boy out for you," he'd said. *What a relief because he's such a trouble,* she thought sarcastically. She didn't let her resentment fester; anyway, the job was done and dusted, thank goodness.

Betty was making signs that she needed the toilet. Oh no, she couldn't go on the street outside the school! Carrie wasn't even sure she had a poo bag. She had to get her to the grass on the other side of the road as soon as possible.

"Hi. You must be the twins' mum?"

Carrie found herself looking into two smouldering eyes filling up in front of her like pools of chocolate. She took in his features: close-cut black hair, high cheek bones, boxer's nose, and a smile as wide as the river. He was about six foot two and dressed casually but immaculately, layered up in lamb's wool, chinos and topped off with a Barbour jacket. Carrie could have happily stared at this perfection all day long.

"Oh, hi. Yes, that's me. Carrie. Nice to meet you."

Betty was looking desperate now.

"I thought so. Dee hasn't stopped going on about them all weekend. They've really welcomed her into the school."

Hmmm, haven't they just! she thought.

"I'm Terry, and who's this?" he asked, crouching down to stroke Betty. Unfortunately, Betty had chosen that moment to excrete. "Oh wow!" he said, backing away.

"Gosh, I'm so sorry," she said, rummaging around in her pockets for a bag. She was standing in front of this god of a man while her dog was practically shitting on his shoes. Parents were giving her dirty looks and tutting. This was not the first time she had been caught short without a bag.

Her face turned crimson. Sensing her predicament, Terry reached into his jacket and gave her a bag.

"Here, we used to have a King Charles spaniel. He died last year, but weirdly, I seem to keep finding these bags in every pocket of every coat." He laughed. "Now we can say hello properly." He resumed fussing over Betty.

"Thanks so much." She efficiently cleaned up the mess and popped it into the bin nearby. "Have you just moved to the area?"

"Yes, from Leeds. My wife got a promotion, so we had to up sticks again. She's the breadwinner." He laughed. "She's a solicitor in the city. Works long hours, and I'm daddy day care, but I love it! Wouldn't have it any other way."

Carrie mused at the role reversal in this relationship and admired how comfortable Terry seemed to be with the unconventional shift. It was refreshing.

"That's great. It's lovely to be there for them when they need us the most, isn't it?" she replied.

"For sure! I do work part-time at a bank, but it's *very* part-time, and I only manage a few accounts. I take it you don't work then?"

"No, I was a staff nurse before I had my kids. I loved it, but sometimes life comes along and changes everything." She sighed.

"You sound a bit sad about that. Would you ever go back to nursing?" he asked.

"Oh yes, but not until the girls have left school. I also have a fifteen-year-old boy who needs keeping on the straight and narrow, so I've got my work cut out!"

"No way! You're not old enough to have a fifteen-year-old! What are you? Thirty-two?"

She choked on her own laughter. "No! Thirty-eight. You?"

His eyes danced, the chocolate swirling before her own, drew her in. "Guess," he teased.

Although he was extremely handsome and in excellent shape, flecks of silver in his beard and hairline gave his age away. She decided to play safe so as not to offend him. "Same as me?"

His smile widened. The river was opening, and she could feel herself on the bank, teetering on the edge, waiting for it to swallow her whole.

"Forty-three but thank you for the compliment. So, what will you be doing with your day today then, Miss Carrie?"

Betty was getting impatient. She was bored of her new friend now that his attention had turned to her owner. She chewed on her lead. Carrie pulled it away.

"Get this one out." She looked down at Betty. "And then back home to do the usual housework, maybe a bit of gardening. We are drowning in leaves."

Just then, a shrill ring sliced through their conversation. Terry's mobile interrupted her.

He groaned as he checked his smartwatch. "I'm so sorry, Carrie, I have to take this. See you soon." He flashed her one last smile and disappeared across the road as quickly as he had arrived.

Carrie looked down at Betty and exhaled slowly. "Well, little one, that certainly cheered up my morning." Betty shook her head and started to chew her lead again. "Come on. We better get away before you decide to redecorate the pavement again."

* * *

Matthew was seated in the reception, waiting for his account handler. He had made the appointment as early as possible and parked his car near the flats at the back of the bank, despite there being ample parking on the high street. He didn't want Carrie to see his car as she would pass this way after walking the girls to school. He wanted to be in and out to confirm his new salary and perhaps negotiate a new overdraft limit to begin diminishing the debt.

The branch was dimly lit for the dark morning— gloomy, dank, and depressing. Matthew wondered why they couldn't make more effort. Banks delivered both good and bad news every day. Why make the environment reflect the negative? He tucked his feet under the cheap, plastic chair and folded his arms. Glancing at the digital clock on the wall, he could see it was nearly nine-thirty. He wanted this done. He had stuff to do.

Reflecting on the weekend, he smiled; it had been good. Although Friday had fallen a little flat, Saturday had been spent with Luke watching United and then a bit of golf. Matthew had seen a few of the lads at the range and had stopped off on the way home for a few beers and a catch-up. He hadn't seen any of them for so long due to his work commitments. Luke had met his friend Lawrence in the pub with his dad, so they escaped outside to kick a football around in the car park before it got too dark.

They got home around 7 p.m. Carrie was not impressed. She tried her best to hide it, but he knew her too well. He bathed the girls and put them to bed to make up for it. He and Luke ate their heated-up dinner, and then he fell asleep in front of the TV.

Sunday was spent on the rugby pitch. Luke had a tournament, so it was an all-day affair. The girls had the time of their lives with the other siblings, running in and out of the trees that lined the pitches. Falling into the mountains of patchy-bronzed leaves that had cascaded down from the sweeping boughs above was great fun, apparently! The tournament was a local event, so there were plenty of familiar faces to chat to. He had even taken a bit of a ribbing from the coach, who claimed he couldn't remember who Matthew was, as he hadn't seen him for so long. Matthew took the hint. Changes were afoot, and family time was on the table again.

He had let Carrie have a lie in. She rarely got the opportunity being up so early with the girls every day. She had, after all, done the letters with them, which must have been awful. She looked tired and worn out. He brought her a cup of tea in bed, and she had beamed back at him. Although she had bed hair and a makeup-free face, she made his heart turn over with that smile. It had set him up for a good day and, hopefully, the week ahead. Perhaps things would be better from now on.

"Mr Pritchard?" the bank clerk called. "Please come this way."

He followed the young girl down another poorly lit corridor to the rear of the branch. Although a little nervous, he was confident that he could convince Graham, the handler, that his current credit rating was in the past, and he was going to erase the outstanding debt. Matthew could be very persuasive when he wanted to be. The girl led him into a small office and gestured for him to sit on another cheap, plastic chair. She then took the seat opposite him.

"Hello, Mr Pritchard, Frankie Reeve. I will be handling your account from now on."

Matthew sighed. Great. This girl looked about two years older than Luke. What did she know about account management and debt? What had happened to Graham? He had been brilliant, extending overdrafts and loans for the past few years whenever Matthew had requested it. He sensed it wouldn't be such an easy ride with Frankie Reeve.

She peered at him over her trendy, circular glasses. "Shall we begin?"

It transpired that Graham had been moved to another office, and Frankie had been brought in, along with a few others, to *'Provide a more productive and efficient service to their customers.'* She was a junior manager, so the account would also be overseen by a senior staff member. Matthew turned on the charm and persuaded her his new revised income could easily erode the deficit.

Over the weekend, he had managed to pay off one of the outstanding credit cards using some inheritance money he had forgotten about, which seemed to help swing her vote. She warned him she would have to run this by her senior but was content with what she had seen. If relief was a drink, he was knocking back the shots! After the successful promotion and now backing from the bank, *luck was finally shining down on him,* he thought.

He managed to escape the bank by ten. Satisfied Carrie hadn't spotted him, he arrived at the office in good time. Stanton-Peake was sitting rigid in his office, waiting for him. Surely Lady Luck hadn't abandoned him already?

* * *

Lunchtime couldn't come around quickly enough for Matthew. Clarissa had been droning on for hours about the sales figures and this year's targets, and now he had a headache. It was difficult to concentrate on what she was saying as the words were firing out of her mouth as fast as a bullet from a gun. She liked to use the latest corporate jargon to show she was current, but Matthew could see right through the façade. She was testing him.

His predecessor, Derek Grant, had been an excellent FD, managing the accounts and nurturing them like his own children. He was not a risk-taker nor a gambler, so although he ran a tight ship, it was always well-stocked and watertight. Last year had been phenomenally successful for the company, and bonuses had been given out just before Christmas. Derek had been a hero. Unfortunately for the company, he'd done such a good job that he was headhunted by a large competitor and whisked away on the promise of a salary package larger than the GDP of a small country.

In a nutshell, Matthew had big boots to fill, and Clarissa Stanton-Peake knew it. She had begun her slow dissection of his capabilities. Thank goodness Johanna had the foresight to suggest sitting in on the meeting. She was diligently taking notes and asking the right questions. Again, Matthew wondered how this absolute gem of a woman had been so overlooked. He knew why, really. She was his, and he didn't want to share her with anyone. Matthew just sat back, absorbing the situation as best he could. He made sure he had scheduled a meeting with Johanna after this morning to catch up on Stanton-Peake's demands.

Finally, Stanton-Peake got up to leave but not before delivering her final shot.

"I presume you know that you are on one year's probation. You won't be privy to *all* the luxuries of a partnership just yet. Your new salary will be increased incrementally with each satisfactory performance review." A slow, satisfying smile slipped across her thin lips as she emphasised the word *satisfactory*. "It takes time to earn *all* of the privileges, you know." Leaving him to soak up her words, she quietly slipped away.

Matthew had to get out, so he left the office for some fresh air. He hadn't banked on a probationary period. Nobody had said anything about that. What did she mean by *"all the luxuries"*? A car? Hospitality events? Salary? Words and figures choked his thoughts. Just when he could see himself climbing out of the financial cesspit, vines of red tape and company regulations were curling around his ankles and yanking him back down.

He had unknowingly lied to the bank. He had assumed he would be paid a similar salary to Derek Grant. Charles Harvey hadn't discussed a probationary period with him when he had offered him the job. Maybe she was making it up. Was this Clarissa's cruel way of keeping him exactly where she wanted him? Either way, he had to know. His family's future depended on it.

Despite the cold, Matthew loosened his tie off as he made his way to the deli on the corner. He would speak to Harvey this afternoon. There was little point worrying about it when he didn't know the truth.

Johanna was outside the deli smoking a cigarette.

"Oh, hi. Give me a sec. I'll grab a wrap and then walk back with you." she said.

"I was actually going to take a walk around the gardens to clear my head. Join me if you want to."

"Sure," she replied. "We can discuss this morning."

Johanna hadn't had a chance to leave his office before Clarissa had informed him of his probation. Even for Clarissa, that was a low blow. Johanna had raised her eyebrows and quickly left the room. Great.

She came out of the deli carrying a coffee and a brown paper bag. Minutes later, they were making their way across the busy intersection to the tranquil urban oasis of the city's public gardens. Although it was a chilly day, and the autumn sun was slunk low between the surrounding buildings, it was still able to stretch out its tendrils of light, illuminating their faces as they settled on an empty bench.

"Wow! What a morning," Johanna started. "Stanton-Peake has really set standards high. I'm not sure that we can meet them again. Last year was a bit of a fluke with us striking those deals in July."

Matthew unwrapped his bacon and brie ciabatta and took his first bite. He looked out into the park watching the approaching greedy pigeons bobbing their heads as they quickly walked, hoping to steal a few stray crumbs from his precious lunch. He was all too aware that he was being watched, not just by the winged rats but by his tall, haughty colleague back at the office.

The irony was not lost on him. Here he was, the FD of a successful firm negotiating terms of his personal loan agreements and inflated credit cards with his account manager only a few hours ago. Did Clarissa Stanton-Peake know? Could she see through his confident exterior to his insecure soul?

"We'll be fine, Jo," was all he could muster as he took another bite.

"I think it was pretty shitty, what she said in there in front of me. That should have been private."

"Yep, doesn't help when you have a mountain of debt to pay off." Out it came before he could stop himself. The burden of the secret that he had carried for years was coming to the surface. What he said should have remained private too.

They sat in silence for a minute or two, and then Johanna said, "How are things with Carrie?"

Matthew smiled at the mention of her name. For the first time in months, he felt like they had begun to reconnect. "Great, thanks." He glanced over at Johanna. He was grateful for the change of subject. She bowed her head fiddling with her packet of crisps. "But you know how it is, great one minute, at each other's throats the next."

It was true. They both seemed to be on opposite ends of the marital spectrum most of the time, but when they did harmonise, it was wonderful.

He didn't know why, but he felt he had to play down how things were with his wife to make Johanna feel better. It was something he had always done. Johanna seemed to live for work and was dedicated. Matthew sometimes wondered whether work was the dominant force in her life and everything else orbited around, like satellites circling the earth. Did she see him as a central figure in this existence? To him, his family was his world, and work was just an unfortunate distraction he must endure. He worked to live. It was just something he had to do. She, on the other hand, *wanted* to do it, and she was bloody good at it too.

It occurred to him that although he confided in her about his marital problems and now his finances, he knew nothing of her situation. She had had a 'partner' for a while, but she didn't seem to mention anything now. Maybe it had just fizzled out. He should make more effort to ask how she was. After all, Johanna was his best friend at the office. He knew she lived in a flat in the city suburbs. He knew she liked to ski in the winter and dive in the summer. He knew she travelled to work on a red Vespa moped and that her dad was Swedish. That was about it.

"How about you? Anyone on the scene?"

"Nope," she answered abruptly. "Just me and the cat."

He tried to engage with her further, but she cut the conversation short. "Time to go back?"

"Yeah."

CHAPTER 5

Remembrance Day was always a poignant time for Carrie. Her male family line was faithful to the forces. Her maternal side bowed to the Royal Navy, and her paternal side was devoted to the British Army for generations. Her father had been injured during the Falklands War and eventually died just short of Carrie's thirteenth birthday. Even though Edward Kevan had been absent since Carrie's childhood, she had adored him. So, she felt it was her duty to represent him, proudly wearing the scarlet poppy on her lapel.

Little Browton Primary School always put on a fantastic service at the local church, St Mark's. Carrie had missed it for the past few years with Luke being at secondary school, but now she could attend again with the twins.

As she didn't know many parents, she found herself a seat in the middle but on the right-hand side of the church. She had a good view of the altar embellished with red poppies that the pupils had drawn. It was cold inside, so she drew her coat firmly around herself and pulled on her woollen gloves.

The church began to fill up. There were rows at the front marked out for the pupils and teachers. Church staff were sweeping around the aisles showing parents to seats and rattling collection boxes for the Royal British Legion.

Mrs Gray, the headteacher, walked down the centre, nodding and smiling at parents as she went. She was quickly followed by a train of pupils who filed off left and right as directed by their teachers. Jen and Hannah, separated by Delilah, were sashaying behind Mr Turner. They were waving frantically to someone on the other side of the church. Carrie followed their gaze to see Terry accompanied by a beautiful woman with the glossiest hair she had ever seen. He was grinning and waving back. The woman even blew a kiss toward Delilah—her mum.

Since meeting Terry, Carrie had fantasised about what his wife must look like. He knew she had to be extremely attractive to be with a man like him. Due to her job as a lawyer, she also deduced that she would be glamorous, but nothing prepared Carrie for the beauty she saw before her. She was transfixed. This woman was a goddess. Alongside the hair, she had delicate features and a show-stopping smile. Like something out of a celebrity magazine, she was perfect for him, and he was perfect for her.

Carrie was suddenly aware of the couples in the room—the *perfect* couples. Next to her, in front of her, behind her. Two halves of a whole. Holding hands, stroking each other's arms, and smiling adoringly into each other's eyes as their beloved offspring read at the lectern or pumped out The Last Post on the recorder. She felt lonely.

She felt like a single parent—a familiar feeling for almost a decade. Matthew hadn't attended one school event or parents' evening with any of the kids. It had niggled at Carrie before, but now it twinged and twisted and gnawed at her cogitation. Now, the reality of her loneliness was being played out for the next generation of perfect couples to see, and she could feel their pity surrounding her like a cloak of fake condolence. She had hoped it would be different this time, but the pattern Matthew had drawn with Luke seemed to be repeating itself with Jen and Hannah. The record of asking, begging and guilt-tripping him to come was very worn out, so Carrie hadn't even bothered to play it again. He was missing out on so much.

As she left the church, Terry called out to her.

"Carrie, hey, this is Corrine, my wife. Corrine, this is Carrie. She's the twins' mum."

Being caught on the hop, Carrie blushed. This woman had such a formidable presence. She must have been nearly five foot ten, and in heels, she towered above Carrie. She had expensive clothes and smelt divine. She oozed sophistication and enchantment. In stark contrast, Carrie had scraped her dirty hair up into a bun, hidden her faded jeans and jumper under a bobbling brown Teddy coat, and she smelt of nothing. The worst kind of smell.

"Hello, Corrine," she mumbled, pushing her glasses back up her nose.

"Well, hello, Carrie. I have heard so much about your girls from Dee. Quite a force to be reckoned with, aren't they?" She had a thick Yorkshire accent, was cheerful, astute, and brimming with self-confidence. She reminded Carrie of Scary Spice.

"Yes, I suppose so."

"Who do they get that from?" Her eyes sparkled, and a smile played across her lips. "I bet you are a feisty one with your beautiful red hair."

"Maybe," was all she could muster, tucking a few whisps of escaped strands behind her ears.

Corrine laughed and linked her arm through her husband's. "Well, now, we must have you round for a playdate thing. I might not be there, but Terry can arrange it. How about after school one night next week?"

Carrie glanced nervously at Terry. She thought he would be mortified, but he was quite taken with the idea.

"Well, ok, if that works?" he replied.

"Absolutely. It's nice for the girls to get together outside of the school environment. We want Dee to develop her social connections positively with her peers in her own space. We want to repel any digital influences for as long as we can. We like to encourage good, old, wholesome activities with our baby." She tightened her grip on Terry and turned her face to his. "She's our world, isn't she, darling?" Terry nodded obligingly, and Corrine loosened her grip. He looked at Carrie.

"Thursday, ok?" he asked. "Should we meet at school, and you can walk back to ours with us?"

"Yes, thank you."

"What about your son, though? Will he need picking up?" Terry quizzed.

"Son? Is he at this school too?" Corrine looked curious.

"No, he's at the high school and gets the bus. Proper little latch-key kid." Carrie snorted apprehensively. She wasn't sure how this admission would go down with these 'coming-of-age' parents.

"No way! You are far too young to have a teenager!" Corrine looked genuinely shocked. Maybe all those makeup-free years were finally paying off for Carrie.

"That's what I said when she told me!" Terry said.

Corrine briefly shot him a stern look which fell to the floor and was replaced by her perfect smile when returning to look at Carrie. "Well then, I look forward to getting to know more about you and yours, Carrie Pritchard."

After they had left the church, Carrie meandered home alone through the leafy lanes. They seemed like a nice couple, but one comment was pestering her at the woman's observance. She couldn't remember telling Corrine her last name.

* * *

Carrie watched Luke pushing the lasagne around his plate. He had eaten about three mouthfuls. He had always loved lasagne, especially her homemade version. She sneakily shoehorned as many vegetables as possible into the mixture. Mushrooms, peppers, and courgettes were expertly chopped to microscopic proportions so as to not give the game away. Jen and Hannah had almost finished their plates and were making encouraging noises for seconds. Maybe he was being a picky teen as she had caught him on several occasions raiding the kitchen cupboards for crisps and crackers after he'd gotten home from school. He had most likely filled himself up from snacks already.

She sighed and glanced across the table to the empty place that had been set for her husband. She had held the kids off for as long as she could, but it was now 6:45 p.m. and too late for two hungry five-year-olds to wait any longer. Matthew was still at the office. This was the second time he had missed the family mealtime this week, and it was only Wednesday. She understood he needed to commit to his new role by putting the hours in. He had worked hard to get this opportunity, so a few absent dinners couldn't be held against him. She just missed him. They all did.

"Who fancies a yoghurt for dessert?" she asked the two eager faces before her.

The girls squealed with delight. Luke dismissed himself to his room. He had muttered something about maths homework, so Carrie let him go making a mental note to check on him later. The girls had to be bathed and then read to. The last few nights had been a later bedtime than planned, but she was determined to get them to sleep by half past seven, or the knock-on effect for the rest of the week would be catastrophic!

She handed the twins their dessert and quickly ran upstairs to start running the bath. They'd be ok for a few minutes. Betty was glued to their side anyway, hoping one of them would give her a final polish of their 'empty' yoghurt pot.

As she turned on the taps and added a flick of bubbles, she thought about tomorrow afternoon. She was excited to be spending a few hours with this handsome stranger. She couldn't deny there was a tiny flutter of attraction between them. He was utterly gorgeous, and she had caught his gaze lingering on her a little longer than was socially acceptable. He had also gone out of his way to speak to her twice. Was she imagining this connection? Was he just being friendly as he was new to the area and his daughter was friends with her daughters, or did he like her? The anticipation of the next day fizzed inside her stomach. She hadn't felt like this for a long time. It almost felt a little naughty going around to another man's house. But his wife knew. *She* had suggested it. Carrie had told Matthew, but she was sure it had gotten lost in his preoccupied monologue of pay reviews and forecast growth.

The bath was done. She retrieved the girls from downstairs after swiftly swiping away the plastic containers from Betty's jaws and depositing them in the bin.

"Come on, girls, we won't be able to read your favourite book if we don't get in the bath soon."

Once the girls were happily splashing around and washing each other's hair, she looked in on Luke. He was immersed in cyber chat, and his illuminated face twisted with confusion as he decoded the content of his phone screen.

"You ok, love? Homework done then?"

She knew she should check it more thoroughly as there were no textbooks or schoolwork on his desk. His school bag lay silently in the hallway, untouched since he'd slung it there at 4:30 p.m. Luke was a good kid. He just needed to be refocused now and again. She'd take a sneaky peek later as she didn't want to risk another argument with Matthew about Luke.

"Uh-hum," he responded, not looking up.

Carrie sighed; her little boy was growing into a man right before her eyes. She felt that she had missed the pre-teen stage and now he was slipping further and further away from her, no longer seeking her reassurance from a compliment or a hug. He was on the threshold of scratching out his own place in the world, and he didn't need her to hold his hand. At that moment, it struck her that her role as a parent was shifting significantly from nurturing to guidance. He needed her in a completely different way. But how? Their conversations would be conducted shoulder-to-shoulder from now on, not with her looking down as she talked to him. He was no longer a child, she would have to accept that, but he was still *her* child. Whatever advice or behaviour she bestowed on him from this point forward would influence his transition into adulthood. She had always done her best with her children, but why did she have this uneasy feeling that it wouldn't be enough?

There was a huge splash from the bathroom. "Mummy!" Jen called out. "Hannah dropped the shampoo in the water!" She had to get back to the girls. She would speak to him after she had put them to bed.

At 7:45 p.m., she went back to Luke, but he was already

asleep in bed, his phone silently pinging, discarded on the windowsill. She took it and slipped it into her pocket to charge downstairs. She then slowly drew the curtains, slipped his limp body under the duvet, kissed his forehead and turned out the light cherishing every second.

* * *

Matthew poured himself a large glass of wine. It had been a long day and was turning into a long week. Stanton-Peake was still on his case, and Johanna had been dragged into her office for an hour this afternoon. When he'd tackled her about the surprise meeting, she said it hadn't been important, but he didn't believe her. Johanna looked shaken.

The kids were already asleep, and Carrie was in the shower. Betty yawned and stretched and peeled herself from the snug arms of the sofa. At least there was one family member still around to welcome him home. He pulled his overcooked lasagne from the oven and began to tuck in without even sitting at the table. He hadn't realised how hungry he was as he attacked his feast like a famished hyena. Betty sniffed at his feet for scraps, and when none came, she retreated to her den.

He poured himself a second glass and joined his dog. She nuzzled her head into his lap, and he turned on the TV. It was after 10 p.m. The news reeled off depressing story after depressing story and did little to lift his mood, so he clicked to a different channel. It was a documentary about police intercepting car thieves. *Excellent*, he thought, putting his feet up on the foot stool. He didn't want to think. He just wanted to be engrossed in a straightforward, good, old-fashioned car chase. His brain was fried, and he wanted to switch off.

Carrie came downstairs.

"Oh, hi," she said. "Did you get your lasagne?"

"Yes, thanks," he replied.

"Hectic day?" she called from the kitchen as she finished filling up the dishwasher.

"Yep."

"Did that meeting go well?"

"Uh, huh." He was getting a little irritated. How could someone make so much noise from over there?

"The kids are ok. The girls brought home a gorgeous painting of a horse, or at least I think it was a horse. It did have a human face but had hooves and a tail, so that's why I'm assuming it was a...."

"Sounds great."

She prattled on. "Luke went to bed early. I think maybe we should look at cutting out one of his sporting activities. I think he's doing too much. What do you think?"

Matthew took a deep breath. "Yeah, maybe."

"I don't know, cricket nets? That's on a Friday evening, and it would be nice for us to get Friday nights back, wouldn't it? Although a lie-in on a Saturday morning from football would be a blessing!"

She really wasn't picking up on the signals.

"Mind you, he's just started basketball., which would be the most logical solution."

Matthew snatched his head away from the screen and glared at her.

"Carrie!" he snapped. "Can't you see I'm tired? I don't want to talk about it. I don't want to talk about anything!" She recoiled as if she had been stung by a wasp.

He knew he had been harsh, especially after last night, but seriously, the body language had been obvious. He didn't want to engage after the afternoon he had had. Charlie Harvey had been out all day, so he couldn't confirm Clarissa's claims about the probationary period. Matthew's money worries had returned like an unwelcome guest, and he knew he had to come clean to the bank. She turned her back on him and walked out of the room.

She'd get over it, he thought, returning to his uncomplicated TV show, casually cutting the cables of the shaky reconciliation bridge without a second thought.

CHAPTER 6

Terry, Corrine and Delilah lived in a pretty cottage nestled in a corner of a cul-de-sac just off the high street. It was a convenient location for amenities but detached from the hustle and bustle of village life. The front garden was filled with burgundy stars of Japanese maple leaves scattered across a tired-looking lawn. Autumnal primroses of orange, purple and pink poked out beneath the weight of yet more burgundy stars accompanied by curling, sepia leaves discarded from an oak tree nearby. A herringbone brick path led to a royal blue front door with a gold letterbox. The doorway was framed by a discoloured wisteria with the remnants of its summer glory still clinging to the odd creeper and in the porch was a decaying Jack O'Lantern.

Carrie liked this house. Even from the outside, it felt warm and inviting. Terry unlocked the door and proceeded into the hallway beyond. The girls flew in but not before Delilah had instructed them to take off their shoes as *'Mummy doesn't like mess.'*

"Come and see my doll's house!" Delilah shrieked, not being able to contain her excitement. She quickly looked for a nod of approval from her father and then promptly disappeared with two equally excited girls in hot pursuit.

Terry laughed. "Sorry, she's not had anyone over to the house yet for a play. She is thrilled that you are all here. Coffee?"

Carrie smiled at him and was immediately catapulted into the chocolate pools again. Blushing, she finally looked away when he released her gaze. "Please."

"All righty then. Come this way."

The kitchen was incredible. From the street, the house looked deceptively small, but at the other end of the cosy hallway was a bright, open-plan family room complete with all the latest accessories you might find in a contemporary city centre flat. She admired the hot water tap, integrated cooker fan and underfloor heating that softly enveloped your feet with every delightful step. Skylights and bifold doors allowed natural light to bounce off every glossy surface, and brightly coloured African art lifted the stark white walls. Carrie was in heaven. It was like being in a photo shoot for an expensive home-styling magazine, absolutely polarizing to her cluttered, worn-out, wood-ridden kitchen.

"Milk? Sugar?" Terry interrupted her dream.

"Neither, thanks. I like it black."

"Me too. Nice and easy then." He grinned. "Please sit down." He gestured towards a pair of striking red bar stools, and Carrie clambered clumsily up. "I'll just go and check on the girls."

Terry soon reappeared, reassuring Carrie that the little ladies were fully absorbed in Delilah's train set.

He scooped up his coffee, and Carrie couldn't help but notice his muscular biceps swell under his shirt as he flexed his arm to take a sip. He caught her looking at him again, and she averted her eyes to the garden.

"Lovely garden, do you get someone in to do it?" she asked.

"No, I do it, although I haven't had a chance to get stuck in properly yet. I enjoy being out in the fresh air and try and do everything myself if I can. Cook, clean, garden, fix stuff when it's broken." He let out a little chuckle. "Corrine is the opposite. She would have a full-time maid, gardener and handyman if she could." *Sounds like Matthew,* Carrie thought to herself. "We had a townhouse in Leeds with a postage stamp plot. So, moving here has been awesome. I am trying to grow some winter onions and garlic. I've got big plans for spring with a rose pergola for Corrine and a summer house for Dee in the corner. I can't wait to get started; I'm hoping to have it done for Christmas. Do you want to see the plans for the summer house?"

"Sure!" Carrie mused, pulling her glasses from her bag, expecting a quick sketch on a scrap of paper.

Terry went over to a desk in the corner and pulled out a huge roll of paper. He unravelled it across the worktop and revealed a sophisticated, schematic diagram of a hexagonal summer house complete with a play kitchen, sofa bed and swing. He included all dimensions and had projected the drawing from all angles. It really was a professional design.

"Wow! This is incredible, Terry."

His eyes lit up at her compliment. "Why, thank you! I used to be an architectural technician before I went into banking. I wanted to be an architect but couldn't afford to put myself through uni for seven years. I ended up on an apprenticeship course and learnt the draughtsman's skills there. I loved it." He drifted away on a faint memory for a moment, then jolted back. "But you know, sometimes these things don't work out."

"You should get started on this right away. It's a big project; if you start it now, you might be ready for summer!"

He smiled, rolling up the blueprint. "Yeah. Corrine isn't keen. She wants to buy one for Christmas."

"No way!" Carrie protested. "You couldn't buy anything this good! You *have* to make it. What a lovely thing to do for your daughter."

Wow! Not only did he look spectacular, but he was talented too. The summer house design was a little girl's dream. How could Corrine just disregard it and overlook his obvious talent? Matthew couldn't even hang a picture straight. She had mastered many DIY skills over the years they had been together. Although they had traditional family roles regarding work, they were reversed when it came to getting your hands dirty with a bit of manual labour. Matthew didn't have time for it, but like Terry, she enjoyed it. Her admiration for him was climbing steeply.

They spent the next hour chatting easily about home improvements, swapping gardening tips, old sporting victories, work goals, and family. It transpired Terry had been a keen runner in his twenties until he sustained an unfortunate knee injury, and he had played rugby at county level. Carrie told him about her gratifying career in nursing and how she had had ambitions to train as a midwife before she got pregnant with Luke. She revealed how her father had died when she was young, and her mother, much to Carrie's confusion, had re-married within a year. She later learned about her mum's perpetual infidelity while her dad was away in the army. Her father never found out, but Carrie hadn't forgiven her and never would. She had revealed so much about herself to a virtual stranger, and yet it had so felt effortless to talk.

"Gosh, it's nearly five o'clock," she announced. "I had better round up the girls and get back."

"Yeah, sure. I need to get dinner on too. Corrine hates eating past six thirty. It messes with her metabolism, apparently." He shrugged. "Will you be ok walking back? There is a ginnel that runs alongside our house, which brings you out in the middle of the high street. It's just a bit hidden from the street by our overgrown holly bush."

"Ginnel?" she questioned.

He laughed. "Oh yeah, sorry. It's Yorkshire for alleyway. I'll show you where it is."

Terry was right. Within seconds of walking down the

damp alley, they were in the heart of the bustling town. It was like entering another world after the tranquillity of his homely cottage. She grabbed the girls' hands and began navigating the rush hour hordes fighting with each other to be the first to get home. Jen and Hannah were glowing with happiness from their afternoon of fun with Delilah, and much of that glow had rubbed off on Carrie too.

* * *

Matthew was already home. He had listened intently as the girls had recalled every fine detail of their playdate at Delilah's, but once the kids had gone to bed, he couldn't help himself. He was beginning to think that Carrie was doing all this on purpose.

"I didn't know the girls were going on a playdate *all* afternoon."

"You did." Carrie laughed apprehensively. "I told you the other day."

"I was too busy then; my head was up my arse for most of it. I don't like the fact that Luke is coming home to an empty house either."

Carrie grimaced. This was how it started. Slow and subtle until exploding into a full-blown argument. She would get upset, apologise, and an eerie calmness would descend over them. If he were satisfied, she would be forgiven. If not, she'd be ignored for days, and so the cycle continued, again and again and again.

"Yes, I know. I did think about that when we got home. But the girls were having such a wonderful time, Matt, and this new girl was so excited to have them over." She was trying to salvage the situation before it grew into an uncontrollable monster. "Luke's fine. He knows where the key is. It's not like we haven't done it before."

That seemed to incense him. He swung his accusing gaze on her. "So, this is not the first time you have left him alone? Do you know what I found when I got home tonight? A slob lying on the sofa gorging on chocolate biscuits when he should have been knuckling down doing his homework. He needs guidance. You need to be here!"

"Matthew, calm down. He's nearly fifteen. At his age, I was always being left on my own." She was desperately trying to keep her composure as her husband amplified a molehill into a mountain.

"That's different. You had no choice. Your mum and Jim had to go out to work with all those mouths to feed. I want it to be different for Luke. He's going to do well at school and forge a fantastic career to set him up for life. He's not going to go off the rails and scrape two or three GCSEs."

She smiled outwardly, but inside, she was furious. His mocking words were sharp as they sliced at her skin, but she kept her composure. Yes, she had passed three GCSEs at grade C. Yes, she had taken her maths GCSE again in college, and yes, she went off the rails a little in her teenage years. Her mother had rejected her after cosying up with her new husband before her dad's body was even cold. Carrie's school persona didn't mimic her home life. Outwardly she was confident and charismatic; inwardly, she had to be clever and streetwise.

She had inherited three gruesome stepbrothers who thought she was their emotional punchbag, so she had found solace in the occasional dalliance in drink and recreational drugs. Matthew had scooped her up and out of that mess, and although she'd be forever grateful, he loved to remind her.

She remained quiet. She wanted to maintain some control but couldn't help crossing her arms defensively. He was picking at her like a stubborn scab refusing to detach itself from the skin. The mask had slipped off again; the other night had meant nothing. He moved his remarks up a notch.

"The girls tell me it was the dad there, not the mum. Weird." He laughed. "A stay-at-home husband. How very 21st century. Is she a 'beard'?"

"No, he is not!" She flared a little too defensively, so retreated to her quietude once again. She didn't want to draw any attention to the fact that she had also had a wonderful time that afternoon.

"He must be a bit of a ponce. What sort of a husband sends his wife out to work while he plays house?"

"He's a qualified architectural technician. It's his choice too. He's just supporting his wife." He was picking, and it was coming. The scab was slowly peeling away, and he knew it.

"You seem to know a lot about him. Had a good old chinwag, did you? Is this how you spend your afternoons whilst I'm hard at work?"

She ignored him and unfolded her arms. "I think I might go to bed."

"Ok, well, that's fine then. I work hard all week, and the one time I'm home early, you go to bed. *I* want to have a good old chinwag with my wife now., Or are you all talked out with your new friend?"

"Matthew, please. I'm tired. I don't want an argument." Carrie attempted to stamp out the fire.

"I don't want an argument either!" he snapped. "I have to deal with stress all day long. The last thing I want is a stressful time when I get home. Oh, for God's sake, just go to bed!"

She wanted to, but something in his voice made her stay. He sounded frustrated, not angry. She slowly got up and sat on the other sofa across from him.

"Is everything ok?" she asked. "Is the new job not going well?" He remained still, staring into the void of the unlit fireplace. "Do you want to talk about it?"

He let out a long sigh. "No, not really." He reached for the remote and switched on the TV, signalling the end of their conversation. She went to bed.

Sensing her master's dismay, Betty leapt onto the sofa next to him. She nuzzled her nose into his lap as he sipped his cool beer. The amber liquid momentarily soothed his troubled mind while the film on the TV temporarily transported him somewhere else entirely. It would soon end, however, and the grey anxiety would close in once again. He was exhausted. Clarissa had him on a tight leash.

She challenged his suggestions and questioned his motives. She knew just how to dig in her claws so that they would leave an invisible dent in his inexperience. She had even whipped up Monsieur Baudelaire to interrupt his afternoons with feeble questions and irrelevant meetings. He jumped through every one of their hoops but increasingly felt like he couldn't breathe under their micromanagement. He could do the job. Why couldn't they just let him get on with it?

The bank was also knocking at his 'door.' Frankie Reeve's supervisor wasn't quite satisfied with his salary credentials and repayment rate and had asked to see Matthew next week. He couldn't negotiate an early meeting this time as the supervisor only worked part-time. Matthew suggested a lunchtime slot instead and decided to work from home in the afternoon. After tonight's events, being at home next week would be a good move. He wouldn't say anything to Carrie. He wanted to keep his eye on her. He felt like he was losing his grip on every corner of his life, and she wasn't helping.

He needed her to manage the home and not disappear for the afternoon mid-week when her son needed her. He had tests next week, and as far as Matthew knew, Luke hadn't done an ounce of revision. She should be on top of this. He didn't ask much of her. These past few weeks had been quite disruptive with Luke not completing homework and the girls fighting. He needed a steady ship here.

Annoyance was rearing its ugly head; he took another sip of beer to quell the feeling. Betty shifted her weight on his lap as he twisted to replace the bottle on the side table. The film had ended, but he couldn't recall what had happened in the one hour and forty-nine minutes he had been mindlessly staring at the screen. He should have been preparing for the pay reviews he had to conduct with his team the next day, but Carrie's inappropriate playdate had thrown him off course.

He finished the beer and let the dog out in the garden. He should go to bed; things would be clearer in the morning. In his pocket, his phone vibrated. It was past midnight; it was a message from Johanna.

"Hey, sorry it's late. Need to talk. Can we get lunch together tomorrow?"

He was intrigued. Questions rushed through him, and he wondered if it was about work or a personal thing. He hoped it was the latter. After all, he had probed into her home life, and she had clammed up. He wanted to know the real Johanna. They worked so closely together every day, but her private life was a closed book. Maybe she was finally going to open up to him, and this could be a welcome distraction.

It would be about work, he told himself. Johanna always conducted herself in a professional way. She would never let her guard down so readily.

"Sure, see you tomorrow." He replied and retired to bed.

CHAPTER 7

December threw down a frost every day in the first week. It was bitterly cold, and the wind whipped its icy tentacles with every gust. Carrie loved it. It made her run faster. This morning, she had reached the top of the hill with Betty at her heels, and now, as she caught her breath, she took in the chilly wilderness below.

The last few weeks had been turbulent. Matthew was working more and becoming increasingly distant when he came home. He seemed to live, sleep, and breathe the office now, but he assured Carrie it was just with the run-up to Christmas. Outwardly, he appeared to be doing well. He had changed his car for a more family-friendly 4x4, treated the children to new clothes and talked about booking some winter sun for them all in February. The sacrifices he was making were commendable, and she knew how much he had wanted this opportunity. She was proud of him.

However, the cracks in their marriage were opening

again and refusing to heal. He was still critical and snappy. They just didn't seem to synchronize anymore. She had decided to try a new tack, shifting her focus from what he was missing out on to what he was achieving. Nonetheless, the positive sentiments slipped away and were left undetected as he marched on with his ignorance of family life. Matthew didn't get the message, and Carrie was becoming more and more resentful. There were only so many times you could make someone tea or coffee, get them a beer, run them a bath, or cook a romantic dinner without a single thank you. When the bitterness bubbled up, she desperately tried to wipe it away. He was only trying to make a better life for them all. He had invested in their future, and they had a superb holiday on the horizon. This was her life now. Her husband was committed to his, and it was hers to pick up the pieces and singlehandedly juggle the day-to-day.

Out of the blue, Betty took off along the trail, fixated on someone running up towards them. She automatically reached for the dog whistle as she didn't want Betty to disappear, but from the dog's body language, she knew who it was. The figure stopped and crouched down to give Betty a fuss, who was rolling around on the frosty ground in delight—it was Terry. He had become a familiar face to Betty as she saw him most mornings and afternoons at school, and he usually had a biscuit for her.

Betty came galloping back to her, quickly followed by Terry, covering the last ascent with ease. Carrie admired his shapely legs and powerful body as he approached. She got the impression he was putting in the extra effort to her impress her, and she was.

"Fancy seeing you here this morning," she called out.

"That's a good climb. I can see why you like it," he said, drawing in the view. "Wow! Carrie, this is incredible! I didn't know you could see all this from here."

His breath eventually returned to normal. "I can't believe I've not been up here before now."

The cold was circling her, and the bite was closing in, but she wanted to cling to this curious connection. She moved closer to him to benefit from some of the heat energy encompassing his warm body. He instinctively put his strong arm around her shoulder.

"Cold?"

She nodded, but she wasn't, not anymore. She breathed in his musky scent, and together, they stood staring out to sea for several minutes. Everything was perfect, from the delicate touch of frost over the hillside to the warmth of his embrace. She could feel the beat of his heart under his running jacket, and it wasn't steadying; they were both aroused by this unexpected intimacy.

A couple of walkers approached from the far side of the ridge, and Terry dropped his arm and suggested that they get back into the warmth. There was a coffee shop that straddled the forest and the wood, and Carrie offered to buy him a warm drink. To her joy, he accepted, and they steadily jogged down towards the welcome lights with Betty leading the way.

Freshly cut spruces and firs were piled up against the café, and the unmistakable fragrance of the needles filled the air. There were Christmas stalls outside selling wreaths and natural Christmas decorations made from pinecones and wooden offcuts. Terry was particularly taken with a wooden reindeer for the front garden, and it was so big that Delilah could have ridden it! He was going to come back to pick it up later after work. They ordered two black Americanos and settled down outside under a patio heater.

The café was decorated in the style of a ski lodge, complete with thick, faux fur covers for their outdoor patrons, which were particularly welcomed by two cool runners after their workout. Even Betty managed to find a furry rug to curl up on under the table. As it was early, people were only just venturing out on their morning walks. It was quiet, but the steady trickle of customers kept a buoyant ambience as they chatted excitedly about the impending holiday.

Carrie settled down under her throw to sip her coffee. Terry spoke first.

"Carrie, this is lovely. I haven't felt so content in a long time." He relaxed back into the bench. She sensed that he wanted to say more, so she waited patiently. "It's true what they say about exercise, it's hard, but you really do feel better afterwards. I like it because I can escape from my thoughts and run away from my drama. Even though my life is pretty uncomplicated, I sometimes wish that I could get a glimpse into Corrine's life, just for a little while. I know it must be stressful, but the excitement of building a case and preparing interviews, the thrill of winning and actually making someone's life better." He laughed. "Not to mention all the posh lunches and dinners you get invited to." He turned to look at her. "Do you know I haven't seen her properly for three days? She's up to her eyes in research and Christmas parties. She didn't even come upstairs to wish Dee goodnight yesterday; my baby was heartbroken. She just seems so preoccupied. It's confusing for Dee."

Carrie was bowled over. The perfect couple, apparently not so perfect after all, but finally, someone knew what she was going through. Even though Carrie felt desperately sorry for their situation, she was startled by the similarities of their family life. Was this normal? Was this the same in every household? What about family life with those parents who both worked full-time? When did those couples even see each other?

He checked himself. "I'm so sorry, Carrie. I haven't come here to burden you with my troubles." Carrie looked into those sad brown eyes. She felt his pain and despair and wanted to smooth away the creases on his furrowed brow.

"You're not burdening me. I'm glad you feel you can talk to me."

"No, no. It's not right. We hardly know each other, and I'm gibbering on." He paused. "It's just so easy to talk to you. I feel you understand."

"Sadly, I do," she replied. "Matthew is the same. He leaves early, comes home late. He doesn't eat dinner with us anymore. We haven't had a proper conversation in weeks. It's like nothing else matters to him but work. Luke is suffering too. They used to spend so much time together at the park or watching football…and the girls, they don't deserve a part-time dad."

They exchanged stories about their other halves for a

good hour. Guilt and betrayal burned slowly in the pit of her stomach, but she couldn't stop herself. She had opened the door into her private life with a stranger, a stranger who understood. The relief of being able to talk freely and with someone so receptive to her feelings was a revelation.

"Thank you, Carrie," he said gently.

"For what?"

"Being so honest. It's lovely to talk with someone who gets it. Just nice to talk to another adult about how I'm feeling. One who listens anyway."

She smiled. "Anytime…and thank you too."

He put his hand over hers and patted it softly. She drew in a sharp breath. She hadn't been touched so tenderly for months.

Carrie's mobile phone rang, it was the school.

"Hello?" she answered.

"Mrs Pritchard, if it wouldn't be too much trouble. Could you please come in? We need to talk to you about a delicate matter involving the girls." Mrs Gray's voice came through the handset.

Carrie was perturbed. "What? Right now? Is everything ok? Are the girls ok?"

"Yes, yes. We just need to inform you of something and agree on the best course of action going forward. Can you be here by, say, 11:30?"

"Of course."

"Great, see you then." Mrs Gray hung up.

Carrie turned to Terry. "I'm sorry, I need to go to the school. The girls have done something, and Mrs Gray needs to see me."

"Right, I hope everything's ok," he said. "Can we do this again?"

"Yes," she replied instinctively. "I'd like that."

* * *

Mrs Gray's office was welcoming, warm, and full of festive cheer. There were clumsily handmade baubles and decorations hanging from the desktop tree, and twinkling fairy lights bordered the window while a candle burned gently on the windowsill delivering notes of cinnamon, ginger, and orange. If Carrie hadn't felt so unsettled by what she had been called in for, she would have been quite happy to stay there all morning.

Mrs Gray was just finishing on the phone with a governor but had ushered Carrie in to sit down. A few moments later, she was done.

"Sorry about that. Just the treasurer questioning why I'd like to buy three extra benches for the canteen. I mean, seriously. He knows we are an expanding school and is an accountant by trade! It doesn't take a genius to work it out." She chuckled and settled back into her broad office chair, sipping her tea. Then a stern look settled on her face. "Now, I'm sorry to call you in here like this, Mrs Pritchard, but a serious matter has come to my attention involving the twins." She replaced her teacup onto the saucer and looked directly at Carrie. "Things have been going missing from the reception classroom, and I have reason to believe Jennifer and Hannah have been 'collecting' them."

"What?" Carrie interjected. "No way. They're only five. Why? How? Why do you think this?"

Mrs Gray took a deep breath. It was clear she was measuring her response carefully. "Mr Turner has noticed bits and pieces going missing from the classroom for weeks now. Rubbers, counting cubes, cotton reels... just little things to start with. Recently, though, it's been the other children's keyrings from their bags and their breaktime snacks."

"Ok, but that doesn't mean it's my girls."

"I'm afraid some of the other children have seen them taking things. When asked by Mr Turner, they both denied it, so I searched their bags and found every missing item this morning."

"Oh."

"I have removed them from their class and placed them with another for the rest of the day as punishment. Jennifer is with the other reception class, and Hannah is with Year 1. Taking them out of their comfort zone can give them an opportunity to reflect on what they have done."

"Right...erm...."

"The thing is, Mrs Pritchard, it's quite unusual

behaviour. Why do you think they are doing it?" Mrs Gray uncrossed her legs and leaned forward in her chair, peering closely at Carrie.

She couldn't believe this. Her two five-year-old girls were feisty little pocket rockets with boundless energy but stealing from their friends? That was planned, calculated, surely? They were only little. No way! This didn't make any sense at all. Her twins? She wanted to see them, ask them, to see it for herself.

"Mrs Gray, are you sure?" she queried.

"Quite," she replied. "I wish I weren't. Mrs Pritchard, we really must investigate this. It is unusual at their age, but children take things for a variety of reasons—jealousy, attention, modelling behaviour that they have seen...." Carrie raised an eyebrow. "...they are feeling threatened, they don't know boundaries...." Carrie had heard enough.

"Mrs Gray, I can assure you that my girls have a *very* happy home life. They aren't spoilt. We treat them all the same. They don't even know what the word steal means! We have very clear boundaries, but we don't restrict them unless we think it's right. I don't know where this has come from. I'll speak to them tonight."

Mrs Gray contemplated her next few words. "Is Mr Pritchard at home?"

Carrie's response shot out of her before she could stop herself. "Yes, of course he is! Why?"

The headteacher paused, slightly taken aback by her response and then asked gingerly. "How much do the girls see him? Do you think they might be missing him? Could this be a reason?" Carrie was offended. The delicate buttons of her relationship were pressing on a raw nerve.

"No!" she said firmly. "He works hard like I'm sure many of the parents in this school do."

"Yes, yes, I'm sure he does."

"And anyway, it could be bullying. What if they are being threatened here in this school? What are you doing about that?" she asked.

"Yes, I've considered this, so I asked Mr Turner and Miss Fuller to study the children's relationships carefully over the last few weeks, and nothing has come to light. They both assure me that the class is very happy and content. The only friction seems to be between the twins." She paused again. "Have you noticed any odd behaviour at home recently?"

"No," Carrie replied defensively but now a little deflated. The girl's behaviour was upsetting the apple cart again. "So, what do you suggest?"

"Mrs Pritchard, I don't have all the answers, but I do know that something is troubling the girls. I can assure you that they are safe at school, and we will do everything in our power to support them. We'll see how the next week goes, and if they don't settle together, maybe we should consider separating them into different classes after Christmas."

This was a sad solution. The girls were best friends and had never been separated. Carrie had remained adamant that she wouldn't dress them the same and would allow their individual identities to surface. They were, after all, two different people, not two halves of the same person. However, splitting them up now could be a disaster. She reminded herself that they were only five, but on the other hand, something wasn't quite right. Perhaps they were grappling to establish their own characters and felt uncomfortable in each other's company at school. Maybe their absent father was having a severe impact on their development. The familiar pangs of guilty parent syndrome pulled at her apron strings, and it fell on her shoulders to sort it out.

Mrs Gray attempted to reduce some ripples of the unforeseen bombshell.

"I'm confident that this will resolve itself with a positive approach on all sides. Talk to Mr Pritchard and see what he thinks. He may have noticed something that you haven't, even just a subtle change."

Carrie looked at the pathetic baubles clinging onto the Christmas tree on Mrs Gray's desktop. They were awful, especially the brown one. She suspected it was intended to be a picture of a robin, but the kid had gotten carried away and continued swirling the paintbrush until the robin now represented something Betty would do in the garden first thing in the morning. Nevertheless, it had pride of place on the headteacher's desk. Mrs Gray was proud to have that imperfect poo picture on her tree, just as Carrie was proud of her imperfect girls. There had been a mistake, and Carrie would prove it.

"Thank you, Mrs Gray, I will."

"I'll ring you in a week, and we can see how things have been." She got to her feet, signalling the end of the conversation. "Thanks for coming in, and we'll sort it out. I'm sure there is a logical explanation."

Carrie stood up and pulled on her coat. "Yes, thank you." She sincerely hoped so.

CHAPTER 8

"So, all you have to do is manipulate this number on the spreadsheet. You can invoice people this amount, but really, it's this amount. Then you pocket the difference. It's such a small amount, no one ever notices."

It was late, and Johanna was sitting with Matthew at his laptop in his office. Since she had admitted her little secret to him, he had agonised about what to do with the startling information. Syphoning off fragments of credit from the company accounts was a criminal offence, and Johanna was his most trusted employee. The cornerstone of his team, crudely stealing from the company right under his nose! He had been floored when she had made the shocking revelation two weeks ago.

However, time had desensitised the crime and part of him had rejected the idea of it being wrong. It transpired she had been heavily in debt due to her ex-partner's lavish spending habits and had been justifying her 'additional earnings' by working long hours at the office. In a way,

Matthew admired her. She was smart, cunning, and clever. She had pulled the wool over his eyes and those of Clarissa Stanton-Peake and Monsieur Baudelaire, and he couldn't help but smile about that too. He didn't even feel sorry for Charlie as he was hardly ever in the office these days. Johanna had told him that she was now debt free and managing to get her life back together. A situation that Matthew desperately wanted for himself.

His meeting at the bank a few weeks ago hadn't gone well. Mr Jennings, the supervisor overseeing Frankie Reeve, was a tough nut to crack. He was sceptical of Matthew's sporadic repayment methods, and he hadn't had three months' pay from his new position yet. He wasn't convinced that Matthew could repay the credit but had been satisfied to give him the opportunity to try for a trial period. Now Johanna was offering him a lifeline. It was a chance to escape the murky waters of endless deficit and pull himself up to where he should be, riding high on the waves of his success.

"Gosh, it really is quite simple, isn't it?" he smirked.

The more he thought about it, the more he made peace with the discovery. It was his ticket out of the doldrums, and he was going to take it. He couldn't let Carrie know that despite all his hard work and her unwavering support, he was just a loser. He wanted to punish Clarissa for all the snide comments and deliberate, steady vandalism of his career. Even though it felt wrong, it felt right, and Matthew felt powerful. Clarissa thought she knew everything and everyone in this business, but clearly not.

"Yes. But don't get greedy. It only works if you take a little bit here and there. It soon adds up, though." Johanna winked.

Since confessing all, Matthew had done the same to her. He had produced his unwanted collection of credit cards and admitted that he didn't even know how much was piled up on which. He had changed his car and booked a holiday to keep up the façade for his family. He wanted them to believe in him. He needed to keep their trust so he could sort out the mess behind the scenes.

"I'm ok now, Matt." Johanna turned to look at him as she sat back in her office chair. "You need this more than me. There can only ever be one of us doing it at any time, as we can't make it obvious."

"I know I shouldn't be saying this, Jo, but thank you."

She smiled. "I know how debt can destroy you and those around you. You deserve to be happy. Just don't abuse the system, ok?"

"I won't." Matthew looked at his watch. "It's nearly eight. I better make a move. I haven't even texted Carrie to tell her I'll be late."

"She hasn't texted you either...you know, to see if you are ok." Johanna pulled a face.

He knew Johanna had a point, but he was aware of how detached he was from his wife right now. She would know better than to pester him. If he couldn't advocate his indiscretion to himself, then he would have been feeling very guilty right now. They barely spoke, and he was in and out of the house. Even the kids had noticed. He missed them, but what good would it be without money to live the lifestyle they had become accustomed to?

"I'll text her now," he said finally. "Do you need a lift?"

"No, no. Thanks. I might stay here for another half an hour, and then I've got my scooter," she replied.

"Ok, see you tomorrow."

"You bet." She smiled.

She watched him leave and then carefully typed the message that would pierce the happy future she'd seen forming in Matthew's head.

'Clarissa,

I am sorry to confirm your suspicions, but I think you were right about Matthew....'

* * *

He got in after nine. The traffic was awful due to the late-night shopping at the retail park. Carrie and Luke were watching the last few kicks of a football match. Betty was curled up on the rug at their feet, snoring loudly. It was an idyllic scene, his perfect family safe and secure, and thanks to Johanna was how it would be from now on. He knew this was a turning point in his misfortune, and he could make it all better. It would take time but right here, right now in this house, was everyone and everything he cared about. He plotted to start the fraudulent acts in the new year. For now, he would just enjoy the moment at last.

"Hey," he called, hanging his coat up on the rack. "I'm sorry I'm late. Busy day again."

"Ok. Have you eaten?" Carrie looked up, relieved that despite the late hour, he seemed to be in a jubilant mood.

"No."

"Oh, sorry, I assumed you would have, so we ate the leftovers. I can put a pizza in for you."

"Sure." He pulled a beer from the fridge and wandered into the living room to join his family. Settling down in an armchair, he reached over to stroke the dog's head. Betty's tail thumped steadily on the laminate, acknowledging his presence. Luke didn't flinch; he was glued to the game.

"Hey, pal," Matthew started. "Who's winning?"

"City."

"Good game?" Luke shrugged. "Who scored?"

"Can't remember."

Matthew took a sip from the bottle and looked across at Carrie in the kitchen.

"Conversations flowing here tonight then," he joked.

She smiled a wry smile. Distracted was an all too familiar feeling with the men in this house. Now Matthew was on the receiving end of some.

"He's tired. He's had assessments all week."

"Oh yeah." Matthew swung round on Luke. "How did they go?"

The match had finished one nil. Luke looked back at him blankly. "What?"

Matthew repeated himself slightly impatiently. "How did they go?"

"Ok, I think." Luke yawned and made a big performance of stretching across the sofa and onto the floor to settle beside Betty. After a few minutes of nothing, he got to his feet. "I'm going to bed."

Matthew despaired as he left the room. "What's got into him?"

Carrie returned to the living room and sat down. Betty shuffled to the rug and rolled over onto her back, front legs flopping, begging for a belly rub. "It's nearly the end of term, Matt. He's flagging."

"Hmm, I know the feeling."

She knew she had to tell him about the meeting yesterday with Mrs Gray, but considering his current mood, she didn't know whether it was the right time. He could react on either side of his personality spectrum—supportive or explosive, and she didn't know if she had the energy to deal with one or the other tonight. Instead, she decided to sleep on it and broach the subject tomorrow. After all, it was Friday, and he would hopefully be in a good mood.

"I thought we could get a takeaway tomorrow night.

You know, after the kids have gone to bed. We can catch up. We haven't had a proper chat in ages," she suggested tentatively.

"What do you want to chat about?" he enquired.

"Oh, nothing really, just don't feel like I've seen you." Oh crikey! Why did she say that? Surely this would raise his hackles, and the defences would go up. She winced, waiting for the sting.

"Yeah, you're right. It would be nice not to talk about work for a change." He patted her leg, and Carrie's heart slid back down her throat and into its rightful place. Slowly its heightened rhythmic pace steadied to a natural beat.

He finished his bottle of beer and relaxed back into the armchair. A contented smile formed on his lips. His smile dazzled amongst the fledgling wrinkles and transported her back to happier times. He could still hook her back in with that smile—arguments, absences, and abruptness long forgotten. She still loved him very much.

"Can I get you another beer, dear?" she teased.

"Absolutely." He winked.

* * *

"Chinese? Thai? Indian?" Carrie asked, flicking through her phone. She was excited about tonight and had already opened the wine. It had been a good day. They had all gone to the park as Matthew had been determined to get Jen riding her bike without stabilisers. She had done it and then spent a few happy hours tearing around with Hannah, squealing in delight as Betty chased their frantic revolving legs in hot pursuit. Luke had come for a little while and then disappeared with some friends to play football on the tennis courts. Carrie didn't mind. She could remember being a teenager, and hanging out with Mum, Dad, and little sisters all day was not cool. When he was with the family, he had been brilliant. Charging after Hannah whilst Matthew concentrated on Jen and her confidence. He then patiently threw the frisbee for Betty so his dad could correct any wobbles his sister had and make sure she knew how to apply the brakes correctly. He had been a rare delight that afternoon, so Carrie did not want to deny him a few hours' freedom with his pals.

Matthew was now absorbed in work emails. Carrie had tried to dissuade him from opening them but had come down from seeing Luke into bed to find him engrossed.

"I know, pizza!" she exclaimed, trying to tease him out of the work trance. Matthew loved pizza. He always ordered it at Lorenzo's, the local Italian restaurant on the high street. Pepperoni, Margarita, Salami, even Hawaiian, any flavour would do. It just had to be thin crust. *'Deep pan detracts you from the flavours and fills you up,'* he would say, and he was right; it did.

There was a muffled response from the other side of the computer.

"What?" Carrie asked.

"Bloody email from Stanton-Peake sent this morning," he grumbled. "Something about an intern coming in to shadow me. Me? Why me? I don't have the time! I'll fob them off onto Johanna or Dave. I'm far too busy. What was she thinking? Stupid cow!"

Carrie felt sad and sat down next to him; he had been in such a good mood. She didn't want the lovely day destroyed by a few bothersome work emails.

"Matthew, it's Saturday night. Try not to let it worry you now. Let's enjoy a nice pizza and the rest of this wine. I'm happy to pop down and pick it up. What flavour do you fancy?"

He continued ignoring her completely. "Bloody hell! He's starting on Monday! *After a brief induction, Jonathan Parker will be assigned to Matthew Pritchard to shadow his duties for three weeks,*" he quoted from the text. "What? She is mental. I have back-to-back meetings online Monday afternoon. I was going to work from home." Carrie sighed. "He's not about to slide in out of nowhere and listen to our financial situation. Why wasn't I even consulted?" He furiously began responding, reciting the email as he typed as if by saying the words aloud, they would carry more weight.

Carrie let him get it out of his system. Better to let him vent now so they could settle down and have a cosy evening together, their first in a long time. However, her conversation with Mrs Gray last Thursday still taunted her. She couldn't leave it any longer to tell him, and he had to know what his little angels had been up to, but she didn't want to tarnish this day. They had all been so happy together. It had felt easy and uncomplicated, just how it used to feel.

Matthew finished his email, slammed his laptop shut and took a swig of beer.

"Sorry," he said, looking at her with a deflated expression. "She knows how to press my buttons that woman, and I'd had such a good week too." He leaned back and lay his arm across the back of the sofa, she obligingly settled in next to him under the crook, but she could still feel him twitching. "We had a good day today, didn't we?" he said softly, stroking her hair. She sensed that he was looking for some reassurance, and she was happy to give it.

"Yes, we did. Thank you for spending the day with us."

They sat in silence for a few minutes, enjoying each other's company and listening to the sound of the winter squall that had blown up a late afternoon hum around the house, gently rattling the windowpanes and whistling through the cracks. Betty was dreaming. Her body flinched and contorted. Her eyes flickered. How wonderful to be a dog! Warm and content, lying by the fire and dreaming of chasing squirrels up trees and rabbits down holes. All was well, so she thought it might be a good time to bring up the stealing issue.

"Hey, I need to talk to you about something," she started. "The girls got in trouble again, and I had to go and see Mrs Gray the other day."

"Mrs Gray?" His arm retracted back to his side as quickly as his body twisted to face hers. "Is it that serious? Was it fighting again?"

"No." Carrie took a deep breath, moving her body to

face him. "Mrs Gray says that the girls have been taking things that don't belong to them."

"Taking things? Like what? Stealing?" He scowled, confused.

The hairs on the back of her neck began to tingle and stood on end. Distant but familiar alarm bells rang in her ears. She knew that look; he was going to erupt when she told him the full story. That work email had triggered it. She wondered if she could diffuse the situation, perhaps play it down. Stealing was a bit difficult to play down. No, it was too late. She was already too far down the destructive dead end. The fuse had been lit, and it was only a matter of time before the explosion blew them to a place neither wanted to be in.

"Carrie! Tell me!" he demanded. Matthew's face was ashen-grey etched with furrows of concern and a fixed solemn stare. His eyes were like a persuasive weapon, peeling away the layers of her secret until she divulged it. "What's going on?"

Again, she breathed hard. She was rapidly trying to make sense of it all so that her words wouldn't unleash a tsunami of incrimination.

"Mrs Gray says that Jen and Hannah have been taking, no, her words were 'collecting' other children's things like rubbers, keyrings, badges. Some of the children saw them do it, so Mrs Gray searched their bags and found all the missing items."

"Searched their bags? Has she got any authority to do that?" Matthew was desperately trying to cling on to the only piece of driftwood in this mess.

"I don't know, Matthew, but it's not the point, is it? She had to find out somehow." Carrie looked down, waiting for the first blast.

Matthew leaned back into the sofa once again and took another sip. "So, what has she done about it?"

"Mrs Gray and Mr Turner have confronted the girls, and Hannah admitted to it. They said they liked them, and that's why they were taking them."

"Confronted?"

"Well, I mean spoken to...."

"But you said confronted. Was it a confrontation? Were our girls put in a threatening situation?"

"I don't think so, Matthew. This is Mrs Gray. She's kind and compassionate. She wouldn't have *confronted* our five-year-old girls in a threatening manner." Matthew snorted his disapproval. "She asked if we knew why they might take the things."

"Kids are like magpies at that age. Anything new and shiny, and they want it."

"Yes, I pretty much said that to her. She thought there might be a deeper reason, though, as they have been quite disruptive recently." Carrie ventured onto the thin ice. She knew that it would crack but speaking to Matthew was often like swallowing truth serum. She couldn't lie or leave any part out. "She said kids can take things for a number of reasons, jealousy, attention…maybe they are missing having you around, and it's their way of getting your attention? Mrs Gray did ask if you were at home…."

Matthew froze. A stark realisation washed over him.

"Oh right…now I know where this is *really* going." Carrie felt his body stiffen as he rose and strode to the fridge to get another beer. "In some warped little twisted way, you have managed to make this my fault, haven't you?" He pulled open the fridge door and angrily snatched a bottle.

"No…no…I'm just telling you what was discussed at our meeting…."

"So, you quite openly discussed our personal lives with the headteacher of our kids' school?"

"No, she suggested you being absent might be a factor. I said that it was ridiculous."

"Really?" Matthew glared at her. "So why am I having a hard time believing that? You'd relish the opportunity to be the hard-done-by little housewife, wouldn't you? How awful that your husband goes to work all hours and you're left all alone. No wonder the five-year-old twins are stealing. It's due to their daddy not being around."

"Matthew, please," she begged. "Just listen. You haven't heard everything yet."

"Oh, I think I've got the gist, Carrie. Bloody hell! We

were having such a lovely weekend too. Why does the balloon have to go up every time with you?"

He slammed his beer bottle on the counter so hard that it made Betty jump. Carrie was surprised it hadn't cracked open. She attempted to back-pedal out of the situation. She had managed to do it on occasion. She just had to calm him down by choosing her words carefully.

"Mrs Gray thinks it would be good for the twins if they were in separate classes. Perhaps it would give them an opportunity to shine as individuals for a bit. I think it's quite a good idea now I've had time to think about it."

"Oh yes, that's right!" The momentum was building again. "You've known about this for a while, haven't you? When was your meeting? Three days ago?"

"Two," she replied, lowering her head. It *had* been a mistake not to tell him straight away.

"Two days! *Two days* you've sat on this. Didn't you think it was important enough to tell me at the time? Maybe give *me* a chance to think about it? Were you wanting to play out the sorry housewife card a little longer?"

"But you've been so busy, and you were quite late back the other night...."

"And there it is. Another arrow through the heart of a hardworking father. Jesus Christ, Carrie! You can be so heartless. You could have picked up the phone or texted. You're not a single parent, you know!"

Before she could stop them, her eyebrows twitched

upwards. Although her mouth hadn't betrayed her, the expression had. He saw it. He had been watching carefully, like a bird of prey waiting to swoop down on any surly response—verbal or non-verbal.

"Well then. Clearly, that's what you think you are! A single parent! Poor hard-done-to Carrie! Bringing up these three feral children on her own without any help or support from her spouse! Isn't she a saint!" The rant continued. "And while I'm at it, why on earth would you want to split our girls up? What gives you the right to make that decision...?"

"I wasn't," Carrie tried to interject.

"They're best friends, Carrie! It would be like ripping them in two from their very core!"

He was quiet for a long time then, occasionally taking a swig of beer, no doubt contemplating what she had said so he could twist the dirty knife of guilt just a little more into her heart. She found the courage from somewhere to look at him. He was staring into the bottom of his beer bottle, twisting it around and around. She studied him carefully and longed to know what he was thinking. She knew he was upset with her for not telling him, and she knew he was cross with himself, but there was something else. What other secrets lay locked away in the vaults of his mind? Carrie wished she had the key to unlock his brooding. Even just a little crack of a window would do, just to peep into his thoughts. He looked lost. Why did he shut her out? She was his wife. They were supposed to be in this together. She opened her mouth to speak, but he was there first.

"You do what you think is best, but know this,

Carrie…." His eyes were bearing down on her now. "If it gets worse for my girls, I'll hold you responsible for this."

With that, he downed his beer and went to bed.

A few moments later, the bathroom door clicked open, and Carrie caught a glimpse of Luke scurrying off to bed. Her heart sank.

CHAPTER 9

Jonathan Parker was about mid-thirties, older than Matthew had expected. He was certainly not the young whipper-snapper Stanton-Peake had made him out to be in her weekend email. He was tall and lean, which irritated Matthew. He had thick brown hair (also irritating to a forty-something balding chap) and a pathetic beard stitched to his chin. The beard did, however, make Matthew feel much better. He knew instantly that he wouldn't like him. Not just from the annoying introduction of him in his inbox on Friday night, nor that Matthew had had to rearrange his day and come into the office instead of working from home, or the fact that Matthew had had a headache from the moment he had woken up three hours earlier. It was the way he was conducting himself in Clarissa's office that was pissing him off. All amateur-dramatic-like with big arm gestures and nodding like an incessant lap dog. What a prick!

Curiously, Johanna was in the office with them. From her face, she didn't look too impressed either. Matthew knew she would gather intel for him on their new colleague, and he would look forward to hearing her observations later. He peeled his eyes away from the glass frontage of Clarissa's office and made his way across the open-plan floor to his own.

He had so much to do. He had lost precious time this weekend. Carrie and her little performance on Saturday night had zapped him of all focus and energy, and he had spent the rest of Sunday hammering balls down the driving range.

His emails were pinging through his smartwatch like an alarm clock reverberating on his wrist. Why had he bothered syncing the two? It was like he never got a break from it all. He was torn between keeping in touch and keeping his steps up to ripping the damn thing off his arm and throwing it in the bin.

He had a mountain of accounts to check over and budgets to review. His head was throbbing. He wished he could have called in sick, but the thought of being here, tucked away in his office, working like he was wading through treacle, was much more appealing than spending the day with *her*.

Johanna was at his door. She gingerly knocked, and he waved her in. As she sat down, he pulled some paracetamol from his laptop bag and chucked them down his throat, followed by a clean swig of water.

"You ok?" Johanna asked. "Decided to come in then?"

"Yeah, yeah." He brushed off her comments as he collapsed into his office chair. "So…what's up? Our new friend, settling in ok?"

Johanna shot him an impatient look. "He's quite full of himself. Not sure why he's an intern. He seems to know everything already." She rolled her eyes, then settled her gaze on the paperwork in front of him. "What's all this? Want some help?"

"No, don't worry. It's my problem. I just need a few hours to smash through it. Why don't you take charge of Jonathan for me today? I can't face it. Show him the team, and accounts, not all of them, obviously. Take him out to lunch, a *long* lunch. I'm sorry, Johanna, but I want to get my head in the game with these. The board of directors want some answers this afternoon from this lot, and I need to provide them quickly."

Johanna sighed quietly and rose. "Ok, boss. But you're having him back tomorrow, ok?"

"Sure, can't wait." He grimaced.

"Thought any more about starting your extra-curricular assignment yet?" she teased.

"I can't say I know what you mean." Matthew flashed her a flirtatious smile, and she disappeared to do his dirty work.

* * *

The day dragged, and so did his headache, plundering his concentration and melting his rationality. He had just about held it together through the difficult meeting with Harvey and the others. They had seemed satisfied that all was in order. Johanna's pint-sized pay cheques remained hidden within the profits, and he was tentatively excited about receiving his own supplementary earnings. He would have to be incredibly careful. Stanton-Peake was sniffing around him like a drug detection dog, quizzing him on every account and personally checking figures herself. It was as if she knew he was up to something, but how could she? She clearly didn't trust or like him and had made that clear since he was promoted. As Head of New Business and Sales, she had a unique interest in checking all the records. He respected her attentiveness and almost admired her intensity, but she unnerved him. He began to doubt whether he could get away with his master plan after all. But what a coup if he did! Just knowing that he had one up on that snooty, cold-hearted bitch would be so satisfying.

It was nearly six. His headache had subsided, and he had to go home. The traffic would have eased, so the journey could take him as little as twenty minutes. But he didn't want to be home in twenty minutes. He wished he could go somewhere else, anywhere else. He longed for his old life, then fantasised about a life he never had but could have if he hadn't met Carrie. She had always been in his life, since they were both fifteen years old. He didn't know anything or anyone else. He wondered what he had missed out on.

His phone vibrated. It was the bank. Shit! He had forgotten about his follow-up meeting. He let it ring out and decided to listen to the voicemail in the car. He'd deal with it tomorrow.

Matthew gathered up his laptop and keys, then left. He decided to drive the 'long way' home to do some thinking. He cruised the streets of the town, taking in the sights. Despite it being a cold Monday night, dozens of jubilant groups were enjoying the early Christmas festivities. His eye glimpsed a sparkle of sequins shimmering under a fur coat, a gaggle of women already staggering on their outrageous heels, trip-trapped their way in front of his car. The trailing blonde caught his gaze and gave him a little wave. He was tempted to park his car up and follow them. He wanted to go into a maze of the unknown and escape the day-to-day more than anything, but something made him drive on.

The town looked pretty. Christmas lights twinkled, enhancing the streetlights illuminating his way. Brash, mundane Christmas music from three decades ago drifted out of the moist, sweaty establishments lining the streets. Merriment was oozing out of every crevice, and Matthew wished he could lose himself amongst it all just for the night. A night off duty from being a father, husband and responsible company director. Tonight, he wanted to be someone else.

As he approached the proverbial crossroads, his mind whirled. One way led to home, while the other to a curious world he yearned to explore. What would he do? Where would he go? A taxi beeped its horn behind him, the traffic light had only been on green for seconds, but Matthew's hesitation was irritating enough for the driver at this crucial time of night.

Matthew turned left. Home

* * *

"I told you, Mum. I'm just not hungry," Luke insisted.

"But you've had football training and fitness today. You need to eat, Luke. I can make you anything you want…pasta, stir fry, bangers and mash? What do you fancy?"

"None of the above." He smiled at her. "Mum, honestly. Don't worry. I don't want to be a bother. I'll just have a bit of toast."

"Beans on toast?" she offered.

"Nah. Dry. I'm just not in the mood. I might go up and have a bath in a bit."

She watched her son slip two slices of wholemeal into the toaster. He was getting so tall and starting to fill out. He was gaining his father's lovely broad shoulders. Not only was he maturing mentally, but his physical appearance was also changing. More signs of the man he was about to become.

"How about some peanut butter?" She placed the jar down on the sideboard in front of him.

"Ok." He winked. "Just a little."

Without warning, Betty came bounding in from the living room. She was sporting an old scarf of Carrie's, which was tucked into her collar, and the girls had coloured in her front claws with felt tip pen.

"Oh god!" exclaimed Carrie. "You poor dog!"

"She loves it, Mummy!" Hannah suddenly appeared in the kitchen. "We've got a beauty shop in the living room. You're our next customer!"

"Really? I'm about to cook tea, actually," she replied, amused.

Luke grabbed his toast from the toaster and escaped upstairs. Carrie stared after her son. She was losing him.

"We do boys, too!" Jen called. "What would you like, Mummy? Nails? Hair? Makeup?"

"Erm, where did you get the makeup from?" Carrie gulped. She wanted to close her eyes as she entered the living room area. She envisaged eye shadow trodden into the rug and mascara wand stripes across the cushions. However, what greeted her was a neatly organised, dare she say, professional set-up. The girls had laid out their felt tip pens in rainbow colour order across the coffee table, alongside sponges, flannels and soap stolen from the bathroom. A mismatch of Carrie's lipsticks sat neatly in a row behind them, accompanied by a nail file. She had to admit that it was impressive for a couple of five-year-olds.

"Wow, girls! This looks great." As she glanced around the room, her eyes settled upon a collection of unfamiliar artefacts on the side table. A flamingo keyring, a sparkly bouncy ball and a handkerchief with a pink initial 'I' stitched into it. "Oh! What are these?" Carrie gestured towards the items. "Are they for sale?"

Jen looked at Hannah and raised her eyebrows. They

both looked back at their mum. Finally, Hannah quietly said, "No. They belong to someone at school."

"Oh. Who?" Carrie asked in her best-surprised voice.

"Imogen," Jen replied. "But she doesn't mind. We're just looking after them for her."

"Oh, right," Carrie said gently, taking the girls by the hand and settling them on the living room floor. The proverbial penny had dropped right through the slot. The moment had presented itself beautifully, and Carrie knew she could nip this in the bud—right here, right now.

"Do you sometimes look after things for other people?"

"Yeah."

"Ok…why?" Carrie looked into the eyes of her innocent girls. It was just a game to them. She knew that now.

"Because…we're playing, Mummy. We need things for our shop," Hannah said as if it was the most obvious thing in the world.

"And where is this shop, Han? Is it at school?"

"Yeah, course it is!" They both laughed.

"Who comes to the shop, girls?" Carrie continued to probe; this was a positive breakthrough.

"Everyone at school."

"How do they pay?" Carrie bit her lip. Did she honestly think that her girls were charging their friends for their own stuff?

"They don't. We just look after it."

"Some shops do that, you know. Dee told us."

"Oh. Does Dee play shops too, then?" Carrie asked.

"No. She likes to play football with the boys, so we just do it on our own. She always asks about it, though, Mummy," Jen explained.

"Yeah. Sometimes, she tells us what the shop needs, so we get it," Hannah pitched in.

"Oh, ok." Carrie's mind raced. This was an interesting development. How should she approach this? "Did Mrs Gray and Mr Turner have a chat with you about it?"

It transpired, unsurprisingly, that Mrs Gray and Mr Turner had blown the whole story way out of proportion. If they had only taken a more delicate approach in investigating the situation, they would have realised it had all just been part of a game. They were not taking other pupils' stuff; they were looking after it. To a five-year-old, there was a big difference. Carrie was so relieved. She knew there must have been more to it. She would call Mrs Gray first thing tomorrow and explain and also talk to Matthew. Hopefully, this would help to settle his concerns, and they could move on. The girls wouldn't need to be spilt up, and he wouldn't blame her for it.

Carrie explained to the twins that taking people's things

without them knowing was not ok, even if it was part of a game. The girls seemed to understand and handled it well. They agreed to only play shops with their own stuff and not to listen to everything another child told them to do.

Carrie thought about the influence little Delilah seemed to have on her two, and something about it didn't sit right with her. She wondered if she should talk to Terry about it tomorrow. Her heart leapt at the thought. It was not a particularly nice topic to speak to him about, but she had to for her girls. She'd suggest the coffee shop on the high street, where they could sit in a secluded corner. It would need to be handled tactfully. After all, Delilah was the twins' best friend. And Terry? Carrie wasn't sure what he was, but she couldn't deny the attraction in these sterile days roughly stitched together to make up her so-called life. Carrie enjoyed the distraction.

Matthew appeared through the front door. Shit! She hadn't even started dinner. He would not be best pleased about that at 6:45 p.m. on a Monday night, but at least she could now explain the girls' unusual behaviour. It would have to be a culinary delight from the freezer tonight.

* * *

Later as she brushed her teeth, she was glad she had talked to Matthew. He was hot-headed and impulsive at times, but once she had explained the situation, the *real* situation, he had understood. Although initially stung by his reaction, she knew her husband was just lashing out. At least this time, he had listened to what she had to say and not tethered her to days of his cold shoulder.

He was exhausted, much like her son, and the Christmas

holidays couldn't come quick enough. Matthew wasn't so keen on encouraging the relationship with Delilah, stating what a bad influence he thought she was, but Carrie was resolute that this was one connection she was not prepared to sever.

She decided not to say anything to Terry about Delilah. There was no need to make it into a big deal. The thought of Terry filled her with warmth, and she knew how much his little girl meant to him. She couldn't upset him with an issue that had been effectively dealt with. If anything else happened, though, she would speak up. She would have to think of another excuse to get Terry out for a coffee tomorrow.

* * *

Matthew couldn't sleep. He was still thinking about what could have been. Confusion clouded his mind. Not only confusion but remorse. He had overreacted. Carrie was doing her best; they all were.

He looked at his wife sleeping peacefully beside him. What would she think of him if she knew his inner thoughts and desires? What would she think of him if she knew how he was planning to pay their debt? Her innocence amplified his deceit. He reached out and touched her hand under the covers; she stirred gently and rolled onto her side. He was sure that she had squeezed his hand back. He suddenly felt a familiar, distant love for his wife and family. He was proud of them and pondered how two green young people, with a naïve view of the world, had created something so wonderful.

Carrie was a fabulous mother. He knew that he didn't

tell her enough, and he should. She had managed the situation with the girls without the merest hint of a ruffle. She had lifted her babies, turned them around and set them back down on the desired direction of socialisation so gently that the five-year-olds understood how to interact with their peers properly without even realising it. His heart melted and then froze again. How could he have unleashed those barbed words on her without trusting her motherly instincts to kick in? He had to control his temper. He knew there were only so many attacks on her character that she was willing to absorb.

She was also a good wife—loving and attentive. He was just trying to do the right thing, and he couldn't let her or his children down. He had to keep the plates spinning. At least he had negotiated some breathing room with this new intern under Johanna's guidance. He could delegate some frivolous tasks to him, so he could concentrate on being a step ahead of Stanton-Peake. The week ahead looked stagnant as he thought of all the meetings he had to chair and bonuses he had to review. It was also the bloody office Christmas party at the end of the week. Now he was Financial Director, he could no longer crack a few jokes with the other staff at the expense of the management or slip away quietly without being seen. He would have to sit with the 'borings' and, as soon as he was able, would leave early. Good plan. He also had to phone the bank. He sighed as he rolled over to switch off the light. Yep, another bloody long week.

CHAPTER 10

The rain was hammering down. Why Luke insisted on playing football on nights like this was beyond Carrie. Matthew called to say he would be late, so she had to bring the twins out past their bedtime to pick Luke up. They were whining and complaining, fighting their overtiredness. Books, dolls, music and even marshmallows couldn't satisfy Hannah. Carrie had had to resort to her mobile and Temple Run app. At least she could have some peace for the last five minutes of training.

Despite the dismal weather that had plagued the day, it had been wonderful. Terry had asked Carrie to go for a coffee after dropping the kids off, and for an hour and a half, she had been lost in his childhood stories and his philosophies of life. He was intriguing and sensitive, the opposite of Matthew. Carrie was heightened by the parallels she could draw between her own marriage and his.

He talked a lot about the highs and lows of his relationship with Corrine. It was clear from his words that he loved her intensely but at the same time seemed so frustrated with her lack of commitment to family life. She wanted the 'mummy stamp' but didn't seem to want all that came with it. Terry described how his heart broke every time he saw his daughter's crest-fallen face as her mother had chosen a work call over baking biscuits with her or a business dinner over movie night. Corrine just didn't get it. She would never get these years back with Delilah. He felt she was already wishing away her childhood to a time when they could be retail therapy buddies and spa mates. Terry cringed when she showered Delilah with expensive gifts from her various trips away. Delilah was young enough to lap it up and thought her mum was fabulous, but it wouldn't be long before she'd see through this fake thoughtfulness to the lazy neglect it really was. They were his words, *'lazy'* and *'neglect'*, harsh but fair, she concluded. He was protecting his daughter, after all. Such a shame it was her mother that he was protecting her from.

Carrie asked about the playhouse, and Terry's eyes lit up again like the disturbed embers of a dying fire. They glowed as he described the painstaking effort of getting the dovetail joints to line up correctly and cutting out the decorative arches of the doorway and shutters. He would be on to painting it by next week, and he had wanted Carrie's opinion on the colour. She was flattered but couldn't help feeling she was stealing the decision from Corrine. He should have been asking his wife's opinion, not hers. However, when she protested this, he insisted, so she suggested a brilliant teal. She had remembered the beautiful garden at the cottage where he lived, bursting with oranges, pinks and purples and the fantastic Japanese maple. The teal playhouse would sit elegantly amongst those pretty tones. Terry was enchanted.

"Wonderful!" he had exclaimed, clasping up his coffee and taking a deep swig. He smiled at her, and she felt her colour rise. "Perfect."

The door of the car suddenly opened, and a sodden, wet, muddy life form slid into the front seat. Carrie wished she had brought a towel for him to sit on, but it was too late now. His waterlogged clothes and pungent odour were seeping into the fabric of the seat, leaving a filthy stain that would take weeks to eradicate. She was about to ask how the session went when there was a tap on her window. It was the coach. He gestured for her to get out for a word. Carrie reluctantly obliged, leaving the warmth of the car to see what he wanted. She pulled up her hood and folded her arms as her friend John Paterson spoke from the shelter of his umbrella.

"Sorry, Carrie. Awful night, isn't it?" She nodded and hoped he would get on with it. "I'm worried about Luke."

Carrie glared at him. "Go on," she urged, desperately wanting to get out of the rain.

Carrie had known John Paterson for years. He had been a friend of her middle stepbrother, Nick, and had always hung around their house during her teenage years, destroying her mother's garden with the football and playing computer games in the front room. Nick had always teased his friend about how he had a soft spot for his stepsister, but she knew it wasn't true. He was just a decent guy, hence why she was anxious now. She could hear the concern in his voice.

"Luke had to sit out a while before you arrived. He was complaining of feeling lightheaded. I've also noticed that he's a bit slower than he usually is. Less reactive to the ball. Is he overdoing it at school?" Carrie stepped under the canopy, embracing its cover from the relentless rain.

"No," she replied. "Quite the opposite." She thought of him lounging around the house and sleeping at every opportunity. "He's certainly *not* overdoing it."

"Oh right, well, maybe he's just off form at the moment," John replied. "He's such a key player in the team, but besides that, I've noticed that he seems withdrawn from his teammates and overreacts when decisions don't go his way. That's not like Luke." He looked directly at Carrie. "It's not drugs, is it?"

"Certainly not," she snapped. However, she couldn't be one hundred per cent sure. Luke was distant and moody. She felt like she hardly knew him anymore. Maybe he was hiding something. She softened her manner towards John; he was only trying to help.

"Thanks, John. I'll talk to him." John nodded and walked her back to the car.

"See you Saturday morning," he called to Luke as Carrie slipped into the driver's seat from under the umbrella. Then he disappeared into the shadows of the dank, soggy evening.

Carrie turned to Luke. He was lost inside the LCD of his mobile phone, oblivious to the shrieks of his sisters squabbling in the back seat. She was shocked at how fragile and gaunt he looked in the screen's glow. She would talk to him later. It was impossible here with the distraction of the girls, who were now about ten seconds from detonating the self-destruct button on themselves. As Carrie pulled off into the road, the head of Hannah's doll became detached from its neck. There was a second of brilliant silence as what had just happened caught up with Hannah's brain, and then wails of agony reverberated around the car so loudly that Carrie was sure one of her eardrums had burst. The noise was excruciating, like her little girl was having her fingernails pulled out one by one with a pair of pliers in some gruesome hostage situation. Suddenly Jen started too. Quarter past eight was no time to have two five-year-olds up on a school night. *Bloody Matthew*, she thought as she waited impatiently to turn right at the junction, mentally arming herself for the battle looming for her with the girls when she got home.

* * *

Luke had a shower, wolfed down some beans on toast and went to bed. He didn't want to talk, despite her protests. Teenagers really were a unique breed. She thought back to when she was a teen and cringed. She had been bloody awful to her mum and stepfather—moody and self-indulgent. She understood that Luke wanted his own space but for John Paterson to have commented on the changes in his character meant she *had* to investigate further. She decided that a little snoop in his room might be a good idea tomorrow, and she would pester him all week until he did talk to her.

She let Betty out in the garden and settled on the sofa with a glass of wine. It had taken ages to calm the girls after they had got home. Even with a warm bubble bath and Carrie's expensive lavender pillow mist, they still fought their slumber. It had taken three stories before seeing their eyelids droop and mouths yawn widely. Carrie was exhausted. She was fighting the tiredness herself, and it was only half past nine. The girls were now far away in the land of nod, and Luke, too, as there was no noise coming from his room. The TV flickered, as did her eyelids. Soon she succumbed to the seduction of sleep and nestled into the old Chesterfield sofa.

When she awoke, it was half past one in the morning. Focusing on her surroundings, she could see Betty had been let in and was snoring sweetly in her basket in the kitchen. Carrie's glass of wine was still on the coffee table but had since been elevated by a coaster, she noted and smiled. The lights were off in the kitchen, and the dishwasher was humming methodically to its own cleaning tune. Matthew's keys were on the kitchen island where he usually left them. He was home. He had not tried to wake her. Instead, he had draped the old woollen throw over her and let her be. A distant warmth drifted around her and settled on her shoulders.

She didn't know that two hours earlier, he had watched her sleeping peacefully for twenty minutes as he let the complications of his day dissolve with every sip of his wine. She didn't know that he had kissed her tenderly on the cheek before retreating upstairs to seek some escape from the worries and burdens that stole him away from his family life. She didn't see it, but it was there, always. He knew it and felt it, but he just couldn't reach out and tell her how much he loved her.

CHAPTER 11

You couldn't describe Luke's room as a bedroom; it was a pit. *A pit of despair,* Carrie thought, as she recalled how she had lovingly tided it up the week before. The clothes she had ironed to within an inch of their life were now overflowing from a newly-broken chest of drawers. Books, papers, and what looked like the entire contents of his pencil case were strewn all over the carpet. His bed was unmade, with the sheet half coming off. The shade on his bedside light was jaunting at an erratic angle, and the smell! Had Betty brought something dead upstairs again and left it in here? She would never know under all this mess! It was like a scene from a gangster movie just after a fight. How would she find anything in here?

Carrie sat on the corner of his bed and took a sharp intake of breath. She had no choice. She had to find out what was on in her son's mind. She recalled her conversation with John Paterson the night before. *"It's not drugs, is it?"* She didn't know. She hadn't a clue. Luke, the beautiful bundle of fun she had welcomed into the world fifteen years ago, had gone. In his place stood a ghost, a vacant outline of the boy she knew.

John was right; he was distracted and withdrawn. He didn't engage in family life, but Carrie had put this down to being a teen and wanting to find his own place in the world. However, the age gap between him and the girls had never been more obvious. Maybe he was just wrestling with the transition from boyhood to manhood. The teenage years were such a difficult time.

Twisting around to pull the bedsheet back over the mattress, an old acquaintance fell out of the covers, Floppy. Carrie bent down to pick up the ragged, threadbare platypus and held him close. She closed her eyes and breathed in the scent of her son.

"Come back to me," she whispered into the fabric of her old friend. After a few moments, she set about righting the wrongs of the room, hoping to uncover a clue from the mysterious agony that was consuming Luke.

The search was fruitless, but at least Luke had a tidy room now. Betty had disturbed Carrie from her troubled thoughts, persuading her to get some fresh air, and gratefully she obliged.

"Run or walk, girl?" she asked her excited pal. "Yes, I quite agree. A run would do us good."

In just over ten minutes, they were out running in the low winter sunshine, heading purposefully for the woods. Betty was leaping in and out of the prickly skeletal clumps of hedging and bushes that scraped across the cold ground. Carrie had to pick her way carefully as the overnight frost had penetrated the path here and there, making it slippery and uneven underfoot. The branches reached and yawned as the figures skipped by while delicate droplets of icy tears glistened and danced in the light. It was eerily quiet, with only the occasional shrill of a winter bird and Carrie's even footsteps drumming through the hushed balance.

She thought of Christmas, her favourite time of year. Special in so many ways with a young family but also woven with nostalgia and tradition from her own childhood. Her father instilled the love of the season in her. He tried so hard to be home for Christmas and do all the normal fatherly things, church on Christmas Eve, decorate the tree, make crepe Christmas crackers out of toilet roll, and bake mince pies. Her memories, although faded and frayed, filled her with love, so she tried to recreate these traditions with her children. They made the dumb crackers, burnt the mince pies, and went to church on Christmas Eve. Her mother was usually drunk for most of the holiday and out at some god-awful party until the small hours. She said it was her 'payback' time for looking after Carrie whilst Edward was away. She also dressed it up by calling it quality time with her dad. Carrie smiled to herself, but that was just it. It really *was* quality time. Her mum couldn't see or appreciate it. Sometimes she felt it was like this with Matthew. He was always chasing something more and couldn't see what was right in front of him.

"Carrie?" A face appeared from the path to her left, making her startle. "Are you mad?"

Even without her glasses, Carrie knew it was Corrine. She looked incredible, wrapped in a long, woollen, camel coat, rich brown leather boots and a cashmere pom-pom hat. In contrast, Carrie must have looked a complete mess—red-faced and puffy in her ill-fitting synthetics, sweating and stinking.

"Why would you run in this weather? You might slip over and hurt yourself." she exclaimed.

As she approached, she looked even more beautiful with cerise pink splashed across her lips and powerful dark eyelashes that could bat away an army. If Carrie didn't have such a crush on her husband, she could easily have one on her.

"Hi, Corrine." She stumbled awkwardly on a rogue pebble.

"See what I mean, girl!" Corrine pouted. "Terry loves all this trail running stuff. Why anyone would want to run outside in the cold and rain when you get the same results on a treadmill is beyond me!"

Carrie bit her lip. She didn't want to go into the benefits of wild running as opposed to 'robot running,' as she called it. She had an inkling that Corrine wouldn't care or even listen anyway.

"I'm just out for a bit of fresh air, though, escaping the laptop for a little while. You know how it is?" Carrie didn't.

"I think they call it a brain break or something," Corrine continued. "Terry's always droning on about this forest, so I thought I'd check it out. Anyway, I'm glad I caught you. I hear the girls have been a little naughty at school."

Carrie was taken aback. She didn't think for one minute that Corrine would have been informed about the 'stealing' incidents. Sensing Corrine wanted a response, she blurted out something about it being a big misunderstanding and how the three of them had just been playing a game.

"Three?" Corrine fired back at her. "I thought it was *your* twins doing the stealing *and* the fighting. That's what I heard anyway. Who else is involved? Do tell!"

Carrie felt uneasy. Where was Corrine getting her information from? She seemed to enjoy extracting idle chatter. Who was the weak link? She shifted her weight from one trainer to the other and folded her arms defensively. Corrine was treating this unfortunate incident like gossip. It most certainly was *not* gossip, but if she wanted to know who, then Carrie felt it was *not* her duty to tell her. She lied. Corinne intimidated her. She felt her towering over her like an inquisitor with her expensive boots and flawless hair framing her perfect face, willing her to answer her demands. Carrie had to think quickly. She noticed the LV initials emblazoned across Corrine's expensive silk scarf tucked beneath the camel coat.

"Louis," she blurted. Carrie didn't even know if there was a Louis at the school, let alone in their class, but she was sure Corrine wouldn't know anyway.

"Well, I'm glad they're sorting it out. No offence, Carrie, but I can't abide stealing, bullying or any other disregard for anyone's property or feelings."

What about your husband's feelings? Carrie thought defensively, then pulled herself out of it. She wouldn't lower herself to bitterness.

"So, what are you doing for Christmas?" Corrine changed the subject, seemingly bored by having failed to obtain the juicy details from the previous conversation.

Carrie was about to reply, "Nothing much," when Corrine began boasting about extending a work trip to London so Terry and Delilah could join her and travel down on the train (first class, of course). They were going to take in a West End show, a shopping trip to Hamleys (Delilah has an unlimited budget there), dinner at a top restaurant, blah, blah, blah! She whined about how she'd be working most of the time and how awful it would be to miss out on the precious time with her daughter, but needs must when you're the breadwinner. At this, she rolled her eyes in an attempt to gain Carrie's sympathy.

"God, I do wish Terry would get a proper job. Now Delilah's at school, he can stop playing the bank clerk and get back up that career ladder."

"Don't you like him at home?" Carrie quizzed. "Meals cooked, washing done, tidy house."

Corrine glared at her. "Do you know how embarrassing it is telling clients about my stay-at-home husband? They think it's hilarious! They all picture this little nancy-of-a-man flouncing about with a feather duster. They can't imagine me being married to a weak man like that."

Carrie flushed with a spark of anger; Corrine really knew how to push her buttons. Terry was not weak, far from it. He had sacrificed his passion and career for his family. How dare she speak about him in this way! She wanted to shout at her and tell her how bloody lucky she was! She wanted to tell her that her own husband made her feel like crap every time she put a foot wrong. She wanted to yell out loud that Terry made her feel alive and not like a doormat. But she didn't. She was the weak one.

"So, you haven't told me about your holiday plans?" Corrine's words snapped her from her angry speculation.

"Us? Oh no. Nothing. Matthew's got his Christmas party on Friday, and we might go out for a meal at The Three Horseshoes...." She drivelled on, even boring herself. "We are going away in February, though." She felt she had to throw some sort of competitive comment into the ring so she didn't sound utterly pathetic.

"Oooh, what a coincidence. It's my Christmas party on Friday, too," she cooed. "What does Matthew do, and who does he work for? I've not even met him yet." She was luring Carrie into something. *Be careful,* Carrie told herself.

"He's the Finance Director at Harvey's in town," she replied quietly hoping that this discrete little business would pass her by like the holiday comment.

"Ah, yes! Clarissa works there! We've done a bit of work with them over the years. Well, maybe our paths will cross at some point then!" She smirked. "In fact, I must give Clarissa a call and catch up with her soon. It's been ages!"

Bugger, thought Carrie. The last thing she needed was Corrine getting her perfectly polished talons into Matthew.

"Right, well, better be off. Working from home can be so distracting, that's why I prefer the office. Bye, Carrie. See you soon."

Carrie watched her go. Corrine didn't pick her way slowly or carefully over the frozen ground, and she didn't need to. Every footstep oozed sophistication and self-assurance. Her confidence was off the chart as opposed to Carrie's, which was so low it might as well be located somewhere in Australia.

She sighed, about to take up her run again, when she suddenly remembered Betty. Where was the dog? Carrie looked around herself frantically.

"Betty! Betty! Betty!" She called over and over. "Betty! Come on, girl!"

She rushed over to the hedges and thickets, but nothing. She retraced her steps along the path to where she thought she had last seen her. Nothing.

"Betty! Betty!" Carrie yelled. She told herself not to panic. The big, black dog often did this and then turned up a few minutes later. The trouble was it had been more than a few minutes later. How long had she been chatting to Corrine? Bloody Corrine! If she hadn't been so distracted…. "Betty!"

Carrie's heart started pounding as the seriousness of the situation started to take hold. *Think, Carrie! Think! Where were the few places a dog would hide?* She reached down to retrieve the whistle from her pocket. *Damn, she'd forgotten it again.*

She decided to try the hilltop. Betty could be up there waiting for her as, for some miraculous reason, she might have realised that was where they had been originally heading. However, when Carrie arrived at the summit minutes later, panting wildly from all the shouting and searching, there was no sign of her. She looked out over the trees hoping that their winter exposure might reveal where her furry black dot of a dog was hiding. Nothing. She searched the maze of houses and streets beyond the trees, retracing her journey back home. Nothing. She turned to look out over the estuary. Maybe Betty had chased a rabbit or fox along the river and ended up at the mouth, lost. To her dismay, a damp sea mist was descending across the water, rapidly enveloping the surrounding land. She would have to go down there herself and continue the search.

* * *

Hours later, Carrie admitted defeat. After looking for nearly three hours, she had come across a red, nylon collar hanging at eye level from a small holly tree—it was Betty's. Tears streamed down her cheeks as she detached it from the branch. She examined it carefully, there was no damage, and the collar had been fastened tightly on a high branch on the tree. Someone had taken it off her and placed it there. Had they done it on purpose? Had Betty been taken?

"Betty! Betty!" she wailed, hugging the collar tightly to her chest, attempting to fill the void that was now developing so rapidly in her heart. Her feet ached, her head was pounding, and her voice was hoarse. Stumbling home, she suddenly thought that Betty could be there. Just sitting casually on the doorstep like she often did in the front garden.

She remembered how the collar had been intentionally attached to the branch. Her mind whirred like a tornado, gathering momentum with every new thought. What if she had slipped her collar and someone had just found it and hung it on there? What if she had run home? She would be cold, tired and frightened. Carrie had to get to her now.

She took a sharp intake of breath and wiped her face with the back of her hand. Although she was exhausted, she quickened her steps. She crossed the road without even looking and continued down her road as fast as she could. Rounding the old privet hedge that provided her living room with some privacy from the nosy pedestrians that walked to the park, she felt her heart skip a beat. Was she there?

No. The step was empty.

Carrie somehow crawled to the front door and sat down on the step where her dog should have been sitting. She delicately lay the collar down next to her like it was as precious as the crown jewels and burst into tears. What should she do now? Get in the car and trail the streets for the rest of the afternoon?

Betty could be anywhere. How was she going to tell the kids? How was she going to tell Matthew? Dread consumed her. She had failed them, and she had failed Betty.

* * *

"Mummy! Mummy! Where were you?"

Carrie looked up to see her daughters running towards her, arms outstretched. She instinctively pulled them to her and buried her tormented face in their hair. She must have lost track of time. Terry had picked up the girls from

143

school along with another friend of Carrie's, Alisha, who lived a few doors down. They were standing at her gate with concerned looks on their faces.

"Everything ok, Carrie?" Alisha asked, coming up the path and clutching her son's hand. Terry and Delilah closely followed her. "We did try and call you. Mr Turner wanted the girls to stay in the library, but we insisted they come with us. Is that ok?"

"Yeah, I hope you don't mind." Terry squatted down to face Carrie. His beautiful eyes met hers, the perfect lines on his face drawn from worry, not age.

The kids were now racing around the garden, taking turns to jump over the path from one side of the little lawn to the other. It was all just a blur, and Carrie didn't really know what was happening. Terry seized the moment and took her hands in his.

"Carrie, you're freezing! What is it?"

She couldn't speak. She couldn't get the words out. Terry said something to Alisha, and the next moment the two of them were alone on the step. He pulled her close to him, and she breathed him in. A faint scent of coffee and lime mixed with his masculine scent filled her with a second of comfort. Then he was probing her again. "Talk to me, Carrie. What's happened?"

She slid her face gently away from his embrace and steadied herself. "Betty, she's gone. I lost her, Terry. I lost her." A lone tear slipped down her cheek. Despite crying all day, the reservoir was still not empty. "I don't know what to do."

Terry pressed her close again reassuringly. "The girls are with Alisha. What about Luke?"

"Erm…." Carrie's maternal instinct kicked in. "Oh god, Terry. How could I forget about my kids? Luke? He's…." She thought frantically. "Training, football training. Is it Wednesday?"

"Yes."

"It's rugby training then. He goes straight from school. Back around five."

"Ok, that gives us about an hour then," he said, glancing at his watch and helping her to her feet. "We'll take my car, go up Summit Road. There's still a little light if we go now."

Carrie nodded gratefully.

Soon there were in his car, scouring the streets, looking for any sign of the missing dog. Methodically they inspected every road, lane and street they could cover in their limited time before heading up the twisting ascent of Summit Road to the peak of the ridge over the estuary.

Terry pulled up, and they both got out. She was shivering when he'd found her on her doorstep, so he had given her an old fleece that he kept in his golf bag in the back of his car. She pulled it firmly around herself as the cold hit, partly for warmth, partly to breathe in his soothing scent. She watched him rush around, searching the viewpoint in the last of the December daylight, but she knew Betty was gone, long gone. Someone had her. She was only four, and she was valuable. A lump formed in her throat as, once again, the grim reality hit. He turned to face her and shrugged.

"I'm so sorry, Carrie. She's not here," he said gently. As he spoke, she watched his words dissipate along with his breath into the bleak evening. It was a hopeless task tonight. "When we get back, why don't you try the local dog's homes? Maybe someone found her and took her there? We can carry on the search tomorrow after school drop-off, if you like? I'm not working tomorrow."

She returned a thin, insincere smile. Suddenly her phone buzzed in her pocket. It was Luke.

"Hello, love," she gasped, unprepared to explain the devastating events of the past few hours.

"Where are you, Mum? I'm freezing, and I haven't got my key."

"Sorry. Be home in a bit. The girls are with Alisha if you want to go there to keep warm?"

"Why are they with Alisha? What's going on, Mum?"

She paused for a moment. She had to tell them all together, not now. "Long story. Tell you when I get back."

"Ok, bye."

"Bye, son."

As the screen returned to normal, she noticed she had five missed calls and voicemails. Four were from Terry, and one was from Matthew. Once they were back in the car, she deleted Terry's voicemails but listened to Matthew's.

"Hiya. Sorry, it's a bit hectic here today. Not going to be back for tea. Can you leave me some, please? Thanks, and hope you've had a good day. Bye." She sighed as she hung up and slipped her phone back into its hiding place in her pocket.

"It will be all right, you know." Terry patted her knee gently. Instinctively she covered his hand with her own and squeezed it tightly. He didn't flinch. He just smiled to himself and entwined her fingers in his. "How did you lose her anyway?"

"I met Corrine in the woods. She was walking, taking a break from her laptop or something...." Carrie replied.

"What? Corrine? Are you sure?" Terry was perplexed. Sharply, he moved his hand back to the steering wheel.

"Yes, of course! I know who your wife is. We had quite a long conversation. Why?" She laughed nervously. Terry was acting a bit weird.

"She told me she would be in London. I've been working overtime all day, so I could get a few days off before the Christmas holidays to finish the summer house." He gripped the steering wheel firmly, trying to make sense of what Carrie had just told him. Even in the darkness, she could see his knuckles blanch. He fell silent, concentrating on the road ahead.

"Maybe you misheard her?" Carrie suggested.

"No." He shook his head. "I saw the train tickets on the table, and she was all dressed up too."

"She was pretty dressed up when I saw her out walking. I started to talk to her, lost track of time and Betty…." Carrie's voice broke at her beloved pet's name.

Terry loosened his grip and smiled sympathetically. He glanced at his passenger slumped in her seat, all dishevelled and broken. What a contrast she was from his glamorous wife, but somehow, right now, he wanted to shield her from this pain more than anything in the world.

"I promise you. We'll find her tomorrow, ok?" he assured her.

This time, he reached over and took his hand in hers. Carrie's phone buzzed again, and she pulled it out from her pocket. It was Luke. Her heart broke again when she read the message.

"Where's Betty?"

CHAPTER 12

It was a shame that the evening turned out the way it did. Matthew had had all good intentions when he left the office early and picked up the bunch of festive flowers and mince pies from the Christmas market on the way back to his car. He had to get out of there that afternoon. Jonathan was a nightmare. He was like an over-enthusiastic puppy, offering to help with every project and sitting in on every meeting to gain experience. Matthew felt like he had a parrot on his shoulder, but instead of repeating everything he said, he tried Matthew's patience with question after question about pointless shit. Matthew would have got more work done from the bottom of the North Sea; this guy did not shut up.

Finally, Johanna had taken him off to do some auditing or something so Matthew could escape. He was going to work late and had even phoned Carrie to prepare her, but he had had enough. He muttered to his secretary about a meeting with the bank and left. The bank meeting was a lie. He hadn't even called them back from the other day.

Maybe he could keep them at bay until after Christmas. Then with his money-back scheme in full swing, he would have a better outlook on his financial situation.

As he pulled up on the driveway, he was met by his son, who looked distressed. Matthew switched off the engine, grabbed his purchases and got out.

"Hi, Luke, what's up?"

"Dunno really…it's all a bit weird…the girls are with Alisha…Mum is out on an urgent mission or something, and I can't find Betty," he reported without taking a breath.

"What? Where has she gone? She's just *left* you? Again?"

Just then, a car pulled up alongside them. Carrie and a gentleman Matthew vaguely recognised got out. He turned to his wife and the man who was strangely familiar.

"What's going on, Carrie? Is everything ok? The girls…?"

The stranger answered. "They're with Alisha, they're fine."

This incensed Matthew. Another man talking about his girls and being in a car alone with his wife. Who the hell was he? All at once, he recognised his face, and it hit him like a brick. This was no stranger; it was the bloody bank clerk holding his purse strings, cavorting with his wife.

Terry caught Matthew's eye and did a double take. Matthew Pritchard, of course. There couldn't be another Matthew Pritchard in Little Browton. He immediately remained in Dad mode so as not to alarm Carrie that they had met before.

"Sorry. I'm Terry, Delilah's dad." He held out his hand to Matthew, but Matthew didn't take it. Instead, he just glared at him, waiting for more answers. "Ok." Terry retracted his hand. "Shall I go and get the girls from Alisha's whilst you guys talk?"

"Yes," said Carrie.

"No!" Matthew interrupted. "Luke will go. I don't know what has happened here yet, but I'm sure you've done enough, Terry." Matthew stared straight ahead. Antagonism was growing between them like an ugly wart. Carrie winced. Oh goodness, there was going to be hell tonight. She stole a glance at Terry, who looked horrified.

"Luke! Go and get the girls, please," he called to his son, who willingly obliged.

"I'll go and get Delilah, then," Terry replied, meeting Carrie's eyes briefly. She smiled at him before quickly looking away.

"You do that." Matthew grimaced, not breaking his sullen expression. He missed the tender moment that had just flickered between his wife and the man holding his future in more ways than one.

When Terry had gone, he turned to look at Carrie. The grimace had gone.

"Inside! Now!" he barked.

* * *

Once the girls and Luke had returned, the interrogation began. Matthew had asked them all to sit in the living room whilst he poured himself a glass of red wine, which he downed like a shot.

They looked like four naughty children waiting outside the headmaster's office. Even the girls knew to remain silent. Luke must have pre-warned them on the short walk home from Alisha's. Something big was about to happen, and it wasn't good.

Matthew calmly walked across the living room to his favourite chair and sat down.

"Right now, Mummy is going to tell us exactly what has happened today. Starting at the very beginning. Go ahead, Mummy." He signalled.

Carrie gingerly began to explain the events of the day. She tried to keep her emotions in check as she described how she had lost their dog in the forest. She told them how she had looked for hours and finally found her collar attached to a tree. She explained how she had stumbled home, and that was when Terry and the girls had appeared. Alisha had taken the girls whilst Terry had offered to help her look for Betty.

Matthew snorted at this. Although he had preconceptions of Terry from their first encounter at the bank, his suspicions of this man contorted and twisted in his mind. He wasn't a stay-at-home ponce or a stuck-up bank clerk. He might prey on the vulnerable mums, projecting the persona of a hero in their hour of need, that kind of guy.

Matthew found this repulsive. He didn't think for one second that Terry had just been trying to help. He tightened his jaw as she carried on.

Carrie explained that they had looked everywhere they could think of in the last of the winter light to find their beloved dog, but it had been futile. His wife's voice broke, and tears were streaming down his little girls' cheeks. Even Luke was solemn, staring at his feet, clenching his fists tightly in his lap. Finally, Matthew's defences began to crack.

He had to be the objective one. There was still hope. It hadn't been twenty-four hours yet. Swallowing his fear and jealousy of Terry, he began formulating a plan. The first thing was to reinstall some belief in his family that Betty would come back.

"Well," he said once Carrie had finished. "She's just lost, and we need to help her find her way home."

"Or a sock?" Hannah interjected.

"Yes, what do we do?" he asked.

"We ask Mummy!" Jen replied triumphantly. Carrie smiled through her heartache, for the first time feeling utterly useless.

"We look harder. We think about where we last had it and retrace our steps," said Luke.

"Exactly," Matthew agreed brightly. "We retrace our steps."

"But I...," Carrie started, but he raised his hand to stop her.

"I will go out there now and have a look. She might be under a bush hiding from the cold. She might have had a fright and is halfway home." He looked around at his frail family unit. "I promise you all, we will find her, ok?" The girls nodded and folded their arms in agreement.

"We could make lost dog posters too, Daddy. Hannah is really good at drawing doggies," Jen piped up.

"Brilliant!"

"And I'd like to come with you, Dad, if that's ok. Two pairs of eyes are better than one, aren't they?" Luke remarked.

"Of course." Matthew smiled gratefully at his son's maturity. Luke hurried off to find a couple of torches and his thick coat.

He turned to look at Carrie; she looked defeated. He had underestimated the toll it must have had on her and the burden of telling her family the awful truth. In an instant, his anger disappeared, and devotion to his family swept over him like a sobering sea of lucidity. He had to step up now. This power struggle he was having with himself was absurd. He pulled her close. She smelt strange. What was she wearing? Was it one of his old, battered fleeces? It didn't matter right now.

"Can you make us something to eat whilst we go out and have a look for an hour or two?" he asked softly. His persona was now laced with a calm benevolence.

"Sure." She forced a smile, and he kissed her forehead.

"We'll be as quick as we can. Girls, get making those posters!" With that, he and Luke pulled on their coats and boots and were out of the door.

* * *

It was nine thirty when they finally trudged back in empty-handed. Carrie had busied herself with scanning the girls' posters and printing them out twenty times or more on their home printer. She had also made a list of all the local dog homes within a ten-mile radius, ready to phone them first thing in the morning. There was a tomato and basil pasta bake left out for them, and the mince pies Matthew had bought hours earlier were warming in the oven.

They hoovered down the food. Even Luke, whose appetite had waned recently, ate hungrily. Then the parents sent their son off to get a hot shower and bed. He was shattered. They all were.

Once the house was quiet, Carrie burst into tears. "I'm so sorry, Matthew. It all happened in a split second…she was just there one minute, and then…."

Matthew reached over and offered Carrie a tissue. "It's no one's fault, Carrie. Her recall was never any good, and she was always going off on her own…."

"Yes, but she always came back." Carrie sniffed.

"And she will come back. We'll find her. I'll take the morning off tomorrow, and we'll go out again once the kids are at school. I have to be back in the office for the afternoon, but at least we can try for a few hours in the morning."

"Ok, are you sure? Thanks," she said appreciatively.

He patted her head gently as she lowered it to his shoulder. This was what mattered; this was what counted. No man was taking his role as protector away from him. Not Stanton-Peake, not Jonathan Parker, and not Terry whatever his name was. His juggling act of work-life balance had got a little harder but seeing his family like this tonight had helped him focus on his priorities. Tomorrow his family must come first.

* * *

"So, you won't be coming in?" Johanna asked in disbelief on the phone the following morning. "But we've got a stack of things to do before the party tomorrow. We stop working at lunchtime, remember?"

"Yes, I know," Matthew said. "I'll be back for one. Something's come up at home."

"Oh, right. What shall I tell Clarissa? We've got another meeting with her to finalise these Christmas figures."

"Just see if we can do it this afternoon, will you? I've got to do this now, Johanna. I'm sorry. See you later." He hung up.

"Ok?" Carrie asked her husband as they walked home from primary school. She knew it wasn't easy for him to rearrange his workday at such short notice. She was grateful. Just as she was grateful for this short frosty walk with her husband by her side, despite the circumstances, it felt lovely to share the parental duty for the first time.

"Yes," he said. "Let's take the bikes. We can cover more ground that way—ground that a dog would cover."

Carrie shivered and rearranged her scarf around her neck. It was cold today and had frozen overnight. As she thrust her red hands further into her coat pockets, Matthew read her thoughts.

"I'm sure Betty found somewhere warm and dry to sleep. Don't worry." He reassured her. "Why don't you try some more animal shelters whilst I get the bikes out of the shed?"

"Good idea," she agreed. Carrie had already called three places before they set off for school. No luck. No one had brought in a black retriever yesterday. They had all taken down her details and promised her they would ring if a dog matching Betty's description came through their doors. One lady suggested Carrie use her social media account to inform a wider audience. She also put her in touch with local people who would help look out for Betty on their own dog walks and recommended that Carrie phone the local vets to check whether she had been taken there. Carrie hadn't even thought of that, so she added the numbers of four local surgeries to the list.

"Don't worry," the lady had said. "Most dogs just turn up on their own, you know."

"Thank you so much for your kindness," Carrie had said.

After a few more unsuccessful calls, they were soon pedalling down the high street towards the woods, carefully following the path that Carrie had taken with their dog the day before.

"Watch out for the black ice!" Matthew yelled behind him as they turned right onto the public footpath leading to the woods. They continued down the track shouting the dog's name into the wintry morning. They split up at the first fork. Matthew took the path that circled the ridge, gradually rising upwards to the top. Carrie turned right, a steeper, more direct route to the summit. They agreed to meet there in twenty minutes and would call if they found anything.

Matthew was hot. He hadn't been riding long, but he was unfit. He pulled up to undo his coat when he caught sight of something running through the woods. As it came into view, his heart sank. It was a man, not a dog. Worst still, it was Terry. He saw Matthew and jogged over.

Matthew was suddenly aware of his chunky mass against the physicality of this athletic model. Lean and toned through his lycra, Terry's muscles rippled with every step. Matthew hated him.

"Hi," Terry said.

"Morning," Matthew offered, not looking up as he carried on fiddling with his coat.

"Out looking for the dog?"

"Yeah."

"Want some help?"

Matthew paused. As much as he wanted to tell Terry to mind his own business, he had to admit that it wouldn't hurt for him to keep a look out whilst he was on his run.

"Sure," he responded. "Thanks."

"No problem. I'm just heading back down. I can take this overgrown trail if you like. I doubt you'll get the bike down there without causing a puncture."

"Sure, whatever." Matthew sniffed, getting back on his bike.

"Ok. If I find her, I'll wait for you at the café."

"Yeah, ok," Matthew said, wanting to get away but knowing he had to address the elephant in the room that was growing larger and more complicated the more they saw each other.

"By the way, my finances stay between us, ok? I know you know my wife, but I'd appreciate it if you kept it under wraps. I've got it under control." Terry just gave him a thumbs up, turned, and started off down the opposite trail.

What a dick, Matthew thought as he continued the steady climb, but he had no choice, he had to put his trust in Terry. His legs ached, but then he thought of his daughters' faces, their sadness haunted him, and it had been a wrench taking them to school this morning.

"Why did Betty run away, Daddy?" Jen asked.

"Doesn't she love us anymore?" Hannah added.

Their innocent questions fuelled his determination as he attacked every ascent. He had tried to provide the answers but was useless at this warm and understanding stuff. That was their mother's domain.

"All I know is, we won't stop looking until we find her," he guaranteed, and that was what he was going to do.

Despite the wintry day, it was a clear morning. The low sun was doing its best to shine through the drab. As the rays touched the earth, they sprinkled the ground with sparkles that lit his way. This lifted his spirits and his legs, pushing him higher towards his destination, all the while calling and scanning the desolate terrain for the dog.

As he rounded the summit, he saw Carrie had just arrived and was leaning her bike against a handy bench at the top. She looked over at him and shrugged.

"Never mind," he said as he approached his wife. "We'll have to head back now anyway, but if you can call those remaining places and put up some posters this afternoon, that would be helpful."

She nodded, keeping her head down. Once again, a lone tear escaped and traced the outline of her cheek. He reached out to catch it and stroked her face.

"It's not your fault," he whispered.

She smiled meekly. *Yes, it is*, she thought.

With Matthew's touch, a cascade of misery was

unleashed, and she sobbed. He pulled her close, and she shuddered within his embrace, releasing some of the tension and pain she felt for him. It felt good to him to hold her again.

"Come on. Let's get a coffee from the café before we go home," he suggested. "We need some thinking time."

* * *

Approaching the café, Matthew sighed inwardly. Thank goodness Terry wasn't there. He couldn't cope with having to measure up against him. Then he checked himself. Why did he need to? *He* was Carrie's husband, not Terry. Why was he letting this petty jealousy get on top of him? Terry was only trying to help, and he had agreed to keep quiet about the debt. After all, if he had been at the café, Betty would have been there too.

Carrie went to the serving window as he locked up the bikes next to a row of Christmas trees. His phone rang, it was Johanna again. Out of earshot, he took the call.

"Hello?"

"Hello, Matt, sorry to bother you, but Stanton- Peake won't wait for these figures. Do you mind if I go over it with her without you?"

"She can't wait? I'll be there by one thirty…," he began.

"No, she's insisting," hissed Johanna.

"Ok, I don't suppose I have a choice then, do I?"

"No, don't worry. I know what I'm doing. See you later."

He hung up. Johanna was a diamond. What would he do without her? She would hold the fort until he got back.

"Everything ok?" Carrie asked, handing him a hot Americano.

"Course." He gave her a wink, and she blushed, just like the schoolgirl he had known all those years ago. Why did he have to go back to work? He wanted to spend the rest of the day with her, soothing her turmoil and making everything that was wrong and had been wrong right again. Why had it taken a family crisis to make him realise how much he still loved her?

* * *

It was early afternoon when he arrived at the office. Jonathan, Johanna and Clarissa had gone out to lunch. *Odd*, he thought but was soon consumed by the flurry of emails and phone calls that had urgently needed his attention since daybreak.

Charlie Harvey was in. Probably because it was the Christmas party tomorrow. He was already full of festive cheer, swinging around the office like the king of the jungle. He was telling the usual pathetic Christmas cracker jokes to the new staff and cementing his solidarity with the rest. Matthew smiled; he was a good bloke. Despite being the captain of the ship, he could put anyone at ease with his quick wit and charm. He had an uncanny ability to nurture talent and bump out waste. Thankfully, he had considered Matthew the former of the two and had drawn him down a path on which Matthew had finally arrived. He did have a twinge of guilt about his new year master plan for embezzling funds out of this man's company, but Harvey had already hinted about retiring next year; he wouldn't even feel a pinch.

Harvey swung open his office door just as Matthew was about to make another demanding call.

"Matty! What kind of motorbike does Santa ride?" he asked, banging the door behind him.

Was he drunk? Matthew replaced the handset and leaned back in his chair.

"Oh gosh, Charlie! I'm sure you told me this one last year!" He played along.

"Possibly." Charlie laughed. "Go on then, tell me!"

Matthew pretended to think. He knew if he waited long enough, Harvey would burst out the punchline; he couldn't resist. Sure enough, after thirty seconds, he did.

"Give up? A Holly Davidson! Ha ha!" Harvey rolled about his office laughing. Matthew did his most convincing fake laugh.

Once he'd steadied himself, he fired again. "Why can't Christmas trees knit?"

Matthew took a deep breath. He was *so* busy, but this was the boss. He had to conform.

"I don't know, sir, *why* don't Christmas trees knit?" he repeated, trying to speed up the process.

"…because they keep dropping their needles!" he roared, plonking himself in the chair opposite Matthew. "How's it going, my old chap? Up to your eyeballs in shit?"

Yes, he had been drinking, Matthew deduced.

"You said it." He puffed out his cheeks. "Trying to get clear before the party tomorrow."

Harvey's eyes lit up. "Oh yes, I'm excited about that. Where is it again?"

"Brown's Hotel on the marina," Matthew replied, daring to focus his attention back to his screen.

"Right, never been there, but I'm sure Chloe's done a fantastic job organising the event as usual." He sat for a few more seconds and then got to his feet. "Sorry, I can see you are busy. Let's have a proper catch-up tomorrow at the bar!" He turned to leave and then added, "By the way, can you check something out for me? I'm a bit confused by some accounts you sent me last night."

"Last night?" Matthew's mind raced. He'd been looking for Betty last night, not at his computer.

"Yes. The Bollington's account and the Clarke and Clarke one," replied Harvey. "Figures don't quite look right to me."

"Oh, ok, sure." Matthew was trying to hide his perplexed expression. What was he talking about?

When he had gone, Matthew checked his outbox. The last email sent was yesterday at 4:08 p.m. to Johanna. He hadn't even opened the Bollington or Clarke and Clarke accounts since last week. He knew that because he rotated all his accounts on a fortnightly basis unless he had to do something specific on them.

He opened the Bollington account and studied the information in front of him. The figures in the columns were, indeed, incorrect. Harvey was right. It was very subtle, but his company had been overcharging for some services and undercharging for others. The amounts were specific to the account, and only a handful of people would know the data. He quickly checked the final amount. Perhaps the overcharging and undercharging would cancel each other out and add up to the correct total on the invoice. They didn't. Bollington's had been overcharged by nearly five hundred pounds.

Matthew fell back into his chair and rubbed his hand across his face. What the hell?

He quickly checked the Clarke account. It was a similar story. They had overpaid by a little over three hundred pounds. Matthew's heart was in his mouth. How many other accounts had been affected, and why did Harvey say that *he* had emailed him the information yesterday afternoon?

Objectional suspicion began to grow like a weed in a flower bed. The only people with the necessary data to manipulate these accounts were himself, Charlie, Clarissa or Johanna. He sighed, Johanna. Really? After a few minutes of contemplating, he couldn't get past it. It must be her, he concluded. Ultimately, she showed him how she had done it the other week. A little here and a little there, however she had told him she was finished. So, why was he here now struggling to make these simple numbers add up to the correct price? And how had Charlie Harvey got hold of them? He had said that he'd received an email from him. *He must be mistaken,* Matthew thought. It must have been Johanna who had sent the email to him, and he had gotten confused.

Quickly, he checked his deleted items. Empty. That didn't mean much as he was sure that the computer system cleared the deleted box at the end of every day anyway. He checked his desktop; nothing looked out of place. He was drawn to his private folder, where he kept his wage slips and other sensitive materials. Within his folder was another folder with a padlock, simply named 'New File'. *What New File?* he wondered. When Matthew was in a rush to leave at the end of the day, he would sometimes forget to name the file, and it would be given this generic name by default, but it wouldn't have a padlock attached to it. The folder could only be unlocked with a password. He couldn't remember seeing this file before, let alone creating a password for it. He tried his usual ones, but the box buzzed back to blank and denied him access each time. Finally, when he had exhausted his technical knowledge, he took his laptop to the IT support team on the floor below.

Ollie was only twenty-one, but he could crack a code quicker than you could crack a nut. It was amazing how rapidly technology was changing day in and day out, and Ollie was all over it. He constantly updated systems and suggested new programs to make their work lives a little easier. Matthew had been involved in his recruitment, so he knew he could ask the young lad to unlock this file without any questions being asked. He was right. Within five minutes, Ollie had opened the file, and soon Matthew was back in his office, clicking through the contents.

CHAPTER 13

"So, no luck then," Alisha ducked under Carrie's umbrella to dodge the drizzle at the school gates.

"No," Carrie replied. "I've put up posters and phoned a few more dog shelters, but nothing."

"I'm sorry. I've asked as many people as I could to keep an eye out."

Alisha had an old Jack Russell whom she walked at a snail's pace once a day. Paddy knew every dog in the town, and Carrie knew how much Alisha loved a good natter, so she was confident that word about Betty's disappearance would spread quickly amongst the dog-owning community.

"Thanks."

"Are you going tomorrow night?" Alisha continued.

"Tomorrow night?" Carrie repeated, puzzled.

"The school Christmas fair? It's from five until about eight. I've got a stall—my knitted dolls. Got Santa's reindeer, elves, the lot this year. You should come and have a look. I'll give you mates' rates." She winked.

Carrie smiled. Alisha was about the only mum she knew at the school now. She felt quite detached from the social side and decided that she should make more of an effort. Besides, Matthew would be at his Christmas party. Why shouldn't they get into the festive spirit too?

"Sounds wonderful. What time did you say it started again?"

"Five till eight. Oh, there's Jeremy. See you tomorrow." Alisha rushed off to scoop up her six-year-old before disappearing through the crowds of waiting parents. As the masses began to disperse, Carrie saw Jen skipping out of the classroom.

"Hi, Mummy! Is Betty home?" Jen asked as she cuddled into her mum's coat.

"I'm sorry, darling. No luck yet, but we'll keep searching," she replied sadly. "I put up your posters today. We'll probably see a few on our way home. How was your day at school? Not long till the Christmas holidays now." She turned to look at Hannah, who was glumly following behind. "Are you ok, Han?"

Hannah remained silent, hands behind her back, kicking the newly formed puddles as she followed her mother and sister home.

"She's sad. She drew a Christmas picture of us all and Delilah scribbled on it," Jenny told her.

"What? Let me see the picture," Carrie demanded.

Under the umbrella, Hannah opened her rucksack and pulled out a crumpled piece of A4 paper. Sure enough, Hannah's picture had a thick red scribble across where Betty had been drawn. *How cruel,* Carrie thought, but she needed to hear the full story.

"Why did she do that?" she asked.

Hannah quietly began to sob, so Carrie pulled her close and looked inquisitively at Jen, who obliged her mother's look and recalled the story. Carrie's initial speculation about Delilah had been right. She couldn't understand it. Delilah knew what had happened to Betty. How could she be so mean? Carrie kept reminding herself that the little girls were only five and couldn't comprehend the situation fully. Right now, she had to comfort her youngest baby again.

"Come on, honey." She squatted to their level, still sheltering her twins from the rain. "How about a hot chocolate on the way home?" This seemed to lift the mood.

"Yeah!" they chorused.

"I'll just text your brother and see if he wants to meet us at the coffee shop."

Moments later, a reply pinged through her phone.

'Training tonight, Mum, then going back to Ashley's for tea. See you around 6:30 p.m.'

Training? What does he do on a Thursday? Carrie had lost track of his sports schedule so close to Christmas. She was glad that he was going back to Ashley's, though. He was a good influence on her grumpy son. Ashley only lived in the next street, so Luke wouldn't have much of a walk home. *I must remember to thank Rachel for having him for tea.* She made a mental note before closing her umbrella and tucking it under her arm. The drizzle had finally stopped, but darkness was creeping in. She grabbed her girls' hands, and they set off for their after-school treat.

* * *

He was at the coffee house with Delilah, sitting on the stripey sofa in the window. Carrie nearly turned for home but surprisingly, Hannah, with the promise of a hot chocolate and no doubt a cake to go with it, had since forgotten about the scribbled picture and was waving violently at her friend as they approached. Kids! She thought, why couldn't adults be so forgiving?

Terry beckoned the girls over as Carrie went to the counter. Delilah shuffled into the middle and began reading or rather making up a story from her picture book about dinosaurs.

"Take out?" the young lad asked.

Carrie exhaled and looked across at the window seat. How could she drag the twins away from their best friend when they looked so settled? Terry wasn't a bad person to spend an hour with on a dark Thursday afternoon, she mused.

Terry got up and quickly pulled a chair across for her from a nearby table. *Matthew wouldn't have done that*, she thought. He would have watched her struggle with three hot drinks and a slice of cake precariously balanced as she found herself a seat. It wouldn't even register with Matthew. It did with Terry. She had to stop comparing them. Matthew was her husband, and he had been so understanding over the Betty incident. He was really trying, and she had to give him more credit.

"Hi." Terry almost purred the word and she melted. Again, she was standing on the trap door between reality and fantasy. How did he make everything feel so right with just one word?

She didn't want to blush, but it was so hot in the café that she couldn't help it. With her Irish colouring, she knew that she would stay a bright crimson for the entire time they would be together. How embarrassing. In contrast, he was as cool as a cucumber.

"How are you? I take it no luck at the ridge?"

She flashed him a confused look.

Terry smiled. "He didn't tell you, did he?" Carrie shook her head. "I saw Matthew along one of the trails this morning."

She glanced over at the kids, who were too engrossed in the dinosaur story to care about what the adults were saying. Sensing her concern, Terry pulled his chair closer to Carrie.

"I was out running and bumped into Matthew. I did look out for Betty, but nothing. I'm sorry she hasn't turned up yet."

He was looking at her, but she couldn't look at him. If she did, she knew she would crumble under the weight of guilt. Guilt from the missing dog and guilt from how he stirred something within her that had been lying dormant for a long time. At that moment, she wanted nothing more than for him to hold her close, but her moral compass dragged her back. She changed the subject.

"Are you going to the Christmas fair tomorrow? I didn't even know about it! So much going on with the run-up to Christmas...," she babbled. "It should be pretty good. Alisha has a stall, and there'll be mulled wine...." He smiled and she stole a look. He was gorgeous.

"Yeah, why not," he said. "Corrine's out *again*." He couldn't hide the irritation in his voice. Carrie knew how he felt.

"Hey!" Delilah suddenly shrieked. "*I'm* telling the story, not *you*!" She snatched the book from Jen and went to sit on her daddy's lap. He promptly lifted her off and turned him to face her.

"Dee. Is that how we speak to people? I thought you were sharing?" She pulled a face at him and threw the book on the floor.

Calmly. He picked it up and gave it back to the twins,

who stared in disbelief at the stroppy behaviour. Carrie didn't know why they were so shocked; they could be three times as bad as this, and there were two of them!

"Delilah Frances, what have I told you about behaving like this? You do know that Santa is watching, don't you?" He remained cool.

"Santa's not even real. Mummy said so." She began to sulk and folded her arms crossly. The twins gasped. Oh goodness, no. How could they remedy this? Carrie didn't think she had the strength.

In one masterful stroke, Terry settled the situation like a diplomatic mediation between two warring countries.

"Oh really, well, that's very sad. It means you've forgotten…."

"Forgotten what?" his daughter asked, intrigued.

"About the magic," he whispered but just loud enough for the twins to hear too. Their eyes were on stalks, and their ears flapped like sails in a high wind. "If you've forgotten about the magic of Christmas, then that means no Christmas for you. Santa doesn't visit people that don't believe."

"I believe!" Hannah chirped up.

"Me too!" agreed Jen. Delilah started to look worried.

"Some parents are so busy; they forget to look for the magic," he continued. "Like the joy of giving presents, family time, the first fall of snow. Christmas wouldn't be

Christmas without Santa. He brings all of this to us. Mummy has just forgotten."

Delilah's eyes were wide as she searched her father's face. "Does that mean Mummy won't get any presents?"

At this, he chuckled and scooped her back onto his lap, squeezing her close. "Of course, she will get presents. We just need to remind her to believe."

"Come on, girls, we need to get back," said Carrie cutting through the loving moment like a knife. His compassion was too much. He was perfect and she was falling in love with him. She had to distance herself before it was too late.

The twins made loud groaning noises but, realising their mum was serious, pulled on their coats. Terry put Delilah down and got to his feet.

"See you tomorrow then?"

"Yes," she muttered, retrieving her girls and disappearing into the crisp evening.

* * *

This was unbelievable! Matthew couldn't understand the extent of the betrayal. The file contained hundreds of doctored spreadsheets linked to his accounts dating back two years, and he hadn't even noticed it hidden in plain sight! Nothing added up right. Not just on the documents themselves, but the times had been altered. He checked his diary over the past six months and compared it to the times on the system. On most occasions, he hadn't even been in the office, or the documents were changed late at night. He was now utterly convinced it was Johanna. Nobody else had exclusive access to his accounts or knew the discreet amounts they charged individuals. But one question consistently hammered away in his head, why?

She was his number two, his right-hand woman. He had trusted her with everything. How could she do this to him? He had been set up.

Carrie was calling. Bloody hell, was it really a quarter to six?

"Hi."

"Oh, hi, sorry, I was just wondering what time you'll be home. I'm about to start cooking tea. Do you want some?"

With all that had happened in the last few days, he just wanted to be with his family, but he knew he had to get to the bottom of this and clear his name. He hadn't noticed that the office had vacated quickly after five o'clock, and Johanna hadn't come back from her lunch with Stanton-Peake and Parker. Interesting.

"Carrie, I'm so sorry. Something major has come up at work. I think I'll be here a while." He closed his eyes to wait for the response. She sounded sad.

"Oh, ok," she paused. "No news on the dog, I'm afraid."

He hung his head. "No, I didn't think so. How are the kids?"

"Fine. Tired. Luke's at Ashley's but will be home soon. Listen, I won't hold you up. See you later."

He sighed and replaced his mobile phone on his desk. Delving back into the swamp of deception before him, questions peppered his already fraught mind. *Were they all in on it? Johanna and Clarissa? Monsieur Baudelaire? Not Charlie Harvey.* He had seemed just as confused as Matthew, so he took him out of the frame. And who was Jonathan Parker? He was too old to be an intern, and the timing of his arrival seemed a bit coincidental. He did ask a lot of questions and wanted to see numerous accounts that were restricted. Was he hiding behind the disguise of wanting to learn the ropes but was gathering intel on him? Was he a fraud investigator? What the fuck!

Like a game of chess, Matthew had to consider his next move carefully. He had no proof that he was being set up. Whoever had done this had been bloody clever, or at least, they thought they had. The files were all on his computer and saved in an unsuspecting folder. According to Harvey, emails had been sent from Matthew's account too. There must be others; the paper trail was deep.

He peeled himself away from the screen and left his office for the first time in hours to make a coffee. The floor was empty, and everyone had gone home. The only light on now was the desk lamp in his office. Suddenly the lift doors opened, and in came Wendy the cleaner, clutching her caddy of cleaning products and dragging her hoover behind her. Matthew liked Wendy. She was eighty-two and as tough as old boots. She smoked like a chimney but was as strong as an ox. She had seventeen grandchildren and thirty-something great-grandchildren. She was amazing.

"Hi Wendy, want a cuppa?"

"Oh my god, Mr Pritchard! You made me jump right out of my skin!" She puffed, dropping the hoover tube to the floor. Once her heart palpitations had settled, she agreed that she would like a cuppa before she got started as she was a little early anyway.

"What are you doing here so late?" she asked, sitting at the cheap table and chairs in the office kitchen.

"Oh, you know, trying to get things out of the way before the party tomorrow."

She nodded. "Ah yes, the party. Can't come this year. Babysitting the great-grandkids. Seems everyone's party is on tomorrow night. I think I've got ten kids to look after. Mr Harvey said I could come in on Saturday to clean instead of tomorrow to save my Henry from minding them on his own. Mr Harvey's good like that."

Matthew could tell she was itching to go out for a cig, but he also knew how much she liked to chat. A thought flashed across his mind, could she be the key to finding out the truth about all the strange goings on?

"Does he often let you clean at the weekend instead, Wendy?" he enquired.

"Oh yes. I've worked here so long; he trusts me with his life. Great man, that."

Matthew agreed, and he ventured further. "Sorry about making you jump before. Bet you're not used to seeing anyone else in the office much after six, are you?"

"Only Johanna." *Jackpot!* he thought. "She works so hard, that girl. Shame she has no one to go home to." She turned to look at him and smiled. "It's so good of you to let her use your office. She can't concentrate with me vacuuming and singing whilst she tries to work. I must put her right off. Especially when she's on the phone." Matthew smiled back, trying to contain his sudden elation. Had he found the evidence he needed?

"How often would you say she's in the office then?"

"Why?" Wendy snapped, finding the line of questioning odd.

Matthew thought quickly. "I'm just worried about her work-life balance. You're right; she's working too hard."

She softened. "That's what I tell her. She was here till gone ten the other night, apparently. The night guard and I were chatting over a ciggie yesterday and he told me."

Brilliant! Keep going, Wendy! he thought.

"Oh no. What night was that?"

"Monday? No, Tuesday. Definitely Tuesday, I know because I do the windows on a Tuesday. She didn't want me bothering her in your office, so I haven't done those for a week or so." She suddenly looked worried. "Sorry, Mr Pritchard."

"It's quite all right, Wendy. It's hard work, isn't it?"

"Yes, but if I stopped, I'd die, just like my sister. Work keeps me going, and the pennies help keep me in ciggies.

Speaking of which, I might just bob down for one now before I get started. Is that ok?" she asked.

"Go ahead. I won't be much longer here, I don't think."

Matthew was satisfied. He had gathered all the information he could for now. He retreated to his office once Wendy had taken the lift. He checked the date and time she had given him against the spreadsheets. Sure enough, four had been altered between the times of seven forty-five and nine-fifteen on Tuesday the thirteenth of December. Matthew was home then. He had left the office at five as he had promised to pick up Luke from basketball. He had *not* changed those spreadsheets, and now he had the screenshots saved, he could prove it.

As the defensive case began to build in his head, so did the cross-examination. What about remote working? It was so easy to work from home these days. How could he show that it was Johanna making the changes and stealing the money, *not* him? She was logging in as him and emailing from his account. All the evidence was pointing his way, and he was running out of time. She had changed almost three-quarters of his accounts, and if Parker were a fraud investigator, they would make their move soon; he knew it. The only thing on his side was the fact that they didn't know he knew the truth. He could dumbly play along, but all the while stealthy setting traps. He had to do his research and execute his plan. For now, though, it was home time. He needed to be with his family. He closed down his computer and left. Battle would commence tomorrow.

CHAPTER 14

Magic was in the air as she stepped into the school hall. The teachers had done a fantastic job repurposing the dull 1960s décor into a shimmering wonderland of discovery. From the artificial snow underfoot to the twinkling rainbow of fairy lights overhead, everywhere screamed Christmas.

The twins were in heaven! Once they had picked their jaws up off the floor, they systematically inspected the array of stalls on offer and settled upon the chocolate tombola being run by Miss Fuller. Carrie felt content for the first time in days. For a few hours at least, she would be able to take her and the kids' minds off the trauma of their missing dog. Luke was meeting them there later, after cricket nets, so she could while away a few happy hours with the girls, getting in the festive spirit.

"Hi, Mrs Pritchard," chirped Miss Fuller above the excited energy pulsating around the room. "Sorry to hear about your dog." She smiled sympathetically at Carrie, then looked down at Jen and Hannah. "Hi, girls, it's 20p a go."

Carrie tipped out a few silver coins from her purse and handed them to the teaching assistant.

"Thank you. That's 80p. How many tickets do you think we can buy with that, girls?" she asked.

Bloody hell! Carrie chortled to herself. This school was only deemed 'adequate' by the government's education department. If they had taught five-year-olds to divide in reception, it would be a miracle.

"A hundred!" yelled Jen.

"Twenty-eight?" asked Hannah.

"Four," answered Miss Fuller. The girls looked slightly disappointed, so Miss Fuller quickly changed tact. "That means two goes each!"

"Yeah!" they both sang, jumping up and down on the spot. Carrie prayed that they would win something small and not the size of a Shetland pony. Two five-year-olds high on sugar and hyped-up about Christmas with ten days to go was not her idea of a great Friday night.

Miss Fuller turned the tombola wheel around and around. The girls' eyes followed every turn until finally, she stopped and asked Hannah to pick out two tickets from inside the barrel.

She unfolded them carefully and screwed her eyes up, trying to read the numbers "Two…, seven…, nine," she read slowly.

"Well done, honey," Carrie said proudly. "What about the other ticket?"

"I can read it! I can read it!" announced Jen.

"Hang on, Jen, you'll get your turn," Carrie assured her.

"Three, five, nothing," Hannah read aloud.

"Three, five, zero!" Jen rolled her eyes. "My go!"

"Hang on. We need to see what she has won." Carrie stopped Jen, grabbing at the paper numbers. Miss Fuller was already looking.

"Oh, I'm sorry, Hannah, those numbers don't match. Shall we see if the next two numbers do?" Miss Fuller turned the barrel again, and soon Jen was reading her own numbers aloud.

"One, four, three." No luck.

"Six, two."

"Sixty-two?" Miss Fuller asked. "Looking around the stall. Here you go."

She extracted a medium-sized pack of chocolate fingers and thrust it into Jen's twitching fingers.

"Yeah! All mine!" She hugged the box tight.

"Share, please," Carrie said, turning her children quickly away from the stall before they got any grand ideas about a second go. Jen pulled a face but promptly ripped open the packet and handed some of the fingers to her sister.

The next half an hour was spent chaperoning the girls around the labyrinth of pop-up shops and haemorrhaging change from a bottomless purse. Carrie had to do her best to reduce the bubble of excitement building inside both of her children. They had won copious amounts of sweets, painted three plastic baubles, of which they had promptly lost one, and made reindeer food. Carrie felt she needed a lie and down, but like Angel Gabriel appearing on Christmas night, Luke popped up beside her.

"I am so glad to see you," she sighed, patting her son's shoulder. "Can you take them around for a bit? They want to see Santa. You just have to stand in the queue with them. Thanks, love."

Luke nodded, dropping his school bags with her, and they went off toward Santa's grotto.

Mulled wine, thought Carrie, sniffing the air. Don't mind if I do, just a small one.

The festive tipple stall was tucked away in a corner of the hall. No doubt Mrs Gray was trying to hide it to avoid any drunk parents getting out of hand. Carrie bought a small cup and leaned against the only available bit of wall nearby to survey the scene. She spotted Alisha behind her stall. Carrie had never seen any of her knitted dolls before, and now she knew why; they were hideous. Alisha was her friend, but how could anyone think these dolls would make cute presents for kids? She had overstuffed some and under-stuffed others. She had clearly run out of red wool at one point, as the Santas were finished in pink, and half of the dolls looked cross-eyed.

"Hi, how's it going?" she asked her friend.

"Slow." Alisha sounded downbeat. "Want anything?"

Carrie took a cursory look around the table. She settled on a small elf keyring that she'd put in Matthew's stocking for a joke.

"Oooh! I'll have this, please," she said enthusiastically. "How much?"

"Five pounds, please," Alisha replied, holding out her hand.

"Wha…? Oh, here you are…." Carrie corrected herself just in time. No wonder she wasn't selling any. They were both hideously ugly and hideously expensive, but Alisha was her friend, and she should support her.

"Thanks. Would you like it gift-wrapped?"

As it would go some way to make up for the inflated price, Carrie said she would. She looked around for her children but instead caught sight of her handsome friend.

He waved when he saw her and ambled over with Delilah in tow.

"Hi," he said, smiling down at her warmly.

"Hi."

She couldn't deny the tenacious spark between them. She felt drawn to him like a magnet to metal, and she was sure he felt the same. All those side glances, stolen touches and comforting words. It was more than a friendship, or maybe that was just what she wanted, needed, and she was blinded by her daydreams. She had never even looked at another man that way, let alone imagined herself being with one. Slowly cracks were beginning to split through her desolated interior.

"Is it any good?"

"What?" She laughed, confused, flicking her hair like an excited schoolgirl.

"The mulled wine?" He joined in, not understanding the joke. "Have you had too much?"

She had to admit, she had gulped it back, but she was enjoying the atmosphere and the present company.

"Hey, Delilah, the girls are in the queue for the grotto. Do you want to join them?" she said.

Delilah's eyes grew wider. "Yes, please!" Carrie gave the little girl her biggest smile. Terry's chat about Santa had brought her back to her childhood, where she belonged.

"Luke's over there. Look, they're waving at you."

Delilah scurried over to them under the watchful eye of her father whilst Carrie bought them both a mulled wine. She turned to ask Alisha if she'd like one, but a flurry of eager teenagers had suddenly appeared at her stall. She was now elbow-deep, digging through her creations to find them the perfect presents.

"What the hell are they?" Terry mouthed, waving his hand towards Alisha's stall. Carrie giggled. "Shall we grab a seat?" he suggested.

They wandered off to the temporary seating area. Thank goodness someone had had the good grace to put tables and chairs out from the junior school and not ant-size ones from the infants. Carrie did think that it would have been amusing to see this huge man sitting on one, looking squashed and folded up like a broken deck chair. They settled at an empty table with a good view of the grotto queue. The girls had gone in, and Luke was hanging about at the other side of the make-shift den chatting to an old teacher who still remembered him.

"How are you doing? It's been a few days since she went missing, hasn't it?"

"Trying not to think about it," Carrie replied honestly. "There's been no sightings and nothing from the shelters. The rain damaged some of the posters, so I'll print out some more and get them out over the weekend."

"Well, just remember, no news is good news, right?" He winked encouragingly.

The optimism was welcome but not felt on both sides. She was disheartened. Matthew had seemingly lost interest. He was wrapped up with something urgent going on at work. She knew it was a distraction for him, but she was getting so tired of the family playing second fiddle to his stringent job.

"Look, I'm working Saturday morning, and I must get on with painting the summer house in the afternoon, but I'm free to help continue the search on Sunday."

Carrie was so grateful but couldn't help thinking it was a waste of time. Betty had gone missing on Wednesday. It was now Friday night, and nothing. Terry seemed to sense her dismay.

"Don't give up, not yet," he said softly. "My mum's cat went missing a few years ago, and he turned up in someone's shed. He had been locked in for a week, and he was ok!"

A whirlwind of five-year-olds descended on the quiet moment.

"Look, Daddy! I got a bubble wand from Santa! Can I open it now?" shrieked Delilah.

Too late, she had unscrewed the wand enthusiastically, and now the contents were spilling all over her pretty dress and onto the floor. Delilah began to cry.

"It's ok, Dee." Her father soothed her tears and stroked her hair. Carrie grabbed a few napkins from the table to try and soak up some of the sticky mixture.

"I want to go home, Daddy!" she cried.

The twins looked mortified, and soon they were sobbing quietly too. It was all getting out of hand.

"Ok, darling. I'll take you home," Terry said.

Carrie smiled sadly, and then a reckless thought crashed into her mind.

"Why don't you come back to ours for a bit? It's closer than your house, and we can lend Delilah some clothes...." Terry put his hand up to protest, but Carrie stammered on. And they can continue playing. I mean, the last thing we both need is grumpy children tonight, and I have mulled wine, or maybe I just have wine?"

Carrie didn't want him to go. She didn't want to go back to an empty house, not when she knew how much fun Matthew would be having at the party. She wanted to enjoy herself too. After all, she'd been through this week, it wasn't too much to ask, was it?

"Please!" the twins begged Terry in unison.

Carrie felt like a hypocrite as she had always told her children not to put parents on the spot in front of friends when it came to getting what they wanted, yet here she was doing it herself. She craved his comforting words and jovial nature. She needed to feel something tonight, anything, anything other than this unrelenting grief. She ached for support. She didn't want to be a lone parent dealing with all the shit again.

Terry pretended to sigh and think for a moment, and then he agreed.

"Yeah!" the girls screamed together.

Luke, who had just joined them, covered his ears with his hands. Once the screams had diminished, he asked if he could stay the night at Ashley's. Under the circumstances, Carrie thought that this would be a good idea.

"He's just texted. His mum says it's fine, and she'll take us to football in the morning."

"Ok," she replied. "Just come back with us to get some clothes and your toothbrush."

They gathered up their coats and purchases and were soon making the short journey on foot to the Pritchard's house. The crisp air stung their faces slightly with its icy, cold hand; however, Carrie felt only warmth as they made their way through the dark streets.

* * *

Was it his fourth or fifth vodka? He couldn't remember. All he knew was that it burnt in all the right places. It was good, and it was what he wanted right now. He tried his best not to stare but armed with this new information, he couldn't help himself.

She looked ridiculous. Nearly sixty but still dressing like a thirty-year-old. She was flouncing about like a flamingo, shaking her tail feather. Matthew hated her, and he hated Johanna. Johanna had been trying to make light conversation with him all night, but he couldn't bring himself to engage. He didn't want to say something that he might later regret, so he replied minimally. She was now on the Stanton-Peake bandwagon, whirling around the dance floor to Wizzard.

He had to formulate a plan to deal with these women and fast, but not now. For now, he would just observe the dynamic from a distance. Like a python, he would wait for the right time to strike.

"Can I get you another?"

Matthew turned to see a strikingly beautiful woman settling herself onto the bar stool next to him. She had the most gorgeous brown eyes and sweeping eyelashes. Her lips were full and enticing, and her body was unbelievable. His attention was immediately redirected. Was she really talking to him? A middle-aged dumpy financial director. Who was she?

"Ok," he mumbled. "Vodka tonic, please."

The goddess indicated to the bartender to make that two and then flicked her glossy mane over her shoulder. She turned to face him.

"Corrine," she held out her perfectly manicured hand.

"Matthew," he replied, taking it. It was so soft, apart from a slight scratch from her scarlet talons. "You don't work for...."

"No," she interrupted. "But I have done some work for you guys, so Clarissa invited me." She turned to look at her friend. "She's not holding back tonight, is she?"

Matthew chuckled. "No, certainly not. What do you do, Corrine?" He liked the sound her name made on his tongue.

"I'm a lawyer. I practice out of London mainly but wanted a nice retreat in the suburbs, so we moved here recently." She sipped her drink seductively. Matthew blinked a few times; he must be imagining it.

"We?"

"My husband, daughter and I." She looked down at her wedding ring. Dominating the band was a diamond as big as the rock of Gibraltar. She twisted it around and around, lost in thought for a moment, then asked, "How about you? Married? Kids?"

"Yeah." He drained his glass just as the fresh drinks arrived. "All of that."

Matthew didn't want to talk about home. He spotted an opportunity to exploit this unexpected drinking partner for all her worth. Matthew was thirsty for ammunition to ambush Clarissa's battle plans and blow her out of the water with a torpedo of truth. He had to remain calm.

"So, how did you meet Clarissa?" he began.

Corrine smirked. "Oh god, friend of the family. She has a thing for black men and was always trying to pull my older brother!" Matthew spat out his drink, which she thought was hilarious. "Your face!" She giggled. "No, seriously, she did fancy Carl, but he was never going to be on the same team, if you know what I mean. Carl is now happily married to Andrew, living in a two-bed apartment in Shepherd's Bush." She reached for her drink. "Once she knew my brother was a no-go, she turned her attention to me." Matthew's eye widened. "Not in that way!" Corrine slapped his leg. "She taught me everything she knew about business, handy when you're in corporate law. She is ruthless! I learned a lot from her. Doesn't mean I have to like her, though." She gave him another flirtatious look with those beautiful feline eyes.

"Hmm. Me either." He watched his nemesis dancing around her ridiculously expensive handbag. God, he *really* hated her. She was the root of all his problems. She was the one blocking his success. Matthew suddenly remembered that he'd just met this woman. He shouldn't get carried away with a few negative words about the wretched Clarissa.

"What's her husband like?" Matthew changed tack.

"Do you mean is he black?" Corrine glared.

"No, no. I didn't mean…."

"I know. I'm playing with you, dummy!" Corrine was enjoying herself. "Well, he is black, actually, but that's beside the point. He's lovely and *long*-suffering! He's a GP. Lovely, lovely man."

"Why do you say long-suffering?"

"Well, could you be married to *that* for nearly thirty years?" Matthew allowed himself a smile, certainly not. "Good, you're warming up too now, baby! We'll have you on that dancefloor in no time." She grinned and continued. "Clarissa is hungry for power. She wants to be top dog. She's been plotting to take down your boss for years." Corrine took a long drink. "She calls him Barmy Harvey. Unsuspecting, too trusting and foolish. Weakness in her eyes. Be careful."

Matthew had heard enough. He wanted to probe

further but was precariously balancing between being nicely drunk and being *very* drunk. One wrong move and he would deal his hand revealing all to this perfect stranger. Drunk as she was, Corrine was smart. She'd see right through him, and even though he was confident that there was no love lost with Clarissa, information could be leaked over the border.

* * *

They sat quietly for a while, watching the waves of colourful co-workers' shimmy and pulsate vigorously to the familiar Christmas beats rolled out every year once the party passed watershed. Matthew decided to offer something back, so broke the silence.

"Don't you find it hard?"

"What?" Corrine swung round on the barstool to face him, her sexy dark legs brushing his own. He drew a sharp breath.

"The whole domestic bliss thing. Managing work, home, kids, marriage. It's hard, isn't it?"

She lowered her eyes to suck him in further. "Yes, but you have to work at it. Especially your marriage. You make choices and decisions for the greater good. For the good of your family and the good of your spouse, whether they appreciate it or not."

"Exactly." Matthew agreed. Was it the drink clouding his judgement, or did his guest understand? You make decisions and choices for the greater good. That's what he was doing! Carrie had given up her career for the good of the family, and he sacrificed home life so he could provide for them.

"I mean, there are perks, but basically, you work to live. I hate being away from my girl but needs must." She took a sip. "Does your wife work?"

"No. She was a nurse, but we decided it would be best for her to become a full-time mum after our son was born."

"A nurse?" Corrine looked surprised.

"Yeah, a bloody good one too. I sometimes wonder if we should have settled on part-time work for her rather than severing all ties completely."

"Oh right, yeah, you mean for the pension?"

"No, although I wish I'd thought of that!" Matthew laughed. "For her own mental health. She gets fed up and lonely."

Corrine shrugged. "Don't we all. My husband works part-time. It doesn't always work out. Sometimes I feel the full weight of the marriage lies heavily on my shoulders. I have all the worry, while he has all the good times with my girl. When I get home, Dee is often in bed or too tired to tell me about her day, but I always make time to go up and stroke her hair whether she is awake or not. I sit with her and allow my hectic schedule to settle. Somehow, she puts everything into perspective." Corrine's eyes glazed over, and her pupils danced in the candlelight. Another silence settled between them as Band-Aid was being screamed out on the dance floor. "Why don't you go home to her? To them? You look miserable here, no offence." She held up her hands. "It is Christmas, after all."

Matthew grinned. He liked Corrine, and she was right.

"You know what, I think I might but promise me, you'll spend a full day with your daughter tomorrow, no work," he chided. "But before I go, one for the road? You've been great company."

"Don't mind if I do." She clinked his now empty glass and settled back on her stool, smiling to herself.

* * *

"The girls have fallen asleep on top of each other under the tepee." Carrie laughed, stumbling back into the living room. "I'm not sure it's a good idea to disturb Delilah now."

Terry was pouring them both another glass of wine. Carrie knew she shouldn't have any more, but Terry had insisted, and they were having a good time. It was Christmas.

"Ok, well, maybe another hour then, if you don't mind?" Terry was knowingly enticing her with his words. Their flirtation had gone up a notch from their usual friendly banter. Carrie was aware of his eyes on her moving steadily across her body, drinking in every curve and crescent, the paleness of her porcelain skin, her vivacious flame-coloured hair, her slender shoulders and delicate neck. As she settled next to him on the sofa, he reached out to touch her thigh, and she thought she might faint. Unknowingly, she had been longing for this moment to happen, and as he slowly slid his hand along her jeans, she quivered.

"Carrie, you are so lovely, and the most beautiful thing about it is you have no idea that you are." He whispered, moving closer towards her. "I'm sorry, but I can't stand seeing you hurting, and I hate that you are going through this all on your own."

The wine was making her head spin, was this reality? Sensuous thoughts of Terry playing out in her daydreams were here, right now, ready for her to reciprocate. Was this what she wanted? Was he what she wanted? She craved comfort from all the heartache of losing Betty, even for just a moment, Terry could make it all go away. She couldn't think straight as confusion clouded her judgement. She just needed a minute. Lowering her head, she gently ran her fingers through her hair. He reached out to touch her chin, lifting it lightly, he turned her face to his. A tear fell from her face and dropped onto the cushion between them. She knew then that it was pointless to resist. She wanted him just as much as he wanted her. Instincts took over, and before she could stop herself, they were kissing. The familiar scent of sandalwood drifted from his collar, he was her poison, and she couldn't get enough of him. She felt his muscular arm move steadily from her face down to her waist, he scooped her up onto his knee, and she felt for the buttons of his shirt.

"What the fuck!"

Matthew was standing in the doorway.

CHAPTER 15

Present Day....

A honeytrap. That's what she had called it. Carrie didn't even know what that was, and to her shame, she had to look it up. Apparently, he had done it before in Leeds, and she had had enough. She said she knew that Carrie was the perfect specimen for her experiment, and it had worked. Flattered by a bit of attention, sucked in by a few kind words. She had been the bait for Corrine to exorcise her demons, and now everything was an empty shell of impracticality. The rusty nail had been hammered right through Carrie's life, and she was paying a heavy price.

It hadn't been very difficult to figure out who was next. The pretty redhead from the Remembrance Day Service had caught his eye as he couldn't stop himself from snatching glances at her in church. A little light detective work from the lady next to Corrine had revealed the redhead to be Carrie Pritchard, the lovely nurse at the hospital that the old lady had taken her sixteen-year-old daughter to when she was a poorly baby. Corrine set up the playdate; she didn't want her instincts to be true, but she couldn't be hit with the dishonesty again. She had Delilah to think of now.

On the train to London the next day, Corrine had Googled Carrie. An article popped up from when she had left the hospital. She read, *"her loving husband Matthew looking forward to starting their own family...."* From this, she could track down Matthew. She needed to know a little about him. He was employed at Harvey's; what a coincidence! So was her good friend Clarissa.

Clarissa loved a gin and tonic, especially strong ones, and after about four, her lips became as loose as a rope of sand. It was clear she despised Matthew, her jealousy of his bond with Charlie Harvey was astronomical. She couldn't stop the train of resentment once it had started tripping so easily from her tongue.

The *'FindMe'* app had also helped and become a daily checking for Corrine to pin down Terry's whereabouts. Even in London, she could see where he was, except when he was up that bloody hill he loved so much.

Corrine hated any outdoor exercise so checking out the signal on that particular day was a necessary evil she had to endure. Seeing Carrie up there had been a shock, but at least she thought she knew why Terry went off-grid so much during the day.

Carrie had looked fit, athletic and healthy; no worries burdened her shoulders. She was the wholesome, popular girl next door, the object of Terry's budding affections.

Despite appearances, Corrine felt sick and couldn't resist a jibe at her twins' behaviour to put Carrie on the back foot.

The collar was another unexpected find. The metal tag had read 'Betty' and was engraved alongside 'Pritchard' and a telephone number. For a moment, Corrine contemplated doing the right thing. Terry had suffered from losing their dog last year. She even considered how it would hurt Carrie's children. But malice captured her fleeting kindness like a familiar enemy and threw it out of her heart. Devastation was coming to them all. Why not throw in another grenade?

Snatching up the collar, she marched along the path to find a bin. Then a wicked thought entered her head. She hung the collar on a nearby tree, slipping in more pain and confusion for good measure. She could hear Carrie in the distance calling the dog's name over and over again. Corrine pouted her flawless lips.

"It's time you had a little destruction in your life, too, Carrie."

The final dose of retribution was administrated through the form of clashing Christmas parties. Terry would be at the school party with Carrie, and through Clarissa's invite, she would be with Matthew.

What an opportunity!

Corrine knew Terry too well. Even with the children there, he would seize the opportunity. It had never bothered him before.

Matthew had to be the one to discover the awful truth.

Just a nudge to the unsuspecting fool to go home to his family. Timed to perfection, the plan had executed both marriages in one fell swoop.

Flattered by a bit of attention, sucked in by a few kind words, now Carrie knew how it felt. She was an empty shell of her former self, and so was Terry.

Corrine had gone to London just before Christmas, taking Delilah with her. Alisha had heard from a friend that the day after the Christmas fair, Corinne had taken a sledgehammer to the summerhouse and smashed it into a million pieces. She intentionally destroyed it in the front garden so everyone could see and hear how wronged she had been. Carrie's name had been mentioned, and now she was gossip fodder. Terry was still at the cottage, although no one had seen sight nor sound of him. The responsibility of the sad situation had been dumped solely on Carrie.

Matthew had moved out, and now Luke was living with him. Carrie hadn't seen her son for two weeks. The girls lived with her during the week and then went to him on weekends. She thought she knew what loneliness was, but once the twins had gone with their father on a Friday night, the house screamed silence, and she was plunged into the depths of her own solitary confinement.

It was only a kiss—a fumbled drunken kiss. Marriages had survived much worse, but evidently, hers couldn't. His mum had called to tell her, in no uncertain terms, what she thought of her. Carrie knew it was the excuse Felicity had been waiting for. The words stung, and they were unfair. Matthew was no angel, but Carrie kept quiet. Who was she to tear a mother from her son?

Her phone rang, and Carrie's heart pounded as she looked at the caller ID. It was John Paterson.

"Hi, John."

"Hi, Carrie. So sorry to bother you but do you know where Luke is? He's not turned up for training tonight, and I can't get hold of Matthew."

"No, John. Luke's not having anything to do with me now since, you know…," she trailed off.

"Since that stupid kiss?" John dismissed it. "This has got way out of hand, by my understanding." Carrie was grateful. At least someone seemed to be on her side. "Look, could you try his mobile again, please? He has been a bit hit and miss these past few weeks anyway and it's going to jeopardise his place in the team."

"Oh really?" Carrie pondered. "I will, and I'll let you know." She hung up. That was strange. Luke loved his sport, and he loved football above all else. She tried his mobile, but it went straight to voicemail, so she tried Matthew's.

"Hello?" he answered.

"Hi, sorry, is Luke with you?" she asked.

"Yes."

"Oh, right, good. It's just he should have been at football tonight. Is everything ok?"

"Yes, why?" He was being rigid.

"John Paterson phoned me. He was worried."

"John? Is he your latest conquest then?" Matthew asked feebly. She imagined him high-fiving himself on his one-up-manship.

"Don't be immature, please. Can you put Luke on the phone?" She heard the handset being passed to her son.

"Hi," Luke said coolly.

"Luke? John says you've missed training."

"So!" he snapped. "I'm tired and not feeling it today, ok?"

"Ok, ok. He's just worried about you, and so am I."

"Oh really." Sarcasm seeped through his words like venom. "You weren't too worried when you were carrying on with that Terry bloke, were you? Did you ever stop and think about us then?"

He hung up.

She tried to call him back, but the mobile just rang out.

Her sentence was cruel, but she accepted it. The twins and Delilah had been in the house when it happened. What if they had walked in on the two of them? They hadn't stopped to think about the consequences; it all happened so quickly. Raw emotion had pulled them together, an unstoppable force of need and lust. They both needed each other on a higher level that night, but their connection had proved catastrophic. After the initial tsunami, successive tidal waves still battered what credibility she had left. How could one poor judgement obliterate fifteen years of near-perfect parenting?

She thought about ringing John back, but she didn't want to be accused of any more meddling, so she left it.

The girls were playing an imaginary game in the living room. Carrie paused to listen. Hannah was making pretend crying noises. "There, there. What's wrong?" Jen said in her a gruff voice.

"My friend won't come back, Mr Policeman. I have been a naughty girl, and I send people away...." Carrie flushed. What was this? She was rooted to the spot, she didn't want to hear it, but she knew she must. Guilt began to bury a knot deep within her stomach. "...nobody wants to play with me anymore. Nobody likes me. I am all alone."

"Where has she gone?"

"To London. That is a *very* long way away."

Carrie couldn't bear it. Tears blurred her vision as she fought her way out of the house and into the front garden. She needed air. Fresh, cold, savage air to burn her; she deserved it. The girls were playing out their feelings in a game mimicking the cruel reality. They had lost their father, brother, pet and best friend. It was all her fault.

She pushed her way out of the door, tripping on a rogue school shoe that had been wedged under a piece of missing skirting board. A bewildered John Paterson was standing on her doorstep. His arm was at an obscure right angle as he was about to press the doorbell but caught her just in time.

"Carrie?" He scooped her up.

"Oh, John, Sorry, sorry…," she mumbled as she righted herself and wiped her face with the back of her hand. She took a moment, then smiled at him. "I'm ok. Thank you for catching me. What can I do for you? We were just on the phone. How did you…."

"Are you ok?" he asked dismissively.

It was then that she realised he was still holding her other hand. He was gently rubbing his thumb across it, attempting to soothe her distress. The roughness of his hand on hers felt strangely tender and familiar. He guided her to the rusty old bench she had long forgotten about next to the garage, sensing that she didn't want to go back inside but wanted to be near enough to hear the girls still playing in the front room. They sat for a moment, taking the chilly surroundings and the bizarre situation they now found themselves in. A frost was already forming around them, and every breath hung in the air. Carrie shivered but rebuffed John's offer of his coat.

"Are you ok?" he placed her hand back on her knee.

"Yes," she said. "I was just having a moment."

"Ah, yes. *The* moment. We all have them."

She smiled gratefully. "Anyway, what brings you to my door, John? Did you hear from Luke or Matthew?"

He shrugged. "I was passing, and I wanted to check in on Luke and you. You didn't sound yourself on the phone."

She brushed off his last words. "I'm fine. You know me, things will get better."

"I do know you, yes. You are a strong woman, Carrie, when you need to be. Just remember that you don't need to fight this alone. Lean on people, let them in. You know...the close ones. Not everyone is on Matthew's side." He reached for her hand again and gave it a squeeze. "You ok now?"

She looked into his kind face, a face she had known most of her life and smiled. "Yes."

"Good." He got up to go, then turned back. The light from the open door illuminated his rugged features; he looked almost saintlike.

"Keep an eye on Luke. I know he's out of reach at the minute, but he's going to need you."

She nodded. "Ok, thanks."

"And by the way." He was stalling; he didn't want to leave her. "There are rumours of a black dog being found in the next town, in a dishevelled state. I can make some enquiries for you."

Hope burnt through her chest.

"Really? Yes, please! Oh my goodness!"

"Now, now, there's the girl I know." He winked. "Be in touch."

Then the modest enigma disappeared, just as he had arrived. His mellow disposition had lifted her spirits above the parapet of turmoil. Finally, a flickering ember of promise had ignited. She closed her eyes and prayed that this was good news. If it was Betty, this could bring them all back together and restore the family to what it once was.

The girls were calling out for her. It was quarter past seven and bedtime. She decided to keep John's revelation to herself for the time being. It was a secret better to be kept safe, like a hidden treasure chest, only exposed at the right time once the facts were established fully. As she left the bench, she looked beyond her garden, down the street, retracing John's path with her eyes. Someone was smoking a cigarette under a streetlight on the fringe of her vision. The figure raised a hand to wave and then was gone. John or Terry? It didn't matter. Someone was on her side. Someone cared.

* * *

The flat was too small with the two of them living there. Matthew had lost count of the times he had slipped on a textbook or tripped over a piece of games kit, but this was his son, the one who had stood by his side when his mother had been so treacherous. He wasn't about to chastise him for being a teenager when he had proven he could be a man.

Matthew had got in late again for the third time this week, and poor Luke had had to fend for himself. However, the kitchen looked untouched, just like Matthew had left it early that morning. One single mug of half-drunk tea sat on the sideboard along with an empty packet of grapes. Was that all he had eaten tonight? Luke was dozing in front of the TV. It was only eight fifteen.

"Sorry, son." Matthew gently shook him awake. "Busy day for you too, then?"

"What?" Luke said groggily. "Yeah, I'm so tired."

Matthew felt awful. He was neglecting his children. No, his veins pulsed with bile. *She* was the one who had been negligent towards all of them. A broken home, siblings split up, parents at each other's throats. He thought back to the last conversation that he had had with Carrie about Luke not showing up for football. The poor boy was exhausted. What kind of a life was this for him, slumming it with his old man in a dreary flat where there wasn't enough room to swing a cat? No wonder he was dispirited and fed up.

It was even worse when the girls came at the weekend. It was impossible to relax with two feisty five-year-olds tearing up the place. Matthew had taken to visiting his parents when the girls were with them. An extra pair of hands evened up the parent-to-child ratio, and Matthew felt he was in control again. His mum spoilt her grandchildren rotten with new clothes, grand days out and copious amounts of sweets.

"We're just making up for lost time," she had remarked when he had suggested that she scale things back. "That woman...," she began.

"You mean their mother," Matthew interjected.

"Yes. She didn't allow me to do anything nice for them." Felicity pouted.

This wasn't true, but Matthew wasn't about to defend *that woman* to his mother, so he remained silent. His dad was a little more forgiving, suggesting that the two of them try and work it out. Matthew couldn't, not yet, perhaps not ever. He was consumed with work and being a good father. His marriage would have to wait.

He turned his attention back to his son. "Did you get yourself some tea? What about homework, Luke?" Luke was dismissive.

"Done, Dad." Stretching himself out on the sofa, his t-shirt rode up, revealing a hollowed stomach and pointy ribs.

Matthew was a little shocked. Luke looked thin. Why hadn't he noticed?

"What did you say you had for tea again, mate?"

"Oh, some fruit and a bag of crisps," his son replied, not looking away from the TV.

Matthew stood up. "Right, well, I'm starving. How about we go the pub on the corner? If we go now, we'll make the last sitting."

"I'm not in the mood…," Luke protested.

"Come on, son. You can have what you want."

Suddenly he was desperate to get out of the flat, it was

suffocating, and he wanted to talk to his boy. *Really* talk to him. He had been so wrapped up with the constant stream of shit at work that he hadn't appreciated the toll this situation was having on Luke. He wondered about the girls. They were so far away from him during the week. How did he know how *she* was treating them? The familiar animosity was gathering tempo, and he clenched his fists to fight it back. Digging his nails deep into the palms of his hands seemed to calm his anger, and the rational side of his brain gave him a slap. This was Carrie; she had put being a mum first before her career and ambitions. He couldn't deny that she was a brilliant mother to their children and, up until a few weeks ago, had never put a foot wrong. She may be a disingenuous adulterer to him, but she wouldn't do anything to harm the children.

No, Luke was his priority now.

"Steak and chips?"

Luke's eyes lit up, and they left.

CHAPTER 16

John picked her up the following morning after she had dropped the girls off at school. He had made some enquiries and was now confident of his lead on Betty.

John was a decorator, and the front seat of his van was covered in paint splodges. She recoiled when she opened the passenger door. He laughed.

"It's all dry. Get in!"

As she closed the door, she caught the eye of several neighbours who had gathered at the park for their morning gossip. Clearly, the content of their conversations hadn't changed. She smiled and said good morning, and they turned away, back to their idle chit-chat.

"Oooh, how exciting! They'll be talking about us now!" John laughed as he pulled away from the kerb.

Carrie didn't laugh. She would never have agreed to get

in a car with another man now unless it was in an emergency, and the possibility of getting back her beloved pet was an emergency in her book. The bystanders could think what they wanted. They obviously had nothing better to do. No amount of protesting or explaining from her would change their minds. She would always be the bad wife, unfit mother, dishonourable neighbour, and there was nothing she could do once they had executed the branding.

"You didn't get back to me about Luke the other day. What's going on, Carrie?"

Carrie sighed. "Trying to get to Luke is like trying to get to Pablo Escobar at the moment, John. He's out of reach and doesn't want anything to do with me. I have to trust that his dad is taking care of him. I have zero influence on him these days."

The turbulent last few weeks had washed Carrie out. She was clinging to survival by her fingernails for the sake of her daughters, her volatile son and a fleeting chance of a reunion with her lost dog, let alone her estranged husband.

John turned left onto the high street, passing Terry's cottage, which looked dark despite the bright day. The curtains were drawn, the garden unkept, and the remnants of the summer house were still strewn across the front garden. It looked as though no one had been near the house for weeks. John caught her looking.

"He has been out and about, you know. I saw him in the pub the other night, drinking quietly in a shady corner. I sat with him for a while. He didn't want to talk but was grateful for me being there when no one else was. He looks a mess."

"Are you trying to make me feel better or worse, John?"

"Come on, Caz. Life is life. Shit things happen, but it's all circumstantial. Things happen for a reason, you'll see." He patted her knee again. She should have chastised him for being overfamiliar, but weirdly, she liked it. "Don't keep the key to your happiness in someone else's pocket."

He looked across at her, and they both burst out laughing.

"Where did you hear that one?

"Just made it up, on the spot," he lied, rubbing his beard and winking at her.

"You're an idiot!"

It felt good to smile and laugh again. The muscles in her face had forgotten how to as they ached from the unfamiliar sensation. They made light conversation as they headed for the motorway, and despite her apprehension about the journey ahead, Carrie was beginning to relax and enjoy herself. John was fun to be around. He didn't take life too seriously and seemed to live one day at a time. He was a bit of a nomad, unmarried, with no children (that he knew about), flitting from decorating jobs to odd jobs and back again. Sometimes, he was busy; sometimes, he spent all day in the pub. He was intriguing, but most of all, he was kind and thoughtful and, right now, a huge rock for Carrie to depend on.

Carrie thought about Betty and what she must have seen these past few weeks. Poor Betty. Carrie had to be strong. She might not be the same dog that she had been before she had gone missing, but Carrie was confident that once she had gotten her home to familiar surroundings, everything would begin to piece itself back together. Slowly but surely, step by step.

"Right, I need to pee," John said gruffly. "Stop here for a break?"

He gestured towards a sign for the services. Carrie agreed. She would love a coffee to steady her nerves as they were getting dangerously close to where Betty was potentially being held. Carrie had waited weeks for answers, and she was about to get them. John had implied that Betty was in a 'dishevelled state.' What did that mean exactly? She had been missing for three weeks and five days. Christmas had come and gone without her, and her family had fallen apart. Was Carrie just taking her dog from one disaster to another, or was she the glue they needed to bring them all back together?

They pulled up and got out of the van. It had just started to snow. Great big powder puff flakes settled gently on the tarmac, flattened and discoloured by any passing vehicle or footprint. It was only a service station on a motorway, but the scene still looked enchanting, and it gave Carrie hope.

"Do you want a hot drink?" John asked as they made their way through the slush to the entrance.

"I'll get them, least I can do as you've driven me here," she replied. "Coffee?"

"Please, Americano, black." He disappeared off to find the toilets.

She meandered to the café and ordered. The services were quiet. Nobody wanted to venture out on a grim day in January. John joined her as she paid for the drinks at the counter.

"Cheers, ma' dears." He lifted the cardboard cup towards hers. "Shall we sit here for five minutes?"

They found a table and sipped. The coffee felt good as it went down her throat. A powerful caffeine injection would give her the boost she needed. The kennels weren't too far from the services, about another half an hour away. Carrie just wanted to get her dog and get back home as soon as possible. She felt it was the first step back on track to her previous life.

"So, I have to tell you something…." John looked down into his drink. *Oh no*, Carrie thought. "It's definitely Betty. My sources have confirmed it from the picture you sent me…."

"But…."

"But she's not at a kennel. She's at a puppy farm."

"What?" Carrie yelled, causing an older lady sitting nearby to jump. She apologised to the women and turned back to John. "A puppy farm?"

"Yeah. You know what that is, don't you?"

"Yes, of course I do! What the hell, John? Why did you

lie to me? How are we going to get her? They won't just hand her over, will they?" Carrie was furious but, most of all, crushed and disappointed. How could he get her hopes up like this? They were never getting her back.

"I didn't tell you because I knew it would upset you. You were the one who wanted to come. I offered to get her for you."

John had, but this was a big deal. Betty coming home would bring them all back. They could forget about what happened and rewind to when it was happier at home. A thought slashed her dream in half. Was it happier at home before all this chaos?

John continued. "It's all set up. A few of the lads will meet me down the road. My contact assures me only one person is working there today. Me and you are going to pretend that we want to buy some puppies, keep them busy whilst Dez and Kyle are going to get Betty, ok?"

Carrie's head was spinning. "What?"

"Just trust me, Carrie. It's going to be ok. We'll get her, but you have to be prepared that she might be...pregnant."

"Pregnant?" Carrie felt lightheaded and a little faint. She breathed in sharply and bit her lip. Slowly she exhaled, trying to fathom this revised information. John reached out to touch her hand and briefly curled his rough fingers around hers. Instinctively she pulled her hand away, but her expression was soft. She looked at him affectionately; she knew he just wanted the best for her.

"Ok. Whatever it takes. Let's go and get her."

* * *

The snow was really starting to come down now, and Matthew was at his office window, mesmerised by it. Little fluffy clouds of frozen water descending from the sky transported him back to being a kid again, sledging down the hills at the back of his parents' cottage. A smile played on his lips; what a happy childhood he'd had. He caught sight of a young lad kicking a snowball around on the pavement, and like being shot with a poisoned arrow, he was reminded of his fragile son. Luke was having a dreadful time. His confidence was rock bottom, he wasn't eating properly, and he couldn't concentrate in school. Since their chat last night, Matthew had been fixated on repairing him. Tonight, he was determined to start rebuilding his little team, starting with his son. He would leave the office early, pick up Luke from school, swing by the shops for supplies and then cook him a hearty vegetable curry. Then he'd tackle the issues of school and sports. He didn't want to overwhelm him, but he had to start somewhere. Luke needed to know that he was Matthew's priority, now and forever.

There was a knock at his office door. It was Johanna. Matthew sighed and was immediately propelled back to his miserable reality. He waved her in, not leaving the security of his window.

"Morning, boss," she said chirpily. "How are you?" She genuinely sounded concerned as she sat on the leather chair on the other side of his desk.

"Same as yesterday and the same as tomorrow," he replied dismissively.

He couldn't be bothered with any of it. He was surrounded by deceitful fakes. All he wanted to do was try to salvage what was left of his family and take care of his children. Whatever she had to say, he didn't care. He had been treading water with his workload for the past fortnight since he had come back to work after the incident. Everyone knew. The whispers from Little Browton had soon reached the city. The first day back in the office was awful. It was like he had been stripped naked and had exposed the staff to every crease and scar of his body. Except it wasn't his body, it was his life, his marriage and most important of all, his family.

Charlie Harvey had been incredible. As soon as the news reached his door, he had immediately shielded Matthew from the prying eyes and done his best to silence the hollow chatter. Matthew didn't know what had been said, but in a few poised words from a benevolent email, Charlie had severed the grapevine before it had grown out of control. He had taken away some of Matthew's workload and reined in Stanton-Peake. He had given Matthew time to just breathe, and he was indebted to him.

In fact, Charlie's acts of pure kindness had pointed Matthew in the right direction of what to do with the information Wendy had revealed before Christmas. For now, however, he'd continue with the mundane, toeing the line and being everyone's mate persona. Why not even play up to the helpless victim they thought he was? He could certainly manipulate Johanna to take the burden out of his day, extracting some sweet revenge for her deception, but recently, somewhere along the line, he'd given up that bitter fight for more important matters.

He looked across the desk towards his colleague. The woman he had mentored, confided in and trusted. She hadn't changed. Same silky blonde hair, honey-kissed skin, full lips pursed tight, seemingly worried about him. She had been his crutch for the past seven years at this firm, and it suddenly hit him like a lightning bolt just how much he had taken her for granted. He'd not thought twice about dumping extra accounts onto her so he could go home a little earlier or how he'd delegated the difficult phone calls and awkward clients because he knew she had a 'special way' with them, or so he told her she did, just to make his life easier. Could he really blame her for setting him up the way she did? Maybe she had changed. Maybe they both had.

"Have you got time to talk about some outstanding accounts?" she asked him hesitantly. He peeled himself away from the snowy scene framed by his window and sat down.

"Yes, of course," he said quietly. "Although, I'd prefer it if we could get Charlie to sit in on these meetings from now on. He has taken over some of these accounts after all."

Johanna looked a little taken aback, then replied sarcastically, "Really? He's very busy, you know, Matt, with his golf trips."

"Is he, though?" Matthew looked directly into her rich brown eyes. "Charlie has had more of a presence these last few weeks than he had in six months last year. I think he's enjoying being more involved. I think he feels he's got his purpose back."

Johanna looked away. For the first time, he saw the mask slip.

Charlie had taken some of Matthew's workload on himself, shunning the offers of his dutiful staff. He had become more engaged with key areas and was authentic in his approach. He had even taken bloody Jonathan Parker off his hands and got him working in his office. They seemed to get on like old pals. The mood of the office had lifted, and Charlie had relegated the vulgar Stanton-Peake to occasional appearances, keeping her busy with social media announcements and public relations.

"Well, I wanted to talk about the Bollington's account and the Clarkes' one. They seem to have been locked down, along with a few others. It seems only you and Charlie have access...."

Matthew was smiling inside. "Well, I wouldn't know about that, Jo. Charlie has taken them off me for now."

She shifted uncomfortably in her seat and sat on her hands. "Oh. How about Bailey's? Matchbox17? Junior Nightingales and Carseras?" Johanna had just listed every account he knew that she had fraudulently plundered. She looked disconcerted.

"Charlie's looking after them. Are these the outstanding accounts you mentioned? Did you want to discuss any others?"

Matthew felt like a steady celestial hand was reaching out and touching his shoulder, reassuring him. He felt calm and, for the first time in a while, in control. Johanna quickly got to her feet.

"No, that's all for now. Thanks, Matthew." She rushed out, glancing towards Clarissa's office as she made her way over to her own desk.

Minutes later, Clarissa was at the coffee machine, quickly followed by Johanna. Matthew busied himself with his inbox, but when he looked up again, they had left the office for an early lunch.

* * *

They arrived at a lock-up of corrugated metal fencing and barbed wire. There was a dirty, dilapidated van parked outside at an awkward angle, obscuring the only visible crack that might expose the grim reality of the puppy farm beyond. The barking and whining tore at Carrie's heartstrings; the dogs were in agony. She wanted to seize John's van and bulldoze the entire farm, releasing them all from their torture, but she knew she had to remain composed if they were to have any hope of rescuing Betty.

Kyle and Dez, John's friends, were ready at the back of the farm, where they had found a way in away from the glare of the makeshift security cameras. Everything was set up. Everyone was ready except for Carrie. She had never done anything like this before, and her heart was beating out of her chest. All she had to do was keep it together for the next half an hour or so, tell a few white lies, and then they'd be out of there with Betty.

John dialled the number and waited for a response.

"Oh, yes, hi. We've come to see some cockapoo puppies you've got for sale...yep...yep...£2,000 was it? We're down Gutterbank Lane…not here? Ok, where? Right…see you soon." He hung up.

John turned to Carrie. "Get back in the van."

Carrie did as she was told, and once they had shut the van doors, he told her about the phone call.

"Well, obviously, they're not going to show us the pups here, are they? We need to go back down the lane to Gutterbank Farm. That's where they are. I'll text Dez and Kyle to let them know. We just need to pretend we like their cockapoo pups, but then, for some reason, I'll come up with a story about why we can't have one, and we'll leave. You can play the disappointed wife, can't you?" He smiled at Carrie. "It's going to be ok. The lads have done this before. They know what they are doing."

Carrie felt reassured by John's confident demeanour. She nodded as he started the van and swung it back towards the farm. This was it! Time to bring the family back once and for all.

* * *

In stark contrast to the lock-up they had just visited, Gutterbank Farm was lovely. It looked like a picture postcard covered in freshly lain snow with a wisp of smoke from a homely fire drifting effortlessly into the grey sky. Carrie wondered how it was possible for the smoke to find a clear path against the frozen flakes wafting relentlessly downwards. A couple stood in the doorway, and the woman waved at them as they approached.

"Come inside," she called as they got out of the van. "You must be frozen. Cup of tea?"

Although they both would have relished a hot drink, they declined. Their getaway had to be clean, not muddled with pleasantries. They had a job to do, a purpose and no amount of kind gestures was going to sway Carrie off course.

They were led through the hallway into a huge farmhouse kitchen. A bottle-green Aga stood in the corner, belching out heat with three or four cats curled up on the surfaces next to it. A large pine table with eight chairs sat on a faded woollen rug that dominated the room. The surfaces were immaculate, not a pot or cup out of place and as clean as a whistle. The two strangers who stood before them were as welcoming as the doorman at The Ritz. They were an old couple in their seventies with friendly faces, not what Carrie had expected at all.

She instinctively took off her coat, John shot her a look, but it was too late.

"Can I take that for you?" the old man asked, reaching out.

"No thanks, I'll hold it," she insisted. The old man backed away.

John took over the situation. "I think we might have just spoken on the phone. We've come to see the cockapoos."

The old woman spoke in a croaky, jagged voice, which suddenly took on a serious, business-like tone. "That was our son-in-law you spoke to. This way, please."

She took them through a side door towards the back of the house. Carrie could hear squealing and shuffling from a cardboard box in the corner.

"Here."

The old lady knelt next to the box where four black and brown furry puppies were blindly dragging themselves over a soft blue towel. The pups looked about three weeks old with no mother in sight. Three seemed quite alert, but one in the corner was not moving.

John leapt into character. "What do you think, babe?" He glanced cheekily across at Carrie.

She was sad. They looked weak and feeble, and they needed their mum. This was such a bizarre situation. How could this couple be harbouring a lock-up of stolen dogs a mile away from this idyllic existence?

"Where's their mother?" Carrie asked the woman. She couldn't help herself. She wanted to test the system. John glared at her again. What was she doing? She didn't know herself.

The old man appeared in the doorway. "Truth be told, she's at the vets. Not feeling too well, a bit loose, you know."

Carrie indicated that she understood and proceeded to play her part. "This little brown one is cute." She pointed to the still one in the corner of the box.

"Oh no, look at the other three. That one is the runt. You don't want the runt. You want a big, strong one. Any preference on gender?" the old lady said.

"Bitch, if possible," John replied. "We are hoping to breed for ourselves."

Carrie saw the old lady wince for a second, but then she righted herself. "Ok, well. This black one is a bitch, quite feisty too," she chuckled. "She sucks your finger, look."

She handed the pup to Carrie, who began cradling it like a newborn. This innocent black ball of fur, with its racing heart beating into the palm of her hand, reminded Carrie of why they were there. Just another ten minutes or so, and it would all be over. They could leave this place and never come back, forgetting about its very existence. Blocking out the memory forever, but Carrie wasn't sure she could do that now.

John was making small talk with the couple, biding his time before teeing up their exit. Carrie had to be ready. Whatever he said, she had to follow.

"So, the deposit is half the amount?" The old man nodded. "It's a bit steep. Usually, it's about £500, isn't it?" John pressed on.

"I'm sorry, son, but that's the price. I can't shift it." The old man seemed genuinely deflated.

"Well, I can't give you £1,000 today, only half. I'm sorry, I thought that was the standard amount."

The old lady steadily got to her feet and whispered something to her husband.

"Wait a minute. I'll call my son-in-law. See what he says." He disappeared out of the room while the old woman smiled at them.

"Weather's closing in. Have you far to travel?"

"Not too far," John said quickly.

She turned to Carrie, who still had the pup. "She likes you. I've called her Martha. I name them all. Breaks my heart every time he sells them, but it's what keeps us on the farm. That's why we can't be flexible on the price, I'm afraid. Perhaps Jason will make an exception if Donald tells him how nice you both are."

Donald appeared in the doorway and shook his head. "I'm sorry, folks. That's the price."

"Ok." John sighed outwardly. "We'll have a think and get back to you. Shall we leave now, darling? This snow might be causing some issues on the motorway. Can I take your number?"

Carrie gently placed the pup back amongst her brothers and sisters and reached out to stroke the still brown one; he was warm. She put her coat back on, and they said their goodbyes.

As they crunched their way over the snow to the van, John checked his phone.

Carrie asked, "Was that all a bit weird? Did you get the impression they were doing all this under duress?"

John said nothing until they were safely back on the glistening lane. Then he pulled over onto the verge.

"I'm so sorry, Carrie. There's been a problem. Betty's gone."

CHAPTER 17

The bank had rung again and again and again. Frankie Reeve was not one to give up easily, so Matthew caved and went to see her the next morning.

He sat in the familiar plastic chair, staring at the familiar faded posters on the familiar dingy walls waiting for the young woman who held his spindly purse strings. Frankie had been honest with him when she called and admitted that she knew what had happened with Terry. She was a local girl, so the village gossip had not managed to escape her ears. Terry hadn't been back to work since, and she was quite sure that he had put in a transfer back to Leeds. All in all, he wouldn't be in the bank today, and that was what Matthew needed to hear. He couldn't face him. He didn't want to see the man who made his wife so happy when he clearly couldn't.

"Hello, Mr Pritchard." Frankie appeared in the doorway. "Shall we go through?"

Matthew nodded and followed her along the gloomy corridor to her office at the back of the bank. She indicated, and he sat down dutifully. She began surprisingly brightly.

"So, I'm happy to report that everything seems to be on track, and you are making the repayments every month, which is excellent."

Matthew smiled but continued looking down at his lap; he was waiting for the conditional 'but' that seemed to be the only conjunctive bank clerks used in positive sentences with him. The 'but' didn't come. He looked up, and she continued.

"…and I was wondering whether you wanted to consider paying off a chunk of the debt with a lump sum, and we, from this, can negotiate lower rates of interest for the rest."

Matthew was confused. "Ms Reeve, I have had a Christmas bonus, but there isn't a chance it's enough to cover a huge part of my debt. I'm paying the rent on a flat in town as well as the mortgage on my semi, so if anything, I'm worse off than before."

Frankie waved away his words and turned the tablet around for him to see his accounts. He had been so distracted lately that he hadn't checked his bank statements since before Christmas. His balance was unusually high. What the…? His Christmas bonus was paid as usual, but a few weeks later, another substantial payment from the firm was almost double the amount. Matthew couldn't believe it. What on earth was going on?

He looked up at Frankie. "I don't understand this."

Frankie reassured Matthew that it was all legitimate. Mr Harvey also banked with this branch, and she had contacted him to check that these and some other recent transactions were correct from his personal account. Charlie Harvey had indeed tripled Matthew's bonus!

"It's a lot to take in, I understand. But Mr Harvey is a wealthy man. He insisted and can do what he likes with his own money. You'll be able to reduce the loan considerably now."

"It's too much." Matthew resisted. "I must speak to him." He left the bank in a daze and drove straight to the office. When he arrived in the car park, he couldn't remember a thing about the journey.

The office was buzzing. Everyone was busy going about their business as efficiently as possible, but with one huge difference, for the first time in months, they were happy.

Charlie Harvey was on the phone in his office with Jonathan Parker sitting at his breakout table typing away on his laptop. The two of them had been working very closely over the last few weeks. That was one thing Matthew *had* noticed. How generous of Charlie, the CEO, to take the time to mentor Parker. Matthew smiled as he crossed the office floor. That was the kind of man he was—reeling off jokes, putting everyone at ease, motivating less experienced staff and tripling bonuses here and there!

Matthew had to see him; it was too much. As soon as he was off the phone, he'd nip in to find out what was going on.

As he reached his office door, he looked across at Johanna's desk to say his usual 'Good morning.' Her head was down at her computer. She didn't even glance up when he opened the door. She had been acting strangely since their conversation the other day about the outstanding accounts.

Brushing it off, he closed the door and hooked his jacket over his chair. He pulled his laptop from his bag and set it up on his desk. As he did so, he surveyed the office. There was certainly a new dynamic. The atmosphere felt lighter somehow.

Monsieur Baudelaire was making his way over to Matthew. He internally groaned before Baudelaire opened the door. Oh, dear God, what did he want?

"Bonjour Matt-hew. I was hoping to catch you earlier." His accent was undoubtedly French and very thick.

Matthew didn't look up. There'd be no point anyway. Monsieur Baudelaire didn't *do* eye contact. "Yeah, sorry. I had to go to the bank."

"It's okay. Charlie and I would like you to come to early dinner with us today. Is that agreeable with you?"

Matthew stopped in his tracks, and this time, he did look up. Jean-Paul Baudelaire was looking him right in the eye. This was all very odd. "Sure, I'll need to text my son. What time?" Matthew stammered out.

"We have booked The Custom House at five. We have much to discuss." He smiled. "Au revoir."

He left the office, and Matthew collapsed in his chair. He really hoped that this discussion involved getting some answers too. It was turning out to be a very weird day. He pulled his mobile out of his jacket pocket to text Luke. Luke. He had forgotten his son. He needed him. Matthew was stuck. If he went to the dinner and left him to his own devices, Luke might feel like the innermost feelings that he had shared with his dad had fallen on deaf ears, and once again, he was putting work before his son. On the flip side, if he didn't go to dinner, he might not find out about the triple bonus or why Monsieur Baudelaire could finally look him in the eye. Matthew was sure Charlie Harvey was the link.

He pondered as his finger hovered over the keypad of his phone. Just then, it rang. It was his mother.

"Hi, Mum."

"Hello, darling," she drawled. "I was hoping you both might like to have dinner with us this evening. Your dad's made a lovely steak pie, but it's enormous! Far too big for the two of us! Six be ok?"

Matthew looked upwards and smiled.

"Perfect, Mum, but I have to go to a last-minute dinner. You couldn't collect Luke for me from training and have him, could you?"

"Of course. Just tell me when and where. I'll send Dad. He'll go and watch too, no doubt, remind him of when he used to watch you."

Matthew finalised the arrangements with her and hung

up. As he texted Luke the plans, he mentally took another step on the road to their recovery. Slowly but surely, the choppy waters were beginning to calm, and he could see a way out after months and months of battle.

* * *

Apathy, like a hungry vulture, picked over the last pieces of her shattered heart. Carrie couldn't do it anymore. The light at the end of the tunnel had burnt out, and despite how many times she shuffled the pack, the last card had already been played. She had lost. Betty was gone, again.

It was cold waiting at the school gates. John had dropped her off after a very sullen drive home from the farm. He tried to reassure her that he would do everything he could to find her dog, but Carrie didn't want to hear it. Her only saving grace was that she hadn't told anyone else about their trip today, so no one else needed to share her bitter disappointment. The door to the reception classroom opened, and Mr Turner stepped out, along with his faction of five-year-olds. Carrie saw Jen, then Hannah, and slowly her heart mended, just a little. This was why she kept going, her wonderful children.

Hannah and Jen waved, and they came skipping over.

"Hi, Mummy!" they both yelled.

"Hello, my darlings!" Carrie buried her face in their hair as she pulled them in close. Tears briefly escaped and buried themselves amongst the wavy locks. She pulled away and wiped away the stragglers before her daughters could see.

"Mrs Pritchard!" A familiar voice boomed across the playground.

"Ah, Mr Turner." Carrie straightened herself up as he approached. She wanted to be ready for the onslaught.

"I just wanted to say how wonderful the girls have been today. They have completed their sticker charts which means they get to go and read to Mrs Gray tomorrow," he said in his dull teacher voice.

How did the kids listen to that all day, she wondered? All the same, she was very proud of them. The girls were now in their fifth month of school and hadn't completed a single sticker chart since September. In comparison, Jeremy, Alisha's boy, had completed four.

"Wow, girls! That's super news!" Carrie found herself copying Mr Turner's inane talk. "Shall we celebrate with a hot chocolate?" She felt she needed another strong caffeine hit or at least a slice of cake.

"Yeah!" they chorused, jumping up and down.

Carrie turned to Mr Turner. "Thank you, I needed to hear this today."

He smiled kindly at her before retreating to the warmth of his classroom. *Perhaps things were slowly going to get better,* she thought as they left for the café.

"Carrie!" Alisha called out. "I heard hot chocolate. Can we come?" She pointed to Jeremy and another little boy she seemed to have collected along the way.

"Of course, the more, the merrier," she replied to the squeals of delight from her girls.

Alisha, along with John, had been the only friends that had supported Carrie during the past few weeks. Jamal, Alisha's husband, had been abandoned on many a weeknight once the children had gone to bed so that she could pop over to Carrie's with a bottle of wine or for a cuppa to cheer her up. Carrie couldn't have been more grateful for the company right now. She hadn't been to the café since the incident but knew she had to move on. Alisha kept telling her to do so.

Jen, Hannah, Jeremy and Clayton, the other little boy Alisha was minding, held hands as they made their way along the high street to the café. They passed Terry's cottage, and Carrie couldn't resist a look. It was in darkness apart from a dim light upstairs in one of the bedroom windows. Carrie stopped at the gate.

"Don't even think about it!" Alisha shot her friend a stern look, grabbed Carrie's arm and pulled her along. "Not on impulse. Let's talk about this."

They reached the café and found a large booth for the six of them to sit in. Alisha pulled out colouring books and pocket board games from her magic handbag, and the kids settled into a contented huddle of activity. As it was quiet, Carrie ventured to the counter and bought the drinks. She handed them out before settling next to her friend.

She sighed. Today had been a huge waste of time. Maybe if she could just talk to Terry, she might be able to salvage something from the day and move forward. However, she wasn't sure how it would help. They had both lost everything at the cost of a stupid kiss. Meeting up with Terry would be like trying to ignite a wet bonfire. The flames had gone out, and so had the intense heat. Over the weeks, Carrie was beginning to realise that it wasn't Terry that she had wanted after all. She had needed comfort, companionship, to be seen and above all, to be heard by someone. He had been the same, and they had found each other in a weak moment. Passion had bewitched them, tricked them into believing that what they were feeling was real. Carrie had to know that it had all been a mistake. She had to see him to know this once and for all. She wanted her family back, the girls, Luke, Matthew, and of course, Betty. If she could conclude her relationship with Terry, she hoped that she could begin building bridges with Matthew, one step at a time.

"Penny for them...," Alisha started.

Carrie smiled and patted her friend's hand. "Have I told you lately what a wonderful friend you have been to me?"

"Only a few times. It's getting boring now."

They both laughed.

"I just feel like I need to talk to Terry and put this whole situation to bed."

"Err, poor choice of words!" Alisha burst out laughing. "Sorry, babe, you've got to see the funny side."

Carrie giggled. "You know what I mean. That night was the right time, right place but with the wrong man."

"Well, he did show up, Carrie, but he was late," Alisha

chirped, still trying to keep the chat light-hearted. However, sensing that her friend wasn't playing anymore, she changed tack.

"If you really want to see him, then do it. If you don't feel like you can move forward without speaking to him, then you have to. He obviously can't move on, judging by the state of that house. This might be therapy for you both."

"Yeah…maybe."

Carrie was lost in thought. Her whole being was yearning to elevate itself from the downward spiral. She hoped that finding Betty was the answer, but maybe this was.

"Listen, there was a light on in the house, so someone must be in," Alisha said. "The girls can come back to mine for tea. I've got Clayton until seven anyway. What's two more? You go and see him. At least then you'll know what's what, won't you?"

"Alisha, thank you. You're right. Are you sure you can manage with four on the way home?" asked Carrie.

"Jamal's coming here in ten minutes. We'll be fine. Now go before you change your mind!"

Carrie kissed the girls as Alisha explained that their mummy had forgotten to get something from the shops. Carrie left the security of the café for the hostile cottage on the high street. She was unarmed and unprotected, but she wasn't scared. She knew deep down this was something that they both needed. One of them just had to make the first move.

* * *

At 16:55 that afternoon, Matthew was standing in the bar of a fashionable city restaurant holding a freshly pulled pint of beer. This was very surreal for a Tuesday, but nothing about this entire day had made sense so far. Charlie and Jean-Paul were making their way to the table, and Matthew followed. The table was set for four, Clarissa, Matthew deduced.

Charlie caught him looking at the empty chair as they sat down. "Jonathan's coming now," he said quietly. "He's had a few loose ends to tie up at the office."

Matthew nodded. He didn't want to start asking questions. Something told him all would be revealed once Parker showed up. Ten minutes later, Jonathan Parker joined them, flustered but jubilant.

"It's done, Charlie," he announced, lifting his beer to clink with his colleagues.

Charlie obliged and thanked Jonathan for all his hard work. Jean-Paul Baudelaire simply bowed his head in acknowledgement. Then they turned to Matthew.

"You're probably wondering what on earth is going on, aren't you?" Charlie smirked. "You see, I knew about the defrauding of the accounts for some time, but I couldn't quite put my finger on who was doing it. The culprits were far too slippery for Jean-Paul and me. They threw out many a red herring, so we hired Jonathan."

They had Matthew's undivided attention; this was a fascinating twist, or was it a test? Were they tricking Matthew into confessing all he knew about Johanna? Matthew decided to stay quiet.

Charlie coolly took a sip of wine. "Jonathan is a fraud investigator. He has been working in the background for months, well two years to be exact...." Two years? That was when Johanna started dabbling in deceit. Had Jonathan been hovering in the shadows all this time? "...it turns out Clarissa is the puppet master, pulling the strings of a few of our most trusted employees. Your number two, Johanna, is one of them and Peter from payroll!"

"What?" Even though Matthew knew about Johanna, this news was shocking. Clarissa behind all of it? No wonder she and Johanna had become as thick as thieves.

"This is insane!" He drank his beer slowly as Charlie continued the story.

"Clarissa has been siphoning off titbits of cash from your accounts but using Johanna to do it under your username. At first, I thought it was you. I had Jonathan watch you under the guise of an intern. He quickly concluded that your activities on the accounts didn't match the rogue activity. I also noticed that you were not being paid your full salary and when I challenged Pete on it, he said Clarissa had you on some probationary period that I hadn't even heard of and certainly never agreed to. That was when I realised you were being set up. You were Clarissa and Johanna's fall guy. After all, why would you take spittle amounts of money at high risk and deny yourself your full salary?"

Matthew's eyes widened. This was more than a can of worms; this was a cesspit of vipers! She had not only stolen from clients but from him too. She had cooked up some story about a probationary period and made his life hell for the past six months jumping through hoop after hoop. Even when she'd heard about Matthew's domestic situation, she had still insisted on that report being completed by the next day and the 8 a.m. meetings when she knew he had to get Luke to school. She was an evil, twisted, manipulative bitch.

"With that in mind. I recently replenished your account with the outstanding earnings. I'm sorry if this has caused you any hardship, Matthew." Charlie leaned across the table. "Things have been tough for you, and we will do everything we can to support you through this time."

"She had me fooled too, Matthew," Jean-Paul added. "She showed me endless examples of your incompetence, which I know now were all her. I haven't been as helpful to you as I could have been. I am sorry for that. Je m'excuse."

Matthew was bowled over. For the first time in his life, he blushed with gratitude. However, one thing was still niggling away at him. Johanna. Why?

It turned out; that Clarissa was blackmailing Johanna. Some time ago, Johanna had bumped into her whilst she was out with her partner, a beautiful woman called Annalise. Clarissa was old friends with Annalise's parents, who were very old-fashioned and wouldn't take too kindly to discover that their only child was a lesbian. Clarissa used this information against the couple until finally, Annalise couldn't take the stress anymore and left for Italy, leaving

Johanna heartbroken. By this point, Johanna was too far into the black widow's web of extortion to escape.

Pieces of the jigsaw began falling into place in Matthew's head. Johanna had never liked talking about her personal life. It also explained why she had thrown herself into work and tried to engage Matthew in the cruel enterprise before Christmas. Johanna had been played. They all had.

"So, what happens now?" Matthew asked.

Jonathan Parker folded his arms and sat back in his chair. "She's gone. We gave her the ultimatum of getting out now with no questions asked or court. Even when she threatened to get some hot-shot city lawyer onto us for unfair dismissal, she could see the holes in her own argument."

"We won't be hearing from her again. My solicitors have taken care of it," Charlie added.

"What about Johanna? And Pete?" Matthew gingerly sipped his beer, looking at Charlie over the distorted rim of his glass.

"Pete's easy. He's just been foolish. He didn't know any better, so he has been reprimanded with a warning. Johanna, though, she could have come to you or me…." Charlie waited for a response from Matthew.

Matthew felt his stare reach right into his conscience to pull out whatever decency he had left in there.

"She did."

Charlie continued to peer at him for what felt like a lifetime, then slowly smiled.

"We know you didn't take the bait. Johanna was just having her strings pulled in all sorts of directions by Clarissa. She's decided to leave us, she's paid back what she owed and is moving back to Sweden." Matthew looked from Charlie to Jonathan and finally to Jean-Paul.

"What about the clients that have been targeted? Do they know?"

Parker puffed himself up in his seat. The irritating intern was finally showing his worth.

"I've dealt with them personally. They all know and will be compensated mostly out of the savings we will make from Johanna's salary, which was terminated as soon as she left."

It seemed all the loose ends had been tied up and that they had all made their peace with the situation, so he felt he must too. What a turn of events! He may have underestimated Johanna, but that was nothing compared to Charlie Harvey. Matthew wasn't sure that if the boot were on the other foot, he would be so forgiving.

The food arrived, and eventually, the dutiful conversation flowed freely. It was strange talking about work without feeling your neck was on the chopping block. His job had been like wading through treacle at times, and as he left the restaurant, he felt the bleak viscosity recede around him, and his shoulders dropped. Finally, he could get on with what he had been employed to do without the pre-set trip wires or inquisitive electric shocks from

Stanton-Peake. He knew the days of constantly looking over his shoulder were over, and trust had been restored.

He thought of Johanna and that he must contact her. She had made a stupid mistake, but she was still his friend. He wanted her to know that he had forgiven her.

He thought of Luke and hoped he was eating a hearty meal with his parents.

He thought of the girls; he missed them so much.

Then he thought of Carrie.

Things were not always so black and white. He hadn't given her time to explain. Perhaps he'd rushed to the wrong conclusion, but she had been in another man's arms. His hands were all over her. What other conclusion could there be? If Matthew hadn't walked in....

He pushed the sordid thought out of his head, but he knew he couldn't avoid the muddy puddle forever. They needed to talk, and he needed to listen; he knew that much.

Hailing a taxi, he decided to go to Little Browton. Luke would be fine with his parents for a few hours, and it was the perfect opportunity to talk to his wife. Butterflies quivered with anticipation inside his stomach, he knew how important this meeting was, and he had to get it right. It was make or break for his marriage. If Charlie Harvey could exonerate him, he could surely try to do the same with Carrie.

He spent the next twenty minutes avoiding insignificant chit-chat with the driver so he could hone his opening words until they were true, and she would know he was being sincere. He thought of how she looked the last time he'd seen her, and the butterflies fluttered a little higher. He missed her. He couldn't be whole without her. Now things seemed to have resolved themselves at work, he could make his family his priority. Their happiness was all that mattered right now.

The driver turned the corner onto the familiar high street, deserted on a typical January evening. He passed the café, dimly lit with a few final customers sipping up the dregs of their coffee before closing time. He passed the bank, no lights on and plunged in gloom and then *his* house, quivering obscurely behind the thick hedge. Something caught his eye, a figure leaving. A slim, petite woman slipping through the garden gate and out under the streetlights. He gasped. His heart dropped like a stone.

"Er...sorry, pal. Can you take me back to the city? Change of plan."

CHAPTER 18

"Hey, Jamal." Carrie smiled as he opened the door.

"Hi, Carrie. Come in. The kids are watching telly. Alisha's just upstairs, but I know she'll want to see you." He winked, stepping aside for her to enter. He knew his wife so well. She was a diamond friend but would also be bursting a blood vessel to find out what had been said between Carrie and Terry.

"Darling! Carrie's here!" he called up the stairs. Within seconds, her friend appeared.

"Hi! Come up, come up!" Alisha waved. Carrie turned and looked at Jamal, who just rolled his eyes and retreated to the living room.

Carrie pulled off her boots, quickly checked in on the kids who didn't stir from their cartoon and made her way upstairs to Alisha's room. She was sitting at her dressing table, fiddling with some fake eyelashes that she had accidentally glued to her finger.

"Do you want some help?" Carrie asked, settling herself on the side of the bed.

"No, I'm going to give up in a minute. But in the meantime, what happened?"

Carrie caught Alisha's eye in the dressing table mirror and burst out laughing.

"I will, but first, please take that hairy caterpillar off your eyelid! You look ridiculous."

They both laughed. "That's the last time I pay £4.99 for fake eye lashes. So?"

Carrie took a deep breath. "Oh gosh, he looks awful. He's missing Delilah so much."

"Well, of course. What about his wife, though?" Alisha tilted her head to listen intently for the reply.

"He didn't mention her much, but I got the impression that she's being difficult."

"Oh, so where does that leave you two?"

Carrie looked down and wiggled her wedding ring with her finger with her thumb. He had been surprised to see her standing on his doorstep. He welcomed her in, and they sat with a coffee on the blood-red stools in the kitchen. She let him speak first. She knew what she wanted out of the conversation, but his intentions were unclear. She needed to be sure.

The cottage was cold and dark. So far away from how it had been on her first visit. A thick layer of dust covered every surface, and no evidence that a little girl had ever lived at the address. No toys, no cute patent leather shoes by the door, no twinkling fairy lights around the mirror in the living room. It was as if Delilah had been wiped out of the picture. Just a sad man, living with his regret.

"I knew then that he felt the same as me. There was no future between us, and there never had been. We were both just looking for affection and a little feeling. We had both suffered rejection and cold shoulders for too long. His true love is Delilah. It's tearing him apart not being with her."

Alisha nodded and allowed her friend to continue.

"He didn't want to talk about what happened. He just kept muttering about ways he could get his little girl back. He's bitter, too, towards Corrine, and she has cut all contact this time. He told me that I was lucky still being able to see my kids. I'd never really thought about it that way. Matthew never denied me access. It must be so hard." Carrie swallowed. "Anyway, he said he was sorry that it had turned out the way it did."

"But he has done this before, hasn't he? Corrine said she'd set a honeytrap for him. You were just caught in the crossfire." Alisha interjected to remind her friend of his betrayal. She sensed Carrie felt sorry for Terry, but he didn't deserve her pity.

"Yes, but this time she has taken Delilah away from him. He is absolutely destroyed."

"Oh, Carrie, you are so forgiving. Do you not feel a bit...used?"

Carrie looked down at her nails and picked at her scruffy cuticles. They were a reminder of how different she and Corrine were. Glamour vs ghastly, confident vs compliant. No wonder Terry didn't want her, not really.

"Yes, I'm transparent all over again, aren't I 'Leesh?" Mundane tears began to fall again. Crying was such a waste of time and energy, but it was her default. It was what she was familiar with. Alisha left the dressing table to comfort her friend on the side of the bed. She put a consoling arm around Carrie's shoulders and pulled her close. Then the sobs came. Carrie was letting everything out, Terry, Matthew, Luke, Betty. She needed the release.

They sat for roughly ten minutes until Carrie's weeping reduced steadily. Damp tissues were scattered across the duvet, and Alisha finally released her friend to gather them and put them in the bin.

"So, how did you leave it with him? I must admit, I thought you'd be gone a lot longer than you were." Alisha said eventually.

"A stupid mistake on all sides. He's thinking about following Corrine to London. He is obsessed with getting Delilah back. I think that's all he's living for right now."

Carrie patted her eyes with the softest part of the tissue that she could find. They were starting to scratch and sting.

"He's out of my life, so I need to focus on rebuilding what I have left."

"Yes, you do. It's going to take time, but I'm here for you." Alisha smiled warmly. "Now, do you fancy a little nightcap before we have to put these little rascals to bed?"

"Sure, why not."

* * *

The taxi pulled up outside his parents' house shortly before nine. He decided to stay a while with his folks, maybe even stay over. He didn't want to be alone with his ugly thoughts tonight. The snow had receded from the driveway but had been replaced by a penetrating frost. Matthew picked his way carefully across the path to the front door. Passing the living room window, he caught sight of his dad and his son laughing together on the sofa. They were watching an old comedy whilst his mum fussed around them with tea and biscuits.

The idyllic scene filled Matthew with mixed emotions. He'd always imagined he'd have the nuclear family he'd grown up with for his own children. Seeing his parents with his son was bittersweet. The tenderness was tinged with sadness for the missing pieces, Jen, Hannah and Carrie. Now the rosy future he'd imagined in the taxi ride to his former home was withering right before his eyes. He thought he could fix everything with a few kind words of clemency. He hadn't banked on Carrie going back to *him*. For the first time, he wasn't angry with her. He was angry with himself for waiting too long and letting her slip through his fingers into the arms of someone else.

He opened the door, and his nostrils filled with the lingering scent of warm apple pie. Despite eating out tonight, he hoped his mother had saved him a piece.

"That you, Matthew?" she called from the living room. "How did it go love?"

She came into the kitchen as he was taking off his coat. He gave her a knowing look, and she knew from his expression not to enquire any further. Experience had taught her not to enquire any further.

"I've saved you a bit of apple pie." His eyes lit up, and there was the little boy she'd known thirty years ago. "Ooh, Luke looked exactly the same way when I mentioned pie for dessert." She chuckled, pulling on her oven gloves and retrieving the goods from the dying warmth of the oven.

"Has he eaten...," Matthew paused, "...well tonight?" He didn't want to worry her with his suspicions about his son.

"Not so keen on the steak pie, but how many fifteen-year-old boys want that, 'eh? Far too good for them. Hoovered up this, though." She cut him a huge slice, plonked it in a bowl and covered it with thick cream. "Here, I think you need it."

He did. He was craving comfort and not just from the food. He wanted his wife. He wanted his girls. He wanted to rewind time to how it had been before.

As he sat down to tuck into the childhood pie, he paused. "Mum, how do you and Dad do it?"

"Do what, love?" His mum replied, loading the dishwasher with the remains of the dirty crockery.

"Marriage. Stay together so long." He put the spoon down as his mum came to join him at the table.

She reached out and patted his arm. "It's not been easy. Your dad is a very stubborn man. Like you really." She laughed. "But we lived a simple life, Matthew. You only played football once a week, not the ton of activities Luke and the girls do. Dad could pick you up on the way home from the printworks."

Her son leapt to her defence. "But you worked too, Mum…," he began. Matthew was quite surprised by what she said next.

"I worked in the post office part-time, and I loved it. I saw a whole host of different people every day, and they all had time for a chat. It was easy to balance family time and work because your dad helped out so much."

"What?" Matthew ate a mouthful of the delicious pie.

"You don't remember?" Matthew shook his head. "He would cook every Wednesday so I could go swimming with Pat after work. He did all the ironing on a Sunday afternoon in front of the football, and he has always changed the bins. I hate that job, so he has always done it. I don't think I have changed a bin in fifty years."

She smiled to herself. "He can be a stick-in-the-mud about some things, but we're a team. We get through it together."

He was confused. "Mum, a bit of ironing, cooking and changing the bins isn't much, is it?"

"Oh, my dear boy. It's not about *what* he did, it's *why* he did it. We both try to make our lives easier. It's the little things like making the other person a cuppa or vacuuming the stairs without being asked. That's the difference."

Matthew couldn't remember the last time he'd made Carrie a cup of tea, and he didn't know where she kept the vacuum. He didn't iron, rarely cooked and never changed the bins. In fact, he didn't do *anything* around the house. He suddenly felt startlingly embarrassed; his sixty-five-year-old father had put him to shame.

A mother's intuition kicked in, and Felicity attempted to soothe her son.

"You're so busy, Matthew. Times have changed since you were a boy. Carrie takes on too much as well. I've lost count of the times I have offered to help her."

He continued to eat the pie, deep in thought. Despite everything, he felt the urge to defend his wife, not for the first time against his mum.

"I could have done more, though. I used work as an excuse and delayed coming home. It was just easier that way. No wonder Carrie was fraught by the time I rolled in at 8 p.m."

"8 p.m.?" Felicity raised her eyebrows.

"She wouldn't accept help from you, Mum, because she is a survivor. She has always had to survive on her own.

Ever since her dad died, she didn't exactly have a role model in her own mother, did she?"

His mum nodded. She remembered the gossip swirling around the post office when Edward had died. Jim O'Grady had quickly got his feet under the table bringing his three sons with him, disrupting poor Carrie's life. How must it have felt to suddenly be a stranger in your own home? Julie Kevan simply 'forgot' about her daughter from that moment on. She hadn't even stayed for Carrie and Matthew's wedding reception. As soon as the cake was cut, she and Jim were nowhere to be seen. She wished the same could have been said for the O'Grady boys, who got devilishly drunk and disruptive and had to be escorted out by the hotel staff. They had wrecked Matthew's night. However, what they had done to Carrie's teenage years must have been catastrophic. They both sighed loudly, caught each other's eyes and let out a simultaneous false laugh.

"None of us is perfect, son. I've misjudged her too. I never thought she was good enough for you, but I don't think anyone ever would have been. She made you happy, and you have such a wonderful little family that needs to be together, not split across a city."

Felicity Pritchard was right; of course, she was. However, she had not witnessed Carrie sneaking out of her lover's house only an hour earlier when Matthew was going over there to offer an olive branch.

The sadness swelled to form a lump in his throat. His preoccupancy and hostility had pushed her away again. Just when one part of his life was righting itself, the other was falling apart.

"Are you bringing the girls over this weekend? I thought we could take them swimming."

Matthew ate another spoonful of the pie and thought carefully about what his mum had asked. A plan was forming in his mind. It was a desperate last chance at saving his marriage from the clutches of divorce. He had only seen Carrie coming out of Terry's house, nothing more. Maybe he was blowing the image he was obsessing over in the taxi way out of context.

"Yeah, maybe. Can I let you know? I might need you on standby for the kids this weekend, if that's ok?"

He finished the last of the dessert and looked up at his mum as she took away his bowl. She gave him a knowing look and squeezed his shoulder.

"Of course, son, you do what you have to do. Now, shall we go in there and see what all this laughter is about? I think the whole street can hear these two 'guffawing goons'!"

CHAPTER 19

It was Friday again, and Carrie needed to think. She pulled on her old friends who hadn't had an outing for weeks, laced them up and grabbed her keys. A run was what she needed now to clear her head. Her mind was bubbling over with possibilities. Matthew would be picking the girls up from school at 3:30 p.m., and she had to intercept his plans before then.

Despite being mid-morning, it was still a little slippery underfoot. Carrie decided to get off the pavements as soon as possible, so she opted for a gentle, rolling route around the ridge and through the woods. She set off at a steady pace as she hadn't run for weeks and didn't want to risk an injury. Music was helping her keep an easy rhythm but hopelessly filling the vacancy of her usual running partner.

Carrie hadn't heard anything from John since their wild goose chase earlier in the week. Sooner or later, she would have to face facts that Betty had gone for good. Even the girls had stopped talking about her. Maybe it was time to move her basket and bowls to the garage. Having them lie empty and unused was just another reminder of Carrie's failures.

She crossed over the road and followed the frozen path into the woods. It was a bleak, habitual day, grey and tedious. Off route, sharp emerald spikes with droopy white shades pierced through the virginal snow, trumpeting the first suggestion of spring. Ducking under the undergrowth, she was grateful to escape the oppressive sky under the shelter of the icy bows and occasional evergreen awning. Being alone with her thoughts was strangely comforting.

So much had happened. Life had shifted the dial and presented a brochure that had appeared enchanting from the outside but, in reality, was not the right destination to find the answers she was looking for.

She didn't have any answers, just questions. Why had this happened to her? Fate suddenly didn't seem so fake. Perhaps this hiccup was *supposed* to happen to shake her out of her humdrum existence.

Carrie decided it was better to be in the present, eager to discover what happens next, rather than grapple with the past and be imprisoned by what might have been. Growth was a result of change, and their relationship had changed in a big way. It was how they responded now that would make the difference. They had to break the cycle and move forward.

She wanted to move forward with him; she wanted her son back. She missed Luke terribly. He was the consistent calm to the girls' ongoing chaos. An oasis of realism when she had needed someone to just be. She yearned for the boy she had nurtured, but he had gone, grown up into a fledgling adult. He was making sense of the world in his own way. She had missed out on too many precious weeks already, and she needed him back where he belonged.

But where did that leave her and Matthew?

Her playlist switched to an upbeat track, and she increased her speed. Soon she was sprinting along the ground, running so fast she could taste her last breath. She wanted to reach the future, touch it, and make sense of it. A culmination was coming, but what? When? Why? How?

Her phone buzzed in her pocket. She stopped sharply, caught her breath for a second and looked at the caller ID. It was John Paterson.

"Hi," she puffed.

"Hi, what *are* you doing?" his voice quizzed through the handset.

"Out running."

"Are you mad? It's like minus three out there today."

She could hear him dragging on a cigarette in between sentences.

"Better than smoking my life away."

"Ok, ok, you win. You're the healthiest, blah, blah, blah!" John teased, and he took another draw.

"What do you want anyway?" she asked, jogging from

one foot to the other to try and maintain some of the body heat she had generated.

"Oh, yes. I've spoken to Donald. You remember the farmer from the puppy farm place?"

"What? Really?" Carrie's mind began to whirl again. "Why?"

"It's a bit delicate. Where are you? Can I meet you somewhere for a chat?"

"Sure. I'm in Blackthorn Woods right now. I could do to get home and…."

"Great, I'm not far from there now. Meet you at the picnic area in five?" He hung up. Shocked, Carrie stared absentmindedly at her phone. She had not been expecting that.

* * *

Five minutes felt more like ten, but eventually, John's clapped-out old van roared into the picnic area car park. Carrie was freezing, so she ran over and hopped into the passenger seat as soon as he had become stationary.

"God, don't you have any heating in here?" She closed the door and immediately started to twist and poke at the buttons on John's dashboard.

"Here, put this over you."

He reached behind his seat and threw an old jumper at her. It stank of turpentine, but she was grateful for some warmth and pulled it over her head. She folded her arms tightly across her chest and tucked up her legs, covering them with the stretched fabric.

"So?" She turned her head slowly to meet John's. She didn't want to let an ounce of heat out of her cocoon.

He switched off the engine, took his hands off the steering wheel and tucked them between his legs. He shifted uncomfortably in his seat. He was thinking carefully about what to say next.

By now, it had started to rain. The slow drumming of raindrops gathered momentum and spattered the van roof, resonating a low humming around the vehicle. Carrie watched droplet after droplet burst its banks and slide down the murky windscreen, occasionally joining up with another, creating an opaque veil across the glass, concealing the outside from view. She was glad nobody was out and about on this dreary morning; Carrie didn't want to be seen. She didn't know what John was about to tell her, and her emotions were already starting to discredit her.

"Cheer up. Your face is as miserable as the weather."

She wanted to shout at him, how dare he! Didn't he remember what she had been through this last month? Yet, she found herself doing the opposite, her mouth curled upward, and she began to smile and then giggle. That was John. He had a gift for defusing difficult situations with pathetic criticism. He began to giggle too, and for a moment, she forgot the reason for their meeting. John hadn't. He put one hand on the steering wheel and started the ignition.

"Shall we go for a drive? I've got so much to tell you."

* * *

Answerphone. He left a message.

"Hi Carrie, it's me. Can we meet up this weekend? Mum and Dad can have the girls and Luke. Please, I promise I won't be difficult. I will listen. Thanks."

He hung up.

He tried Johanna again. Answerphone too.

"Hi Johanna, it's Matthew. Look, I know everything, and I want you to know I don't hold you responsible. I know what it's like to be in an impossible situation. Anyway, call me if you want a chat."

He hung up and sat back in the car seat. The wheels had been set in motion, and hopefully, his plan would play out just how he intended.

Finally, he texted Luke. He wanted his son to meet him at the Greek restaurant opposite the flat as a treat. The girls had been doing well in school, and Luke had recently been more like his old self. He had big news and wanted to share it with them all together.

Last night had been the kick up the backside he'd needed to sort things out. His mother had sprinkled a wholesome dose of clarity on the situation and made him see things from a new perspective. It wasn't all Carrie's fault; he knew he had driven her to it as he'd been a ghost in their marriage for far too long. He had always thought he was the cement keeping the family bonds together, but he was just funding it. The genuine hard work was being done by her. Years and years of self-sacrifice, faithful integrity and bottomless patience were the backbone of his family, and he'd ripped the heart out of it.

The girls would be thrilled with the news, but Luke was as loyal as a guard dog when it came to Matthew. A gentle, slow approach would be what was needed. They had time. These things couldn't be rushed.

He was doing so much better since Matthew intervened, digging him out of his hideaway and encouraging him to be positive. He was going to start football again when he felt strong enough, basketball was back on at school and Felicity had helped feed him up. Solely concentrating on Luke without the distraction of the twins had been good for them both. Matthew missed his angels like mad during the week, but he couldn't deny that he enjoyed the bonding time with his only son. He was starting to feel optimistic; an irregular adolescent crisis had been snuffed out before it had time to fester.

He got out of the car and headed to the office. For the first time in months, he was looking forward to it. Like a young child returning to school after the summer, he was determined to do his best and make those who mattered proud. All at once, he felt that the dials on the axis of his life had shifted towards priority. Money, career progression, succession, none of it mattered anymore. It was all about family now.

* * *

"John. I'm not up for this. Where are you taking me?"

Carrie was starting to get worried as they turned onto the dual carriageway heading out of Little Browton. He flicked the indicator off with his left hand and changed gear to accelerate from the slip road to join the main flow of traffic. Once he'd manoeuvred safely and settled at a steady 60 mph, he replied.

"Remember Donald and Aggie, the old couple from the farm we went to on Monday?"

"Of course." She nodded, intrigued, unwrapping herself from the jumper and sitting up in her seat. The trail on Betty hadn't gone cold after all.

"Well. I did a bit of digging when I heard that Betty had just 'gone', but despite trying all my trusted sources, there were no leads. I suspected that they might have sold her on."

"Oh." Carrie deflated again.

"So…something niggled me to ring the farm. I remembered what you said about feeling like the old couple was under duress. It just didn't sit right with me that they were involved in this puppy farm. Remember that Aggie said selling puppies was what kept them on the farm?"

"Yes, yes, go on." Carrie was getting impatient.

"I made up an excuse to ring them, said that I thought I'd left my hat there or something. Anyway, we got talking. You know what old folks are like, they love a good chat. Aggie let slip that her son-in-law, this Jason bloke, had quite the business selling overpriced puppies. I must have caught her on a bad day because she went on to say that she and

Donald hated it but because Jason had bought the farm from them after their daughter died, he needed them to help him do the selling. Basically, he manages the lock-up, and they 'front out' the selling bit."

Carrie frowned. Where was he going with this? John sensed her bewilderment.

"Bear with me, Carrie. There's more. The floodgates must have opened because she went on to say that many, many dogs had passed through their hands over the years, and it made her desperately upset to know that these dogs were taken to order and then bred from. I let her get it all out of her system. She just wanted to talk to someone about it. She said what a lovely couple we were, said that I must cherish you. You reminded her of her daughter Lesley."

Carrie smiled at John. "Poor woman, she must really miss her daughter. He sounds like a brute, that Jason guy."

"Yes, yes, well, as I said, she had confided so much in me, I decided to push it and ask about Betty. She couldn't remember her but said that Jason did most of his business on the phone. He takes pictures of the dogs and places adverts on some website or other. As soon as the dog has been sold, he pulls down the advert, so the record is deleted from the web, no comeback. She didn't really understand the process but said she was sure he kept a record of the dogs and buyers somewhere."

"Right." Carrie's interest was spiking again. "Has she anything on Betty?"

Just then, her phone rang. It was Matthew.

"It's Matthew."

"Well, get it then," John urged.

She pressed the phone's green button. "Hi."

"Hi, did you get my voicemail?"

Over the noise of the van's engine, Carrie couldn't detect his mood or the manner in which he was asking her. Was it loaded or just a genuine question? The last time they had spoken, he had been awful, accusing her of sleeping with John. How would he react if she knew that she was with him now?

"Sorry, no. I've been out running," she said tentatively.

"Oh, right. Where are you now?"

Oh no, how should she respond? She was at a crossroads. She could lie, tell him that she was shopping in the town, or she could tell him the truth. She decided in an instant to tell him the truth.

"I'm with John…John Paterson. We're in his van, going…."

"Oh right, I get it…sorry I bothered you," he snapped.

"No, Matt, you don't understand. We think we might have…."

He had hung up. He'd made up his mind without hearing the facts.

Carrie held the phone away from her ear and stared at the empty screen, searching for some way of retracting what had just happened. She glanced at John; the pain etched in her expression was as void as the blank handset in her hand. She really didn't know what to say.

"Ring him back. He needs to know the truth," he urged.

She did, but there was no answer.

"Leave a message," John insisted.

She did, but she didn't mention Betty as she wanted to know more first. Replacing the phone in her pocket, she turned back to the matter in hand.

"So? Betty?"

John took a deep breath. "Yes. Betty was there. They re-sold her to a family, she thought, on the other side of the city. In fact, we are going there now. Aggie and I have organised the whole thing. You're getting Betty back today, Carrie!" he exclaimed.

"What?!" she yelled. "That's crazy! How?" Carrie had so many questions.

"Listen, we'll be there in thirty minutes. We're going to meet the lady who's had Betty for the last few weeks."

"Oh no. How does she feel about just handing Betty over? Do we need to buy her back? I hope she isn't going to be too disappointed." Carrie's mind was in turmoil, her family would be getting their pet back, but they would be losing theirs.

"Trust me, Carrie, it's all going to work out." John did one of his famous winks at her, and she couldn't help but have renewed faith. She did trust him; she knew things would be all right.

John started singing to an old song she recognised on the radio, and before she knew it, she was humming along too, tapping out the beat with her fingers on the arm of the passenger side door. She didn't know what to expect but judging by John's mood, they would be fine.

Soon, they arrived at a nondescript semi-detached house in Callingworth. John expertly parked the van into a small gap on the roadside and they got out. Aggie waved from the window as they approached, and a cheery petite lady was waiting at the door.

"Hello, you must be John and Carrie." She held out her hand, and they shook it lightly one after the other. "I'm Yvonne. Please come into my home." She stepped to the left to let them in and then told them to go through to the living room where Aggie was waiting.

Aggie beamed again at them. "Hello."

"Please sit down. Has John told you everything?" Yvonne asked, choosing to remain standing.

Carrie glanced from Yvonne to John and back. "Well, I think he has," she said.

"Oh gosh, sorry, where are my manners? Do you want a tea or coffee before we start?"

Although Carrie trusted John and the vibe she was

picking up in the room was genuine, she was impatient to learn more.

"Thank you, Yvonne, but can someone fill me in first, perhaps?" she asked gently. She didn't want to offend anyone or flatten the mood; however, she needed to know.

"Of course. I expect you want to see Jet, sorry, I mean Betty, don't you?" Yvonne's eyes sparkled like she was delivering presents on Christmas morning. "Sorry, we called her Jet." Carrie smiled weakly at her. "Here, come with me, Carrie. She's in the kitchen."

Carrie followed Yvonne out of the living room and along her small hall. Her heart was pounding out of her chest as they approached the kitchen door. Betty must have picked up on her scent as she began scratching and squealing as they drew closer. Yvonne laughed.

"She knows you're here! Better stand back!"

She opened the door, and Betty flew out whining loudly, waggling her bottom back and forwards uncontrollably. Carrie collapsed on the floor, pulling her dog close.

"Oh, my girl, I've missed you! How are you? I love you so much!" Carrie repeated over and over. Tears of joy streamed down her face. Betty rolled onto her belly for Carrie to tickle her. She leant over the dog and buried her face in her fur, breathing in the unmistakable scent of her dog. Here she was, alive and well. Carrie's unpleasant thoughts about Betty, which had plagued her for a month, were finally extinguished; Betty was in her arms.

Once the mad reunion began to wane, Carrie wiped her

face and turned to Yvonne, who had been joined by Aggie and John.

"Thank you, thank you so very much!" she managed to utter. Aggie and Yvonne had tears in their eyes.

"That's all I needed to see to convince me that I was doing the right thing," Aggie said tenderly.

"Me too," agreed Yvonne. "Now, who wants a cuppa? Then we can fill in the gaps."

They retreated into the living room, where Betty joined them, curling up on Carrie's knee once she had settled into an armchair. She was so big that she was practically sitting on Carrie's chest. Carrie wasn't about to move her, though; she was never letting her go again.

They made polite conversation until Yvonne returned with a tea tray and chocolate biscuits. John dived straight in, stealing more than his fair share.

"Shall I be mother?" he said with a mouthful of biscuit. He picked up the teapot and began to pour. Yvonne settled herself opposite Carrie and began.

"Oh, Carrie. It melts my heart to see you two together. She is a wonderful dog, and I promise you that I took good care of her."

Carrie grinned. "I can tell. Thank you, Yvonne." She turned to Aggie. "But…how? When? What happened?"

Aggie accepted her tea from John and took a steady sip.

"Carrie, this was all meant to be. Donald and I have been trapped for two years in that farmhouse, doing our son-in-law's bidding. He was blackmailing us into helping him with this wretched business in return for buying the farm for us. We lost a lot of money trying to diversify a few years ago. Our gamble didn't pay off, and then when we lost our daughter, we hit rock bottom." She paused to look out of the window. After a few moments, she carried on. "At first, we thought Jason was running a legitimate business selling dogs and puppies, but then the police called round and started asking strange questions about papers and vet assessments. Jason lied to them repeatedly. We couldn't believe how he'd got away with it. We wanted to tell the police the truth, but Jason told us that he'd sell the farm under us. The house was full of so many memories of Lesley. We couldn't bring ourselves to leave." She sipped her tea again, then glanced at John. "But John here made us see that the house was just bricks and mortar, really. It was our hearts that held the memories. We had to stand up to him, so we phoned the police. We told them everything. In fact, Donald is down at the station now, providing more evidence."

Carrie raised her eyebrows in disbelief. "Wow! I can't believe how brave you've been, Aggie."

"No, not really. We just needed a push to know that we didn't need Jason to be our crutch anymore. Donald and I have each other, and we must make the most of what time we have left. We can't live in fear of *him* anymore."

John reached out and patted her shoulder. "So much has happened in a week, but you are doing the right thing." He glanced at Yvonne. "And so are you."

269

"I know." She smiled. "I can see that. Betty belongs with you and your family, Carrie."

Carrie gulped at the mention of her family. Having Betty home was the missing piece. She couldn't believe that after all this time, she had the most fantastic news. She couldn't wait to tell them all together.

She turned to Yvonne. "How did you end up with her then?" She ruffled her big dog's coat as she spoke.

Yvonne smiled. "I lost my husband Jeff last year. We always talked about having a big dog to walk in our retirement. My son, Steve, saw the advert about Betty and bought her for me. It's as simple as that. I've only had her a week, but she is a joy, Carrie. I will miss her company."

Carrie felt a pang of sadness. In the jubilation of their reunion, Carrie had forgotten that this lonely woman would soon be on her own again. Suddenly a thought struck her.

"Aggie, what happened to the other dogs?"

"They all got seized, Carrie. They are now in dog kennels or veterinary care," Aggie replied.

"Oh," Carrie said sadly.

"Except for one," Aggie added. "I couldn't let them take Martha; she was too sick, so I hid her upstairs with the cats."

John interjected. "You remember, Carrie, the little sad black puppy in the box, the one that sucked your finger."

"Yes, I do."

"Well, I'm going to take care of her from now on." Yvonne beamed. "She is going to be my very own Jet, just as soon as we get all clear from my vet. She's there now having some tests done."

Carrie could burst. "Oh, my goodness, I'm sure little Martha is going to be fine. What wonderful news! Aggie, you have made us all so happy. I really hope it works out for you."

Aggie nodded. "In time, in time. Right now, we must cooperate with the police as much as possible and get that awful man out of our lives. I'm so grateful to Donald for keeping notes of all conversations and dealings we had with Jason so the police could see we were being manipulated and used. I don't think it will be plain sailing, but we'll tackle it together. We always do."

She smiled inwardly, hugging her secret to a good marriage tightly. Aggie had complete faith in Donald, and no doubt he did in her. A warm glow flushed over Carrie. She wanted to feel how Aggie felt. Self-assured, secure and satisfied. Wasn't that what marriage was in the golden years, both fighting the good fight, on the same page, supporting each other when things got tough? She wasn't sure she could have or ever did have that with Matthew.

Betty shifted and turned around on Carrie's lap to get more comfortable; she let out a happy sigh as she settled back into her new position on her favourite person. She was as heavy as an elephant, but Carrie could feel the stress and anxiety Betty had felt was now leaving her weary bones and slipping away forever. Carrie pulled her a little closer, still in disbelief that she finally had her back in her arms, where she belonged.

Leaving Yvonne's house with Betty at her side was a surreal but beautiful moment. She jumped effortlessly into the middle seat in John's van, and Carrie climbed in beside her. She turned to John.

"John, I can't thank you enough...," she started.

He held up his hand to stop her. "It was fate or serendipity, that's all. What was meant to be, will be." He started the engine.

Carrie grinned back at him, then secured the seat belt through Betty's harness. The dog fell asleep in her lap again as they drove away.

"Don't forget, you need to speak to Matthew. He needs to know what happened today."

Carrie agreed, but right now, she felt very tired from all the emotion. Before she knew it, her eyelids were closing, and just like Betty, she fell into a peaceful sleep.

CHAPTER 20

Carrie had said she'd been on an urgent mission with John and would explain all tomorrow. Matthew knew John well, and he trusted him. He was the one who had called Matthew after the breakup and taken him out for a pint. He also looked out for Luke on and off the football pitch. He had snapped earlier, he knew nothing was going on between John and Carrie, but he was intrigued to know what they had been doing. Her message said again how sorry she was and how she felt that things could get better if he would give her another chance. He softened; even the sound of her voice soothed him. He had to get his family back together. It wasn't just about him and her. The gossip was that Terry had gone back to Yorkshire. Surely, he was out of the picture now, but Matthew had decided to drive past his cottage for signs of life just in case. To his delight, a 'To Let' sign had appeared in the front garden. They had to move past this.

Carrie wouldn't be there tonight; however, he carried on regardless. Hannah and Jen came flying across the

273

playground straight into his arms. Their unconditional love bowled him over again and again. It was so easy with his children, so why could it not be with his wife?

"What are we doing this weekend, Daddy?" Jen looked up at him, wonder sparkling in her eyes.

"Well, right now, we're going back to the flat so you two can get changed. Then we're meeting Luke at the restaurant you like," he replied. "…and I have a surprise!"

"Ooooh! Is it a Kinder egg?" Hannah chipped in.

"No…."

"Horse riding lessons? We've been asking Mummy for ages," asked Jen.

"Erm, no. Wait and see."

He took each daughter by the hand and skipped with them down the road to his car. The girls squealed with delight at their silly daddy. He didn't feel silly. He felt optimistic and ready for the future. Despite Carrie not being there, he was going to crack on with the original plan. Deep down, he knew she'd want it too. The way she dressed up every Sunday evening for him told him so. She knew she'd made a mistake; she'd come back to him, and he would forgive her. The remainder of the journey back to the flat was spent in his head planning how he would tell his three wonderful children that they were going to be a family again.

* * *

Several hours later, after multiple games of shop, three jigsaws and an indoor football tournament with a tennis ball, the fragile little family was sitting around the table of the Greek restaurant enjoying lamb kebabs and halloumi salad. Matthew, with a beer in hand, decided to make the announcement.

"So, kids, what would make you really happy?" he quizzed.

"Ice cream?" Jen said.

"Ok, but what about something even better that involves Mummy?"

Matthew was almost bursting. He had never been more certain that this was the right thing to do. Luke, however, was not. He slammed down his knife and fork and folded his arms tightly.

"Luke?" Matthew was shocked by the outburst. "What's going on?"

Luke continued to stare blankly in front of him, pursing his lips together tightly. Although they were five, the girls knew it wasn't a good idea to say anything. They nibbled nervously on their kebabs and chatted about school. Matthew slid his mobile phone across to them and then pulled his chair round towards his son. He lowered his head to talk to him quietly.

"Don't you want your mum and I to give things another go?" Luke shook his head. "Why not, son?" Matthew detected intense resistance. He knew Luke had taken the breakup badly, but he thought a little time could build bridges or at least a dam. He hadn't anticipated there being a leak. He hoped that this was just Luke being overprotective again.

"She doesn't deserve it, Dad, and all you ever do is argue. I can't stand it," Luke sulked.

Matthew took a deep breath. Luke was straddling childhood and manhood, but he knew this had to be a man-to-man chat. He looked across at his daughters. They were engaged in a cartoon they had found on his phone, so he seized his opportunity.

"Luke, I love your mum very much. We got together when we were about your age, and I've never met anyone who ever came close to her. She made a mistake, and she is very sorry. I know that. I'm ready to forgive her, so it's time you did too. Don't you want to go home?" Luke remained silent. "Can you try and do this, son, for me?" Matthew begged.

Luke turned and looked at his dad and suddenly saw his innocent little boy again. Matthew felt a rush of love and simultaneous embarrassment. They had caused this confusion and hurt; they had placed this burden on Luke's shoulders, but now it was time to forgive. Matthew had to show him how.

"People make mistakes, Luke. We learn from them, and we move on. Forgiving someone is hard, but if you don't, you'll always be carrying anger and bitterness around with you. If you're not careful, it can consume you. We all have to work through this together, don't we?"

As he gently patted his son's arm, Matthew realised how

far he had come. A month ago, he would not have even contemplated forgiving Carrie; however, much had changed in his life over the past few weeks, and it had left its mark.

After a few minutes, Luke nodded and replied. "Ok, Dad, I'll try."

The girls had finished their cartoon, so Matthew decided to announce that their mum and dad were getting back together. The girls stared at him blankly. They thought that Daddy was having a little holiday from Mummy and Luke was staying with him, they didn't realise they had separated. Carrie had been careful to shield them from any mudslinging, determined to keep things as normal as possible. Even after Luke had left, she kept up the façade that everything was going to be ok. This hadn't even occurred to Matthew. It was another masterstroke from Carrie, defending the girls from the axe of divorce swinging precariously above her head. He took a deep breath and chose his next words very carefully.

* * *

Carrie made a cup of tea and settled in her favourite seat; her old companion curled up next to her, blissfully sleeping. She had told a little white lie, as she didn't think she could deal with it all tonight. Her perfect little secret could remain hidden for a little longer. She stroked her beautiful dog's black fur and Betty purred like a cat, stretching out her paws and arching her back. One piece left to put in the puzzle, and it would all be all right again.

* * *

February arrived the next day, and finally, colour was returning to the landscape. Wild primrose and crocuses infused the arid ground, illuminated by a low sun desperately trying to warm the inhabitants of the weary world. The gentle glow-tinged trees battered by winter stretched and yawned across the park as the luminosity reached out to touch the faces of the people and was welcomed with a humble smile.

When the girls came to stay, Matthew had to sleep on the sofa. He hadn't had the best night's sleep, but that wasn't down to the sleeping arrangements but more to the anticipation of the conversation he would be having with his wife in a few hours.

They had agreed to meet at Luke's football match and then go back to the house to talk. Matthew was determined for the kids' sake to see they were serious about being a family again; supporting Luke would be the first step. He took the girls over to the swings in the park not far from the football pitch. Luke was getting warmed up as the opposition began to arrive in dribs and drabs. John Paterson came over.

"Matthew, good to see you," he said, slapping his back. "Thanks for getting Luke back on track. He's playing like his old self again."

Matthew smiled and remembered that John had been with Carrie yesterday. He still didn't know why. He was about to ask when the girls called to him to push them again. John had to get back to the impending match but said he'd see him after the game.

The match had started, so Matthew gathered the girls

and trudged across to watch. Jen and Hannah were delighted to see a few familiar faces around the touchline, and soon, a raucous game of tag broke out. Matthew and a few other parents had to shepherd the little flock further away from the pitch to avoid disturbing the intense game. Ashley, Luke's best friend, was playing brilliantly and had narrowly missed scoring two goals already. Luke, on the other hand, looked tired. He was pale and sluggish, missing easy tackles and passes. Matthew offered a few words of encouragement when he was near. Luke gave him a thumbs up but continued to play in the same way.

Had Matthew been a little hasty in orchestrating this family reunion? A short while later, John came over.

"Sorry, Matt, I think I'm going to have to bring Luke off at half-time. That fire he had has gone out again, and he's missed some really easy shots," John said, shaking his head.

"Yeah, I know. Not sure what's up with him. Might be feeling unwell, I suppose."

The whistle blew for half-time. The opposition were a goal up, and Luke's team were frustrated. Matthew watched his son walk off the pitch with his head down, failing to make eye contact, and his heart went out to him. He had been there, and he knew how it felt. Luke grabbed his water bottle and threw himself to the ground. Matthew was about to go over when John crouched down and put his hand on Luke's shoulder. After a few moments, Luke got up, pulled on his training top, and made his way over to Matthew.

"Sorry, Dad, I just can't seem to get into the game

today." He shrugged. "First time you and the girls come to watch in ages, and I let you down."

"Don't be silly. Everyone has an off day, even David Beckham!" Matthew joked. "What did John say to you?" Luke tugged at his sleeves, the blanket of warm adrenaline had been lifted, and the cold was creeping in.

"Not much. He just said he was proud of how I conducted myself on the pitch. He said I could have lost my head and gotten angry with myself, but I didn't. He said it was better for me to rest now, ready for the cup game mid-week, and I'm happy with that. I am tired." John was right. Luke had remained calm under pressure, and that had to be commended. He put his arm around his son.

"You look frozen. Shall we all get a hot chocolate and come back for the second half?"

"I thought you said Mum was coming. Bet she's going to let us down *again*," Luke huffed.

Matthew turned to call the girls to go to the café, and as he did so, something caught his eye. A familiar silhouette of a woman walking briskly across the field being pulled by a huge black dog. Jen and Hannah saw it too and screamed.

"Mummy! Betty!"

The girls bolted across like racehorses freshly out of the stalls. Matthew gulped and tears prickled in his eyes. Was it really Betty? As Carrie approached, she was grinning from ear to ear. The girls threw themselves on Betty and smothered her in kisses and cuddles. The dog whined and wiggled with sheer delight, then rolled onto her back for a belly rub. Yes, it was Betty!

Matthew looked across at Luke, who was staring but frozen to the spot. He was clenching and unclenching his fists tightly, digging his nails so hard into the palms of his hands that his knuckles were white. His breath became rapid, and a lone tear fell from his eye.

Instinctively, Matthew pulled him closer. "Come on. Everything's going to be ok now."

Carrie unclipped Betty from the lead, and she raced over to them, followed by the twins. The big dog couldn't keep still, fussing around them like a mother hen. Finally, she rolled on the floor at their feet, making a mollifying purring noise declaring her contentment.

She brushed up against Luke, and he reached out to touch her. Suddenly all bravado was lost, and he collapsed on the ground pulling Betty into his arms. Tears of joy splashed down onto her jet-black coat.

"Betty! Betty! I can't believe it's you," he repeated, burying his face into her fur.

Matthew looked at Carrie, who was staring adoringly at the scene, her eyes shimmering on the verge of spilling over too. "How, what? Why?" he gabbled. She smiled, releasing the tears of pure joy.

"Come back to the house. I'll tell you everything."

He hadn't known what to expect, but despite his absence, everything in the house was just the same. Same non-descript cushions on the sofa, same pictures on the walls, same pile of muddled board games and jigsaws discreetly hidden behind the living room door. In spite of so many changes in the past few months, everything here was as it should be. Carrie made tea, and once the novelty of Betty had worn off, the girls disappeared upstairs to their room. Betty settled into her old basket next to the fireplace. Only Luke looked agitated. He was sitting on his hands, gently rocking backwards and forwards, lost in his thoughts. Matthew decided not to tackle him, he would just let the situation play out, and hopefully, Luke would reveal how he felt when he was ready.

Carrie returned to the room. "Sorry, no sugar. I don't tend to buy it anymore." That was one difference then.

She looked down as she handed Matthew a mug, then held Luke's out to him. He didn't move, so Carrie calmly placed it on the side table within reach. She went to retrieve her mug from the kitchen and then settled in an armchair facing the pair. Slow, soft snores could be heard coming from the basket and the occasional giggle rebounded from upstairs. Other than that, the awkward silence was deafening. Matthew attempted to shrink the void.

"So, what happened? How did you get her back?"

Carrie rubbed her hand across her face and tucked her hair behind her ears. She shuffled in her seat and sat with her legs underneath her. "Oh wow, long story." She smiled coyly.

Matthew waited for her to continue. Luke carried on staring at the floor, fixed like a statue.

"Well, that's why I was with John Paterson. He found her and helped me get her back." Luke's ears pricked up at the sound of John's name. Matthew let out an undetected, internal sigh, then nodded, encouraging her to go on. "You know what he's like, knows everyone, hears everything…well…he heard about a black dog someone was selling matching Betty's description, he took a punt, made some enquiries and tracked her down to this puppy farm nearby.

"Puppy farm? What!" Matthew was in disbelief. "How on earth did she end up there?"

Carrie began to retell the story, much to the disbelief of her audience. She described the dreadful puppy farm, and the poor old couple caught up in the dodgy dealings. How John had thought he'd found Betty only to receive the heart-breaking call that she had gone.

"John didn't give up, though. He kept making enquiries, and by the end of the week, with Donald and Aggie's help, he had narrowed down the search and found a lady called Yvonne on the other side of the city. That's where we were when you called the other day. We were going to get her."

"So, this Yvonne, she just *handed* her over?" asked Matthew.

There was still the faintest layer of suspicion within the question. Luke sat up a little straighter on the sofa, waiting for the reply, briefly lifting his gaze to his mother and then back down again.

"Well, yes. She'd been given Betty as a gift from her son. She'd lost her husband and was lonely. He'd seen the ad for her and bought her. She'd only had Betty a week." Luke stared blankly into space, and Matthew didn't respond, so Carrie continued. "…when Yvonne saw me and Betty together, she just knew that it was the right thing to do to give her up. In fact, weirdly, it all turned out all right. Aggie had secretly kept one of the sickly puppies behind and she gave her to Yvonne. Hopefully, when the little mite comes back from the vets, she'll be ok."

Carrie took a sip of tea. Matthew took a few moments to take in the story.

"What happened to this Jason chap? And Donald and Aggie. Are they just going to carry on?" Carrie grinned, replacing her mug on its coaster.

"Oh yes, so they shopped Jason to the police. He won't be hurting any more animals. They were being blackmailed. I don't think they'll get off scot-free, but they did the right thing."

Matthew rubbed his forehead and leaned forward to grab his drink. "Wow, what a chain of events." He crouched beside the basket and stroked his old friend tenderly.

"All seems a little too perfect, doesn't it?" Luke snipped, folding his arms across his chest tightly and putting his feet up on the footstool. "Betty back, you and Dad back together, that lady just happened to get another dog, the bad guy is going to jail…."

Carrie blushed like a ripe cherry catching Matthew's eye. "But we haven't talked about anything…." Matthew quickly butted in.

"Luke, your mum and I need to talk, but yes, it looks that way." He smiled sheepishly at his wife. "We both want to try again, don't we?"

Carrie put on an anaemic smile. Everything she had wanted back in her life was now right in front of her. She should reach out and grab it with both hands, hold it close and never fuck it up again. However, somewhere a red flag was flying—something wasn't quite right.

CHAPTER 21

It had been three months. Matthew and Luke had moved back in, and life had returned to some sort of normal. Betty had also settled into her old routine and was regularly accompanying Carrie on her morning runs. Mr Turner was thrilled with the twins' progress at school. Tidal waves of stickers flooded home every Friday, sometimes with the odd certificate; Carrie couldn't have been prouder. Luke, on the other hand, was more distant than ever. All sport had been replaced by video games and hiding out in his room. It was as though he'd turned himself inside out and gone from being a social butterfly to a reclusive, nocturnal moth.

There had been two major outbursts with Matthew since, and she had suffered.

He hadn't forgotten and couldn't move past it yet, but he always assured her that he would try, so she put up with it. She busied herself with the kids, specifically the girls, as

Luke drifted away from the homeland like an unanchored boat.

Work was all-consuming for Matthew. One of the partners had announced that he was leaving at the end of June, so an opportunity and more responsibility had presented itself. His competitive streak was in overdrive. He was living, breathing, and dreaming about this new role. Conversations at home revolved around him travelling abroad and the salary increase. Talk of everyday matters was cut short or ignored completely, but Carrie knew this was how it had to be. She had to shut up and put up, so they could all move forward as a family. Bruises and emotional scars faded with time.

Alisha had invited her round for a coffee at ten, but she was running late. It was a glorious day in mid-May, and Carrie had decided to take Betty for a walk rather than a run to savour the beauty of it. When she ran, she often concentrated on her next step or breathing or whether she'd make it to the next mile, not the rolling landscape surrounding her or the burst of jolly colour decorating her journey. She missed the subtle detail of the seasons; they gave her comfort and hope that things would be all right. The gnawing hadn't gone away, her inner voice was screaming, but her sense of duty and guilt kept her fingers firmly in her ears. It would get better; it had to.

It was half past ten when she arrived at Alisha's. She found her sitting out in the garden, listening to Don Henley with her chin tilted upwards, soaking up the early summer rays. She had a flamboyant headscarf tied around her thick black hair and a cappuccino lounging in the palm of her hand.

As Carrie approached, Alisha peered at her over her ridiculously oversized sunglasses. "You're late," she chided. "Your coffee's gone cold."

"Sorry, my walk took me a little further than I thought. What a glorious day."

"Absolutely." Her friend pushed her sunglasses back up her nose. "I'm pretending I'm in the South of France."

They both laughed. Little Browton was certainly *not* the South of France. Alisha was a call handler for the police. She often worked nights but found it difficult to sleep in this heat, so coffee and good music would see her through until evening.

"I suppose you want a fresh coffee then, huh?"

"I'd love a cold drink. Lemonade or water would be great, thanks," replied Carrie.

"No problem." Alisha calmly picked up her phone and pushed a few buttons. Soon her husband's voice could be heard at the other end.

"Hello?"

"Hello, darling. Carrie's here. Please, could you bring out a lemonade?" she wheedled.

"I'm about to go on an important call, Leesha," Jamal protested.

"Please, darling. You know how tired I am from last night...." She trailed off and winked at Carrie, who wasn't sure if she was referring to her work or something else that happened last night.

"Ok, give me five minutes."

Alisha hung up and grinned. "Little diamond, that one." He certainly was. Carrie couldn't imagine Matthew doing that. In fact, she wouldn't have even asked him. "So, how are things?" Alisha stretched her long legs out on the patio furniture.

"Fine."

"*Fine*? I thought you were going to tell me it was better than *fine*. It's been a few months now. Have you rekindled your young love?"

Carrie found herself laughing in nervous response. "Something like that."

Jamal appeared with his mobile nestled into the crook of his neck, handed Carrie her drink and smiled, then retreated indoors all the while, negotiating some deal or other with a foreign buyer.

Alisha rolled her eyes. "He's getting a lot of grief from Romania. I switch off; it bores me to tears." Carrie nodded, and a sedate quietness floated on the breeze. Eventually, Alisha caught it and broke it with both hands. "Jeremy said something odd the other day."

"Oh?"

"Yes, he said that Jen had called Hannah an ungraceful war. They had been arguing over the coloured pencils.

Apparently, Hannah had been hogging the red one."

Carrie started to laugh, but Alisha didn't. She turned and looked at her friend, pushing her sunglasses back on her head, revealing a concerned expression, "She didn't mean ungraceful war, did she? She meant ungrateful whore." Carrie's eyes started to swim. "Is that what he calls you?"

Carrie went cold. Alisha took her hands in hers and shuffled across to her friend.

"What's going on? Talk to me. What else does he say, Carrie? What has he done?"

Carrie couldn't speak. What right did she have for her friend's pity, though everything within her was sobbing, *"Help me!"*

Alisha patiently waited for more, and then it came. A tsunami of indignity endured over a lifetime.

"He controls my life. He knows where I am, what I do, how much money I spend. My only freedom is my morning runs. That's my only escape." Carrie sniffed. "I'll have to phone him at lunchtime to tell him about meeting you; otherwise, I'll face the inquisition tonight." Alisha listened without judgement. She just stroked Carrie's hands and silently encouraged her to talk. "The trust has gone; he tells me I have to build it back up. That's why he keeps me on a tight leash. There's a work event coming up soon, and he's even told me what to wear. The worst of it all is I don't think he even realises what he's like. I'm trapped, like a fly in a web. I made a mistake and must pay for it with my happiness."

"And the children…? asked Alisha, desperately trying to absorb some of Carrie's pain.

"I thought the girls were oblivious, apparently not. As for Luke, who knows! He barely speaks to me; he barely speaks to anyone anymore. He doesn't engage. I haven't had a decent conversation with him for months. I blame myself; it's all my stupid fault!" she wailed.

"No, Carrie," Alisha whispered. "No, it is not." Alisha's reassurance gave Carrie strength, and soon her breathing returned to normal. "What do you want, Carrie?"

After several moments, she replied in a robotic tone. "I want us to be a happy family."

"No, Carrie, you didn't answer my question. What do *you* want?" Alisha wrapped her hands around her friend's and squeezed tightly.

Carrie looked deeply into her eyes and saw her own soul splintering into tiny fragments. Tears fell, again and again, soaking her cheeks despite the heat of the sun.

Eventually, she whispered, "Leave. Get out. I want…no, I *have* to leave."

* * *

Life was great. Work, home, kids, wife, all running like clockwork. Matthew was feeling pleased with himself, and the cherry on the cake was about to be bitten off. Jean-Claude Baudelaire had announced his retirement. He wanted to go home, back to France and enjoy his home country before it was too late.

This was a huge opportunity for Matthew and Charlie was not only opening doors for his apprentice, but he was literally holding them open for him. They had developed a preferential partnership, with Harvey relinquishing more and more responsibility to him. Matthew lapped it up. He had to repay the favour of faith that Charlie had in him. Jean-Claude was the company secretary on paper, but he undertook far more duties than that. They would have to replace him eventually, but for now, Matthew would be taking on his role through the remainder of the summer. He couldn't deny that he wasn't relishing in the new status he had been given. He had a new number two, who he was whipping into shape, and he'd be heavily involved in recruiting Stanton-Peake's replacement which he naturally used to his advantage.

Carrie was behaving herself, but he wished she'd cheer up a bit. She had everything she'd ever wanted back, but it still didn't seem like enough to her. Matthew knew from their limited conversations that Luke was playing on her mind. He was worrying Matthew, too, and he had been wrestling with telling Carrie about their conversation back in January. Luke hadn't gotten any better, his grades were still low, and he wasn't getting into his sports again. John had dropped him to the subs bench, but Matthew knew he was only still on the team because of John's childhood friendship with Carrie.

Surely, she must have noticed. Why wasn't she putting in more effort with him? The girls were doing brilliantly and chomping at the bit to go into year 1. Luke was fading away into the shadows, and he might disappear entirely before September of year 11 dawned. Matthew decided to talk with Carrie tonight and sound her out on it. He wanted to know what she was going to do about it. He typed a reminder into his phone's calendar and sent her an invite. He wanted her to have time to prepare.

His phone rang and he was propelled back into the corporate world he loved so much, bossing around all the little people at his beck and call.

* * *

"Don't do anything yet. You need a plan, a carefully thought-out plan."

Alisha was adjusting the umbrella of her patio furniture to offer them a little shade from the permeating heat. Carrie felt the benefit instantly as the sun was interrupted by the protective canvas overhead. She nodded as Alisha settled back on her lounger and sipped her lemonade.

"If you're serious, you need to get good legal representation too. I know some people."

Carrie gulped. Had she really said those words out loud? *Leave. Leave.* Be released. That's what it felt like. She was being released from her sentence, and Alisha knew a way out.

Then the doubts came. Jibes and snarls filled her head. *"You can't do that!" "You're not strong enough!" "What about the children?" "Who do you think you are!"* Before she knew it, she'd released them into the air.

"Carrie, you are an emotionally battered woman. You deserve so much better and so do your kids."

She knew her friend was right, but this was it, finality. This would be the end of her marriage, but this time, on her terms. She would be strong; she had to be for her three kids. She was their role model, after all. She owed them not to be downtrodden and dismissed by their own father.

Her phone rang. It was Luke's school.

"Hello? …Yes, this is she…What…Collapsed? When? Ok, I'll go there right now. Thank you."

In a split second, she'd been split open from exposing her own fragility to mustering whatever she had left to save her son. She hung up and turned to Alisha.

"It's Luke. They're taking him to St Margaret's. He collapsed in PE just now. I need to go…," she trailed off in a daze.

"I'll drive you. Give me a sec to tell Jamal. Meet me out front."

Within minutes, the ladies were making their way to the hospital. Carrie was frantically trying to get through to Matthew, but as usual, it just cut to voicemail.

"Just keep leaving messages, Carrie. He'll see them and know something is up." Alisha suggested.

"Yeah, I know, but I think four is enough, don't you? I'd better call his parents too. He'll be cross if I don't." Again, her true thoughts betrayed her relationship, spilling into reality instead of staying cooped up in her brain. She was just so used to talking to herself in her loneliness.

"Why? Wouldn't it just cause unnecessary worry for all of you? Let's just get there first and suss out the situation, don't you think?" Alisha was the voice of reason. Carrie couldn't think straight, but she knew she had to focus on her son right now, not her in-laws' feelings.

"Yes, you're right. Oh god, what has happened? Why wouldn't he open up to me? I have been so useless these past few months. I should have been stricter, made him engage. Oh, Alisha!" She buried her head in her hands, and once again, the tears fell.

"Come on now! This could have happened to any of us. All the things that have happened to you happen to people every single day. It's how you deal with them now that counts. You can't change what's happened, but you can be proactive for the future and learn from all this shit. Luke's your focus now, Carrie. Save your energy for him."

Alisha was right, and it was what Carrie needed to hear. Carrie acknowledged her friend's advice with a hasty smile and then drove in silence for the rest of the journey.

On reaching the hospital, they were directed to a children's ward, where from outside a small room, she could see her weak boy lying withering on the bed. He was connected to various machines, from his nose to his wrists. The beeping and humming were deafening. Three or four medics in an array of different coloured uniforms were fussing around him. They had been told to wait outside whilst the examination was taking place. Alisha sat on one of the empty chairs in the little reception area. Carrie couldn't tear herself away from the window. She couldn't take her eyes off her beautiful baby, who she no longer recognised.

One nurse dressed in pink and helped by another in white slowly propped him up. He slumped over like a drunk while a third had to hold his head still to support him further. Carrie couldn't believe what she was seeing. Carefully the pink nurse took off his school uniform, blazer, jumper, tie and shirt. Carrie gasped and fell against the window. There was nothing left of him. Just skin hanging on bones.

CHAPTER 22

"It's anorexia," Carrie told Matthew on the phone. "He's anorexic."

"No! That's a girl's thing, isn't it? Like periods and breast cancer. Boys don't get that. Ask them again." She took a deep breath. This was it, the time to be strong, really strong, stronger than she had ever been.

"No, you are wrong, and the doctors are right. He has an eating disorder. He's had it for about a year, they think."

"Well, I need to speak to them myself. I'll be there in twenty minutes. Have you called my mum?"

Here we go, stay strong, Carrie, she told herself.

"No, I've only just finished speaking to the professionals, Matthew. Then I called you again."

"Ok, ok, I know they'll be worried, that's all," he snapped.

"Well, that's why I didn't call them. I also think it's best coming from you. Your mum is still very frosty with me." This was part of Carrie's strategy, to push back some of the parenting responsibility onto him. She wished it didn't have to be this way at a time like this, but she had to be direct to cut out the unnecessary crap to protect Luke.

"What about the girls?" he asked.

"Alisha was with me this morning when I got the call. She's going to get them and give them some tea back at hers." She heard him sigh.

"Ok, good. Thanks, and sorry, I've been in and out of meetings all day. It shouldn't take you five calls to reach me in an emergency."

Carrie softened a little. "It's ok. See you soon."

She hung up and looked in through the blinds of her son's room. He was awake, and he smiled sadly when he saw her. She entered and took the low seat next to his bed. Slowly he turned his head and tried to speak, but it was raspy and unclear. Carrie took his frail hand in hers; it was as cold as ice, so she willed all her body heat to radiate through him from this gentle touch. She could see the fear in his eyes, the uncertainty and all the questions he had. She saw the word sorry on his lips without a flicker of movement, and she told him everything would be all right with a simple kiss on the forehead. He was weak, but he managed to squeeze her hand in response. A year of conflict was forgotten in a moment; this was a mother protecting her son with everything she had left.

"I'll never leave you again, son. I'm here for you. Now and always."

She wiped a tear from his cheek and gave him her best reassuring smile, although inside, she was furious with herself. How had she missed the signs? Playing with his food, eating in his bedroom, losing interest in sports. They had all been there for her to read, but she had been too fixated on her own problems to notice. She was a bloody nurse, after all! Luke had been to hell, and his parents had put him there, but as she looked at his frail body wheezing with every rise and fall of his chest, she vowed never to neglect her children again, whatever the cost.

Matthew arrived, and Luke did his best to sit up like a private responding to his sergeant major. Carrie frowned. Until a few weeks ago, her immediate action would have been exactly the same.

"Oh, my boy! What on earth...?" Matthew took a moment to take in the sight before him. Carrie noted an extraordinarily long pause before he spoke again. Odd, she thought.

"D...d...," Luke started to whisper. Carrie squeezed his hand. She wanted him to know that he didn't have to say anything.

"No, Luke, you rest." Matthew grabbed a chair and placed it on the opposite side to Carrie. "You'll be all right."

They sat in awkward silence for several minutes, exchanging the odd pitiful glance and staring at the floor. All the while, Carrie was on the defence, stroking Luke's hand and ready to shield him at any moment from the barrage of questions that she knew were accumulating in his father's head.

A doctor appeared at the door accompanied by a few nurses that Carrie recognised from earlier. They needed to ask Luke some questions and carry out tests on him. One parent was allowed to stay, Matthew quickly volunteered, and Luke quietly agreed after casting his mum a woeful look. Carrie nodded and turned away before her son could see the tear betraying her courage.

As the door closed behind her, she felt compelled to go outside and take in some fresh air, but something made her stay, instinct spoke loudly from her inner being, and she remained entrenched, watching closely from behind the window. This was how it had to be from now on. She was a she-wolf protecting all that mattered.

CHAPTER 23

They had decided to move Luke into the office when he came home. It was smaller, more manageable for him, and it was closer to their bedroom. Carrie wanted him close. She didn't want him to face anything like this on his own ever again.

In between hospital visits, school drop-offs and pickups, and evenings over the summer holidays, Carrie tidied the office, preparing it for her son's arrival. She allowed herself to be a little excited. He had been admitted in May; she just wanted her baby home safe now.

She made herself a cup of tea and took Betty upstairs with her. It was going to be a long job. Felicity had taken the girls for the morning, and despite the odd barbed comment thrown her way on occasion, Carrie couldn't deny what a godsend her in-laws had been over the last few months. They had managed to set aside (almost) any ill feelings and move forward positively for Luke's sake.

Carrie was grateful. They were trying, which was a darned sight more than her own mother did.

Carrie took a deep breath and got to work. Today she was tackling his desk. Matthew hadn't used this room as an office since before the incident, and mountains of paperwork covered the small desk in an incoherent order. She decided to try and sort it into piles of similar, if not the same content; it would be a start anyway. Old invoices, receipts, statements with the company header or address in one pile, anything else would be assumed to be personal, so that would go in another. After ten minutes, she hadn't even made a noticeable dent. Betty, who had curled up in the old armchair in the corner, looked up and sighed.

Carrie read her mind. "Yes, girl, exactly."

Sitting back against the wall, sipping the last of her cold tea, something caught her eye under Matthew's desk drawers. She leant forward and slid her flattened hand under the narrow gap between the carpet and the bottom drawer. Her hand clasped around a plastic folder, and she slipped it out from the crack. Intrigued, she unzipped it and pulled out the contents. Bank statements, she said to herself dismissively, but before casually tossing them onto the designated personal pile, the words 'Final reminder' drew her attention for a second look. The statement suggested that Matthew was horrifically overdrawn on his credit card, thousands and thousands of pounds overdrawn and on a card that Carrie wasn't familiar with. She checked the date; it was nearly two years ago. Surely it was settled by now? Matthew had had so many promotions recently and was doing so well at the company it couldn't be anything to worry about, but when she delved further into the folder, the same pattern of bad news was woven into every page. Credit card after credit card, loan after loan, the debt and deceit were immeasurable.

Once again, she leaned against the office wall, letting out a jaded sigh; she had no idea. Years and years of lies were laid out before her in black and white. How did she not know and why had Matthew kept this all to himself? In her head, she flipped from anger to pity to forgiveness and back again. She thought she knew her husband, but she had thought she had known herself. No wonder he'd been wound up like a coiled spring these past few years, but why hadn't he told her? They were a couple, a team who had always faced things together head-on. Maybe she was wrong, and it had always been a counterfeit connection.

The doorbell rang, and Betty shot off the chair, barking loudly. Since coming home, she had become more vocal and unsettled. Carrie shuddered to think about what she must have been through on that awful puppy farm. She opened the front door, partially blocking the threshold with her leg to stop Betty from rushing out. It was the postman.

"Hiya. Parcel for you to sign for, I'm afraid." He grinned from behind oversized sunglasses. "Lovely day, isn't it?"

"Yes, I hadn't noticed, to be honest." Carrie handed back the tablet after scrawling her pathetic signature over it.

"Oh right, well, be sure to make the most of it. Rain tomorrow."

He turned and left her, flicking through the wad of envelopes he had handed her after the parcel. One was from the bank addressed to Matthew. Closing the door gently, she took the parcel and letters into the kitchen and switched on the kettle. The envelope from the bank was willing her to open it, like Pandora's box testing her resolve. The last statement she had found, dated 29th November, still showed tens of thousands of pounds in debt. If she opened this one, it might give her the answer she needed to settle her troubled mind and let sleeping dogs lie, or she could see if her husband was still lying after all they had been through these past few turbulent months.

She stared at the envelope; its secrets had her transfixed. Should she do the right thing and leave it for Matthew, carefully watching his expression as he opened it up, searching for signs of apprehension? Trust had been obliterated, and their relationship had been pushed to the extreme. Ripping open an envelope wouldn't make any difference now anyway.

As the kettle came to the boil, she paced the kitchen, agonising over her decision. She knew once she had made it, she couldn't go back. She snatched it up and peeled back the seal. Unravelling its contents, she sighed with relief. No debt, no minus; everything looked healthy! Carrie knew this was just one account, but the signs were encouraging until she noticed whose name was at the bottom of the letter.

Terence Jennings.

CHAPTER 24

It was late summer when Luke came home. The unit had agreed that he was well enough, providing he came back twice a week for an appointment with the psychiatrist. The outside world was a daunting place for him. Flinching at loud noises and avoiding eye contact with people was the new normal. Carrie's heart broke to see how her confident, fun-loving son had been reduced to a sallow shadow, but her guilt had been replaced by redemption.

Whilst Luke had been away, she had taken the opportunity to focus on herself and the girls. Early morning running had reasserted itself in her weekly routine, as well as a coffee with Alisha on a Wednesday morning. These two activities were Carrie's salvation and kept her feet firmly on the ground. The running cleared her mind and allowed her space to breathe. Alisha, her most trusted ally, listened and restored her faith that she wasn't crazy or mad or out of touch, that she had a point, her opinion mattered and was relevant. This gave her the courage to defend herself when she needed to.

She never brought up the letter she had found a few weeks ago when clearing out Matthew's office. She had been too shocked to react. Alisha said she should, but she couldn't.

Prior to the discovery, she had been gearing up to leave him. Her mind had been made up, and she had been ready. Luke and the twins were her world—Matthew was not, not anymore. However, the letter rocked her to the core. Not only had her husband been lying about the finances, but her alleged 'fancy man' had known everything. The letter outlined a summary of the payments made and how long he had been making them. Terry had written about meetings and conversations they had had to manage the debt. When Matthew met Terry back in the autumn, he had acted like he didn't know him at all and Terry the same— lies from men that she had trusted. Integrity was clearly out of fashion. How stupid and foolish she'd been. They had both played her like a fiddle, dancing to their own selfish tune.

But something remarkable had happened to her. She had survived her ordeal and somehow come out stronger. Her children had become her reason for getting up every day and putting one foot in front of the other when she yearned to hide away. Their welfare had become her welfare, and her atonement was about widening the lens beyond her marriage, which she had once thought was her core. In all honesty, she felt like she had frittered away the past five years of her life and, more importantly, the children's. Striving for perfection had robbed her of her memories, Hannah's first steps, Jen's first words, Luke's first day at secondary school. She'd been trapped in a fog of compliance, acknowledgement and recognition. Like the shy school kid waiting for that one positive remark from their teacher, Carrie had followed Matthew around like a besotted puppy, waiting for a pat on the head from her master. Matthew was not her master, he was her equal; she knew that now.

The girls were playing in the paddling pool in the garden, squealing and splashing around like seals. Luke was under the parasol next to her, slowly sipping lemonade. He wasn't better, but he wasn't any worse, either. The doctor had said to just take it one day at a time. Being at home helped him. Carrie could feel him relax, and she even thought sometimes that he was happy. He'd started to retake an interest in life, just simple things like watching football on the TV or playing chess with her. He hadn't left the house since he'd come home, but that was part of his journey back. It would come in time.

John had paid him a few visits in hospital over the summer, chatting about the football team and recalling hilarious stories of his painting and decorating jobs. Carrie couldn't leave them as she felt Luke's invisible hand in hers. Even though it was John, Luke wasn't ready to be on his own just yet. When her son was sleeping, John looked in on her too. He was like the big brother she never had, and although she couldn't bring herself to confide in him, she knew he'd always be there for her like a comforting blanket.

August was stretching and yawing out its long balmy days and sticky nights. Although the summer seemed endless, she knew it couldn't last forever and had to decide before school loomed like a dark shadow in September. Matthew was hardly ever home now, snatching days here and there over the weekend, but it seemed to suit them both. Would it really make a difference if he weren't home at all?

Luke adjusted the parasol to get some sun on his legs. Carrie smiled, another huge step. His vampiric existence was quietly being forced into the light on his own authority. Luke caught her expression.

"I feel better, Mum. Today is a good day."

Again, a crack appeared in Carrie's heart, but it was instantly cemented over with pride. This was her boy, how far he had come!

There was a loud scream from the paddling pool, followed by a huge splash. Carrie and Luke looked over to see a black furry mess flopping over the side, spilling out oceans of water onto the lawn. Betty, suffering from her many bouts of missing out, had leapt into the pool, catching her back end on the side. The girls were now lolling around in the remains of the water, shrieking with delight, splashing the dog as she frolicked and bayed. Betty was in her element. This was Carrie's essence. Family, this century's remedy. It was in this moment that she realised that minimalization allowed every object to take centre stage. She had to scale down, starting with her husband.

* * *

Another weekend away at a conference, Matthew sat in the dreary hotel room. Thank goodness for the air conditioning; without it, he'd be boiling. He dragged himself away from his laptop to the murky window and looked out over the concrete scene before him. The city was unusually quiet for a Saturday afternoon. There was just a handful of people below, milling about doing their own thing. In the distance, he could hear the penetrating shrill of an ice cream van calling children from all corners of the streets. He thought of his own children and wondered what they were doing. He reached for his phone to call them but remembered that he had to get a report finished this afternoon; otherwise, he wouldn't be able to attend the networking event tonight, and he needed to make those new connections. The pressure of repaying his debt to Charlie was mounting, he knew he had to bring in some new business and it had to be big. He couldn't hang off Jean-Claude's coat-tails forever.

He let out a huge sigh and returned to his desk. This report on the current state of the markets was, without a doubt, the most boring thing he'd ever written. He rubbed his forehead with his hand and reached for his soft drink. It didn't help that he hadn't gotten in until 4 a.m. He couldn't remember much of the night, but they had certainly been at a casino; the receipts in his wallet had told him that. He cringed at the thought of how much he'd lost last night but assured himself that it would be worth it in the long run. He had had to impress his guests.

Something pinged through to his mobile; it was from Carrie. A photo of the girls and Betty bathing in the paddling pool and Luke sunbathing with shorts on! Matthew chuckled, he ached to be with them, yet this was why he did what he did, so they could do that.

Carrie hadn't captioned the pictures, and he wondered how she was. He should have called her last night, but events distracted him after dinner. He had simply run out of time. She understood how it was. She'd texted him shortly after eleven to say goodnight. With a stab of guilt, he knew he should have replied. It hadn't escaped him that she was holding the fort at home so he could dispense his time as he pleased. They seemed to have reached some quiet, mutual understanding, he did his job, and she did hers. They accepted this; excuses stunted progress.

Matthew thought of his parents and what his mother had told him about their relationship, sharing duties and responsibilities. That was what he and Carrie were doing, except it wasn't just mundane tasks like washing up and vacuuming. It was important stuff like making money and managing the house. He didn't bother her with the minute details of his role, and she didn't with him. As far as he was concerned, it worked, although he did think that he should get home tomorrow if possible.

He turned his phone over and contemplated a message back to his family. Seconds later, a message came through.

'Thanks for your help last night! Coming down for a swift one before the dinner tonight?'

A smile played on his lips. Johanna.

It had been a good idea to invite her to the conference. She had been quite hesitant initially, but once he had explained the grand plan to her, she came. Expanding the business overseas had always been an idea Matthew was bouncing around behind the scenes.

After all, Charlie was making noises about his retirement next year, and Sweden seemed as good a place as any to grow.

Trust was important, though. Even after everything that had happened, Charlie had put his trust in Matthew and in turn, he felt he could do the same with Johanna. She wasn't a bad person; she deserved a second chance. He thought of all the times he had stolen her limelight, making her do all the donkey work so he could shine. He wasn't proud of how he had treated her; she was good, too good at what she was doing now. He had an opportunity here to do the right thing, so he should take it.

He was excited, and his family would be so proud of him. He was becoming a leader, perhaps soon even a global leader. He leaned back in his chair and breathed in deeply. Satisfied with the decision, he punched in a reply, 'Of course, see you in ten.'

* * *

Throwing shade never made anyone look brighter, and although Carrie wanted to send a sarcastic text, she didn't. His silence had helped her make her mind up, and it was time to move on. She thought about the noose hanging around her neck for too long and decided to tie up loose ends with it instead of hanging herself. Matthew's ambition was once again sliding family life down the agenda. It was an all too familiar story, and after the chaos of the past year, Carrie couldn't allow that to happen. She had built a fortress for her babies and was standing guard, even if that meant against their own father. No one could hurt them now.

Her thoughts turned to her childhood and how she had longed for her mother to be on her side instead of everybody else's. The death of her dad had left a deep scar that would never heal. It would be different for her own children. Carrie would be the parent she needed when she was little. No one would ever come before her kids, not now, not ever.

Luke had fallen asleep in the haze of the late afternoon sun. The girls were lying on the lawn patting the drenched turf with their hands whilst Betty leapt and barked on command. She had everything she needed right here, right now. She knew it wouldn't be easy, but every day made her stronger and more confident that she could do this on her own.

She thought of the story her father used to tell her about the fishermen facing wave after wave battering their tiny boat as they went about their business. But they went out the next day and the next and the next. Sometimes the waters would be choppy and challenging and sometimes calm and serene. Her father's voice was in her head again, 'The storm will always pass.'

All this time, it was Carrie who had been blocking her own escape, taking on the storm but never allowing it to take its own course. She knew now that the past could no longer hold her captive.

Letting go wasn't the end of the world.

It was a fresh start; the future was waiting for her.

ACKNOWLEDGEMENTS

Simon, Sam and Em, you are my everything.

Katherine, for reading my raw scribbles and bigging me up when the doubt crept in.

Catherine, for letting me confide in you. You have helped me more than you know.

Estelle, for giving me the kick up the backside I needed.

.

ABOUT THE AUTHOR

Bella Roane is a married mother of two. A proud Yorkshire woman, she is living a happy life in rural Cheshire with her family and ginger dog, Stan.

Facebook: @bellaroaneauthor

Instagram: @bellaroaneauthor

TAUK
Publishing

TAUK Publishing is an established assisted publisher for independent authors in the UK.

With over 200 titles including novels, non-fiction and children's books, TAUK Publishing is a collaborative-based team providing step-by-step guidance for authors of all genres and formats.

To sign-up to our newsletter or submit an enquiry, visit:

https://taukpublishing.co.uk/contact/

For a one-to-one advice, consider scheduling a Book Clinic:
https://taukpublishing.co.uk/book-clinic/

Connect with us!

Facebook: @TAUKPublishing
Twitter:@TeamAuthorUK
Instagram:@TAUKPublishing
Pinterest:@TeamAuthorUK

We love to hear from new or established authors wanting support in navigating the world of self-publishing. Visit our website for more details on ways we can help you.

https://taukpublishing.co.uk/

SCAN ME

Printed in Great Britain
by Amazon

12622231R00183